DEATH LIST

Robert McKew

ATHENA PRESS
LONDON

DEATH LIST
Copyright © Robert McKew 1979

ISBN 1 84401 282 4

First Published 1979 by
FUTURA PUBLICATIONS
110 Warner Road, Camberwell
London, SE5

Published 2004 by
ATHENA PRESS
Queen's House, 2 Holly Road
Twickenham, TW1 4EG
United Kingdom

Printed for Athena Press

DEATH LIST

For Sir Stanley Baker, without whose help and encouragement this book would never have been written

PROLOGUE

B LAKE SWITCHED ON THE WINDSHIELD WIPERS. NAGY MUTTERED, 'How far do we have to go?'

Blake slowed down for a sharp curve, then stepped on it. 'About twenty kilometres.'

Nagy was worried. 'For God's sake, be careful. We could go off the road, it's slippery out there.' He wore thick horn-rimmed bifocals which magnified his watery eyes, reminding Blake of fish in bowls. It was very weird.

It was a nasty night and the driving rain made it difficult to see the road, but he couldn't slow down, there simply wasn't time. If they arrived late the crossing would have to be postponed, and that – especially now – would be dangerous.

The Hungarian sat there fidgeting, doing restless little things with his hands. 'Are you sure you know the crossing place?'

'I ought to, I've done it enough times,' Blake replied, careful to keep the impatience out of his voice. They were all the same, even the experienced ones; they all got the wind up on the final stretch.

Nagy was shaking his head, working himself up to another of those passionate outbursts, like the one back at the Hotel Wurzel. It had happened right in the middle of the foyer and Nagy had been too far gone to care who heard him. Blake shuddered. Even the thought of it was enough to bring on the sweat. And the wonder of it all was that no one had paid the slightest attention. Once again pure blind luck had intervened to save their undeserving skins.

'But why now,' Nagy moaned, 'just when it was beginning to look good? That's what I can't understand – why now?'

'You might have been blown,' Blake said gently.

'Never!'

'But you don't know?'

Nagy hesitated, but only for a moment. 'I would know!' he insisted belligerently.

5

'…possibly too late. Centre couldn't take that chance.' He didn't add that the *Abteilung* had already rolled up six of their best agents in East Germany, which was practically next door, and it could well snowball to other parts of the Network. The red light was blinking and they weren't taking any chances. It took too long to recruit and train reliable people. It was better to get them out now before it was too late.

The road narrowed slightly and Blake stuck his head out of the side window. He could just discern the deeper shadows of the high pine that grew right up to the road and he also noticed that the downpour was beginning to slacken off. He slowed down because if he remembered correctly the turning should be somewhere up ahead on the left.

'That's your trouble,' Nagy was mumbling. 'Centre is too far from the field of operations… you Americans could learn something from the Russians.'

Blake grinned. 'They've been at it longer than we have.'

Nagy hadn't taken his eyes away from him for some time now and it was unnerving, that steady myopic stare. One could almost read his mind. Could he trust him, the Hungarian was asking himself. Was Blake who he pretended to be or was he something else, someone from KGB Counter-intelligence perhaps? It was the great guessing game in all the Satellites: could you trust him or could you not? The great collective obsession.

'This is the turning,' Blake said, voicing the thought out loud. He swung the car into a couple of narrow muddy ruts and black walls of foliage rose up steeply on either side. Their luck was still holding, but then he reminded himself that they still had a long way to go.

Nagy gazed at him suspiciously, the magnified whites of his eyes gleaming in the dim light of the dashboard. 'How do we get through the minefield?'

'You follow me.'

'What do we do with this damned car?'

'We leave it.'

'But it will be traced. Any fool knows that!' He started to mutter to himself, this time in Hungarian. 'God, what have I got myself into?'

Blake was becoming irritated. He cut him short harshly. 'There's someone else there. He will drive it back to Budapest. Satisfied?'

Nagy was teetering right on the edge, one tiny shove and he would blow. 'Like hell!' he blurted. 'And now perhaps you will explain how we are expected to cross a minefield in pitch darkness?'

Blake knew he had to be patient. Careful to keep the anger out of his voice, he replied, 'We crawl. The corridor is marked with tapes on either side.'

Nagy looked younger than he actually was, not more than thirty. But to Blake's personal knowledge he had been out in the field for over ten years, so he must have been older than that. Blake wondered why the thought hadn't occurred to him earlier.

'You had better be right,' Nagy spluttered. He was feeling very sorry for himself. 'Or it's kaput for both of us.' He stiffened, suddenly remembering something else. 'And what about the watch towers? Christ, what about those? The searchlights – we don't have a chance!'

Nagy was desperate now, he might do anything. Try to run for it, even shoot it out. It wouldn't be the first time that blind, unreasoning panic had happened, even to hard-shell agents like this one. Blake knew he had to say something fast. 'We've arranged an electricity failure,' he said evenly, 'there won't be any lights.' He put a hand out to steady him.

'You're sure?'

Blake nodded. Nagy's flesh felt like ice.

'You better be.' Nagy slumped weakly back into the seat.

Blake checked his watch then stopped the car, switching off the headlights. 'We wait here for about five minutes, then get out and start walking. The clearing is about three kilometres up ahead. After that it's the minefield.'

Nagy took a deep breath. 'May I smoke?'

'Yes, but use the lighter on the dashboard.'

They sat there waiting in the dark and Blake could feel Nagy's fear, almost smell it as if it had an odour. Presently, apparently regaining control of himself, he said in a flat voice, 'So you're Control!'

'What makes you think that?'

'I often wondered what you'd look like.'

Blake didn't reply. He sat there trying to think up a convincing lie.

'Well, aren't you?'

'No.'

Nagy even managed a laugh, but it wasn't entirely successful because it didn't hide the fear. That was always with them; they wore it like some hideous facial disfigurement the moment they stepped into the field. Blake checked his watch again then opened the door and stepped out. Nagy scurried out behind him like a child afraid of being left behind and they started to move up the road. The going was difficult because of the mud.

'Can we talk?'

'For the moment, yes,' Blake said softly. 'I'll tell you when we can't.' His voice sounded casual, a sentiment he was far from feeling. He had done everything he could. Farkis had sworn that the frontier guards up in the watch towers were his men and that another had fixed the generator, but there could be a slip-up. He felt it all right, the tightening of that fear ball down in his gut, weakening his knees and spreading to his head. They kept walking, struggling in the soft clinging mud.

'Well, you wanted to talk, so talk.'

Nagy was breathing heavily then Blake realised he was as well. 'If I don't get out of this,' the Hungarian finally managed, 'I mean, if something happens… there's someone in Buda. They have her details at your embassy, not that she's any relation or anything.' He clutched Blake's arm for a moment. 'Could you get her out?'

Blake pulled up and turned to him. 'Nothing is going to happen,' he said, the bland tone of his own voice revealing how expert a liar he had become, but then he was an old survivor and to be that you had to master the craft.

Nagy persisted, his voice rising. 'Can you get her out?'

'Yes.'

'You're sure?'

'I'm sure.'

He seemed better after that and they trudged on in silence. They walked for just under half an hour and, finally, Blake edged over to the side of the road. 'This is the path,' he whispered. 'No talking from now on and stay as close behind me as you can. If you find you have to say something – whisper.'

They turned into the path and moved cautiously under the trees. They could have been at the bottom of a mineshaft in total darkness, and there was a lot of stumbling and groping from tree branch to tree branch as they felt their way step by step, grateful that they had left the mud behind out on the road.

Blake lifted the luminous dial of his watch up to his nose, then whispered, 'We will rest here for a moment.'

'How close are we?' Nagy asked softly, the tell-tale tremor back in his voice.

'Not far.'

Nagy joined him on the soft carpet of wet pine needles. It smelled good.

'You've never done this before?' Blake asked presently. He said it so softly that the other couldn't hear him.

'What?'

Blake put his mouth right up to his ear. 'Have you ever crossed a minefield?'

'Once.' Nagy exhaled heavily. 'And I promised myself never to do it again.'

'Just stay close behind me, I know where the tapes are. You will be all right if you stay close.'

'I'll be breathing right up your backside,' Nagy whispered hoarsely.

When they finally reached the clearing it was as silent as the grave. They lay down just within the shelter of the trees, squinting in an effort to see the high wire fence that lay just beyond the freshly ploughed field which they knew contained some two hundred yards of mines. This stretched the entire length of the frontier and it made the mind boggle to think of it. Blake whispered, 'Remember, they're placed in very shallow holes so don't move outside the tapes. I don't know how wide the field is, they keep changing it.'

'Fine time to tell me.'

'One thing is going right anyway, the lights *are* out.'

Blake checked his watch for the last time and knew it was the moment to move out into the field.

'I'm going out to find the tapes, they should be just on the left of us. If you want to stop, grab my ankle, otherwise we keep moving until we're across.'

'For God's sake – go!' the Hungarian gasped and they began to crawl slowly along the edge of the ploughed field.

Blake had a moment of blind panic when his hand pushed down on something which felt alarmingly metallic. He froze, could hear Nagy's laboured breathing just behind his ear, then he realised that it was nothing but a large flat stone. He took a deep breath and started to crawl again, running a hand just above the ground, blindly searching for the tape. Suppose he couldn't find it, what would he do then? Had he already passed it? He kept going, willing it to be there. Then he felt it, his fingers closing gently on the taut cord. He had to stop for a moment to catch his breath, feeling the sweat rolling down the back of his neck and dripping down under his collar. It had been a close thing. After a moment, he lifted it gently then lowered it an inch or two until he was sure that this was it. As he took his first tentative step (they were crawling on all fours) out into the ploughed ground he could hear Nagy whispering to himself in frantic Hungarian, probably praying. They rested a moment then started to move along the bottom of a ploughed furrow.

They kept going for what seemed a very long time and once Blake lifted his head, but the vague outline of the fence seemed as far away as it was before they started. This wasn't so good. He had neglected to tell Nagy that they only had fifteen minutes to reach the fence and find the tunnel and if they didn't keep to the schedule the lights might come on again. Suppose Farkis's men were changed by a relief detail or the man handling the generator was discovered? Blake shut it out of his mind and continued to crawl, speeding up the pace, his fingers brushing lightly along the cord. One false step and they were dead. If the mines didn't finish them the guards in the tower would, even if they were Farkis's men. If they didn't they would betray themselves.

It seemed an age since they had crawled down into the furrow. Hands, elbows and knees caked in heavy chunks of mud, Blake kept going and Nagy followed close behind him, first one knee, then the other, the sharp pain in their lungs reminding them that they couldn't go further without stopping to rest. When at last he lifted his head, Blake saw the fence. It was clearly discernible and not more than fifty yards ahead.

Blake felt slightly ridiculous. A man of his age crawling around in a ploughed field in the middle of a wet Hungarian spring. Was this the career he had chosen for himself? Could it be dignified by such a label? A man without a name or a profession he could admit to, choosing to live among the dregs of the earth where truth was a monstrous mirage, treachery mere routine and a nameless grave the probable end. For what? Political ideologies? How many had come and gone since the beginning, as numerous as the sands of the desert and sinking without memory or trace to be replaced by more of the same because people never changed and never would if he was any judge.

He was only aware that they had reached the fence when he bumped his head against the hard wire, and where the tape ended there was the tunnel. He knew one thing, the current really was shut off or he would have been fried the moment his head had touched the fence. So far so good.

'What now?' Nagy wheezed.

'When we clear the tunnel,' Blake whispered, 'we've got another hundred yards to go. But that's over neutral ground and there are no mines. When we cross that we're in Austria. There's a car waiting about half a kilometre from there.'

When they started to crawl through the tunnel, they found that their arms were submerged up to the elbows in icy water. Blake could hear Nagy splashing behind him, cursing the mother that had brought him into the world. Blake envied him, his own cold detachment precluding even that small comfort.

Thus far everything had gone according to plan and when they emerged from the tunnel they lay doggo for a minute or two to allow the circulation to return to their frozen limbs. Ahead lay the last hundred yards.

They looked up at the nearest tower which loomed out of the darkness some fifty yards to the left, its Auschwitz platform stretching up into the mute blackness of the hut itself. Then Blake was on his feet and running.

The sudden light was blinding. He threw up his hands to cover his face. Nagy started to scream a moment before the bullets struck him. There were only two shots fired from a high-powered rifle that was probably fitted with a telescopic sight.

Blake turned back to look at him. He knew he was dead. Nagy lay there on his young face, the bifocals still in place on the bridge of his nose, half his skull shot away, his back oozing with the bloodstain that was spreading around the hole between his shoulder blades.

It was unpleasant to see a man killed. In reflective moments Blake often speculated on his lack of feeling whenever he witnessed it; or more particularly when, as in the present case, he himself was the instrument by which it was accomplished.

But then, counter-intelligence by its very nature was difficult to assess in terms of loyalty. Often it was necessary for a man such as Nagy to supply real information to establish credibility with the other side. In extreme cases this action might be considered indistinguishable from that of a genuine traitor.

Unfortunately in this instance both sides had decided to dispense with his services at the same time, and this was the inevitable fate of the double-agent.

Blake looked up at the tower, waiting for the lights to be switched off again. Then, with an inward shudder, he turned and started to move slowly towards the road beyond the neutral ground.

CHAPTER ONE

I

BLAKE LAY LUXURIATING IN THE STEAMY WATER THINKING how good it was to be alive and reminding himself that he had much to be thankful for. Centre had been generous in granting him six weeks extended leave and he was looking forward to all those days he would have to become reacquainted with his daughter, who at that moment was only a few feet away in her bedroom happily packing for their first real summer vacation together.

The dark areas, that part of his life that came under the heading of 'work', he had long since learned to push out of his mind. Conscience – if that was the word – had lost its meaning and all he asked of the world now was a bit more hot water. Grunting happily, he lifted a foot and opened the hot-water tap with his toes. It would be good to see Cape Cod again, to laze through the long summer days, to stop the clock, to let the static moments engrave themselves on his memory so that at some future time he might bring them back to comfort him.

Janis had turned out well. England suited her. All things considered the transition from a small New England college to London University had been effortless. It was amazing how quickly young people these days seemed to adapt themselves to alien surroundings, slightly aggravating, too, their bland acceptance of the fact that the world and everything in it was theirs for the asking. Youth like love was blind and perhaps that was the way it should be. There she was, nineteen, full of vitamins, the devil in her eyes, breastwork that brought out the best in sweaters, *brand spanking new*, none of it second-hand, and to top it all – just plain nice.

Sam sighed. It wasn't altogether a satisfying thought,

reminding him that all that was behind him; he had been down too many roads, there were no surprises around any of the bends. You were only young once.

He recalled the moment he stepped into the apartment the night before: a sudden girlish squeal and the soft weight of her body catching him off balance as he came through the door.

'Daddy. Oh, Daddy... darling.'

Arms no longer chubby encircling his neck, excited lips ravaging his unshaven cheeks. Hand in hand, leading him into the room.

'You look so thin. What have you been doing to yourself? Here, let me fix you a drink.'

A slim figure like her mother's, and lovely long legs with thoroughbred ankles, encased in shredded tennis shoes. 'I'd better get rid of that first,' he had said, unaccountably embarrassed, indicating his bag abandoned after the first assault out in the hall. He hadn't realised until then how much he had missed her, how much she meant to him, how never again must he stay away so long. The joy of it, the delight, noting the transition from child to woman in the flick of an eyelash. It wasn't possible. Time was merciless.

Regret? Time they could have shared. 'You damned fool!' Blake protested to the steam-beaded walls. 'You damned, damned fool!'

Outside, the object of all Blake's soul-searching stood in her bedroom exuberantly zipping up the last of the luggage, then she lugged it out to the hall. Monica Riley sat placidly on the living room sofa, crossed her elegant legs and smiled. Janis made an appealing picture and Monica wasn't above a little soul-searching herself. 'Looking forward to it, honey?' she asked languidly, ignoring the drink Janis had hurriedly prepared for her a few minutes earlier.

Janis skipped back into the room, fell into a chair and tilted her head distractedly. 'What?'

'How long has he been away this time?'

Janis wrinkled her nose. 'Oh, months as usual. I'd have seen as much of him back home.' She gazed admiringly at the older woman and blurted impulsively, 'God, how lovely you look. I've never once seen you when you didn't look like you'd just stepped out of a Saks Fifth Avenue window.'

Monica laughed. 'Rather dates me, doesn't it?'

Janis rarely answered questions because she didn't often listen. She went on, 'I mean, all the time you've gone with Daddy, I've never seen you with cold cream on your face or your hair up in curlers.' She wrinkled her pretty forehead. 'How do you find the time, writing all that stuff for newspapers and magazines... where're you off to?'

Monica had risen, picked up her drink and was heading for the bathroom. 'Just checking. He's been awfully quiet in there.' She gave the door a single knock and nudged it open. 'Sam?'

'Uhuh?'

She edged around the door, put the glass in his hand, beat a hasty retreat and returned unscathed to the sofa as Janis was saying, 'Wouldn't it be great if he had a job in one place for a while? They need international lawyers here the same as anywhere else don't they? Or maybe something outside the government, in a university or something... he'd make a fabulous lecturer, he's so altogether the chicks would all flock to law school.'

Monica found herself coughing. 'They might at that.'

'We could even get to know each other. What good is it having a super guy like him for a dad when he's away all the time?' Janis suddenly fixed her with an unblinking stare. 'Oh, what the hell!' she exclaimed suddenly, 'What am I talking about? When are you two going to get married, that's what I want to know?'

Monica slowly smoothed the folds of her skirt then managed gently, 'You'd like that, wouldn't you?'

Janis nodded impatiently. 'It's about time, isn't it?'

'I didn't think your age group cared all that much about things like that?'

Janis sat there, erect, very still, regarding Monica with an unblinking stare; it was a solemn moment for her.

'Why is it so important to you?' the older woman prompted softly.

Janis's gaze didn't waver. She replied solemnly, 'Oh, I don't know. It's been so long now, and you've been marvellous... all those years; I was only nine when Daddy met you, Mother had been dead for so long…'

'Five years,' Monica cut in quickly, immediately regretting the outburst.

'…I hardly remembered her, and ever since,' the girl went on, her voice wavering slightly, 'you were always there when it mattered.' There was no embarrassment, rather a sudden relieved smile. 'Sometimes lately I have found myself wondering how you did it considering how busy you always are.'

Suddenly Monica wanted to reassure her, she seemed so vulnerable. Leaning forward, she took her hand in both of hers. 'Some time, I hope soon,' she began gently, 'we fully intend to marry and settle down, in another year or two – does that answer your question?'

The smile was a delight, the youthful spirit fully restored. Impulsively throwing her arms around her friend's neck, Janis kissed her hard on the cheek, then on a sudden thought she broke away, blurting anxiously, 'But why wait two whole years?'

Monica favoured her with one of those adult smiles. 'It will take that long to tie up all the loose ends. Your father might retire a little earlier than usual and I'll give up my job. There's a farm up in New England that would suit us both admirably…'

Blake finished shaving and a few minutes later appeared fully-dressed in the living room. Janis glanced at her watch and breezing past him chirped, 'I'd better get a face on.'

Blake reached out and pulled her to him. 'Haven't you forgotten something?'

'Oh, Daddy…?'

He pushed out a clean-shaven cheek. 'Put it right there.' He reached into a pocket, brought forth a beribboned package and left it in the palm of her hand. Janis eagerly tore it open, lifted out a heavy golden chain together with a medallion made of the same precious metal. Reduced to strangled exclamations, she finally managed to gasp, 'Monica, do come and look.'

He solemnly lifted it out of her hand and clasped it around her neck.

'Daddy, you shouldn't have,' she stood there, unable to decide whether to laugh or cry. In the end she accomplished both.

Monica exclaimed. 'Darling, it's lovely,' and kissed her.

Janis half-sobbed, 'My birthday isn't until November. He's months early.'

She had looked so like her mother at the same age. Blake didn't trust himself to speak, instead he nudged her gently towards her bedroom door. 'Aren't you supposed to be packing?'

When they were alone, Monica observed quietly, 'You've made her very happy. About time, too. What prompted it?'

'Guilt.'

'Why now?' she asked moving close.

'Neglected you both long enough. From now on I'm going to be a good boy.'

She said softly, 'She means a lot to you, doesn't she?'

'So do you.'

'Sam?'

'I'm right here.'

Monica faltered, dropping her eyes.

'Something the matter?'

'Don't hold onto her too hard. She'll be meeting someone one of these days.'

He grinned. 'If she doesn't – and pretty damn soon by the look of her – I'll be surprised.'

Relieved at his reaction, she recaptured her customary sparkle.

For his part, Blake was appraising her hard. 'My, my, don't you look good,' he decided at last.

She laughed brightly, wanting him, remembering the last time she saw him. 'You look pretty good yourself,' she said turning back towards her chair.

It took him three strides to reach her and sweep her into his arms and when he released her he saw that her lipstick wasn't even smudged.

'Wow!' she gasped.

'Ditto.'

'Where did they send you this time?'

'How about one for the road,' he said moving to the drinks tray on a sideboard. 'Usual swing,' he added, popping a couple of large green olives into the glasses. Returning with the drinks he settled beside her on the sofa. 'Budapest, Vienna, that circuit.' He found her hand and squeezed. 'I've taken a house on the Cape for six weeks, think you can manage a week or two? ...plenty of room.'

She pecked his cheek. 'I'd love to, but not until late in August.'

'Coming to see us off at the airport?'

'Can't, I'm up to my eyes.' She reached for her bag and stood up. 'We'll say our goodbyes right here.'

She stuck her head around Janis's door to say goodbye. He thought of delaying the trip for a day or two and started to suggest it.

She read his mind. 'It won't be long, darling, in no time at all you'll be walking my legs off on that lovely beach. Oh, and tell Janis that I won't forget to send my maid over here to keep things tidy until you get back.' She leaned close, put her arms around his neck and kissed him hard. 'Bye for now,' she whispered.

He stood there staring at the door for some time after she had gone.

II

As Blake paid off the taxi in front of Terminal 3 at Heathrow Airport, a bus pulled up behind and started to unload its passengers. Three young men – all in their early twenties – hurried around to where porters were already lifting out the luggage. Long-haired, and all wearing tight and faded jeans, they found their bags and joined the crush moving into the building.

Inside, Janis found an empty Pan-Am check-in counter and Sam struggled up with the luggage and handed the girl their tickets.

'Flight three-one-six to New York,' he wheezed, 'are we in time?'

The hostess weighed their bags, stamped the luggage stubs on their tickets and pointed to an escalator at the end of the hall. Janis grabbed his arm and dragged him off.

Outside the terminal a private car pulled up and three more youngsters – replicas of the first trio – piled out and headed for the door. One was a Japanese. Lightly burdened with holdalls and duffel bags, they hurried inside. Then a taxi drove up and another pair got out. One looked German with a square unshaven face and long yellow hair and the other had contrived to look like Che Guevara. They both slung backpacks over their shoulders and raced inside.

Upstairs, just inside the departure lounge, people were having their passports checked.

The first three young men appeared, followed by other arrivals, then Blake and Janis rushed in.

Janis clapped her hands like a schoolgirl and exclaimed, 'Just think! Six whole weeks to do nothing but get to know each other all over again!' She nestled close and lay her head on his shoulder. 'We seem to keep doing that, don't we?'

There it was again. A simple gesture and memories of things past came flooding back to remind him of so many things he should have done and hadn't. A thoughtful gesture, a kind word to bring joy to a hopeful young heart. By God, it wouldn't happen again, not to the child. Time. Well, if there wasn't any, he'd have to make it. From now on out she would come first. Not the same mistakes all over again. That was past. 'All that's going to stop,' he murmured squeezing her shoulder. 'You'll see – we're going to get to know each other. Every time you turn around, who'll be there – me.'

A young official handed Blake their passports and he took Janis firmly by the arm and crossed over to the end of the line at the Customs counter where hand luggage was being checked. He managed a grin. 'You've got some studying to do, remember?' But nothing could contain her that morning, life was sweet.

One of the young men had all but reached the head of the line, there were only two people in front of him. Easing the shoulder straps of the heavy duffel bag, he turned to catch the eye of his friends who were standing three or four places behind. One was wearing a bright orange T-shirt, the other a black sweatshirt under a shapeless, loose-fitting and shabby raincoat. He stood very still, both hands buried deep in his pockets. The face was delicate, thinly boned and unusually pale. He didn't look well. A young mother with a small child cradled over her shoulder stood just ahead of him, and as she inched forward the child smiled and shook its rattle in his face. He hardly noticed, he had something else on his mind; unlike the others his face was clean-shaven.

Back at the Passport Control, the German and 'Che Guevara' appeared, followed by the Jap and two others. After having their passports checked they split up, gravitating separately towards the four corners of the hall.

At the head of the Customs queue, the first young man stood just behind an angry matron who was having an abrasive exchange with the officer over her hand luggage. He looked anxiously around the hall, oblivious to what was happening in front of him. Further back his friends were so preoccupied they failed to notice a large fat man who waddled up and pushed ahead of them in the line.

Blake was insisting, 'Remember, the first three days all I do is sleep. There's plenty for you to do without me tagging along... lots of unattached young men, too.'

Eyes sparkling, Janis laughed, 'I'm quite satisfied with the one I've already got, thank you.'

The young German stood in one of the corners nervously fingering the strings on his duffle bag. In another corner the Jap dropped his pack on the floor and squatted on it. 'Che Guevara' lounged beside the corridor leading into the loading bay. None had gone through Customs to have their hand luggage checked.

At the head of the queue the angry matron flounced off and the Customs Officer motioned the first young man to open his duffel bag.

The young man seemed unable to respond.

'Open up, please.'

There was a sudden, frenzied cry. The officer's jaw fell, he found himself staring into the muzzle of a machine pistol. The burst caught him in the centre of the chest.

Then everything happened at once: a shrill scream, a welter of cries, stuttering machine pistols, stampeding feet. People were running, colliding blindly with others, tripping, falling, being trampled on in their mindless will to live, to escape.

Blake grabbed Janis, flung her over the counter, dived over behind her. She gaped at him, her lovely face twisted with bewilderment, then she saw the gun in his hand. She made a move to get to her feet and the man she didn't really know pushed her roughly back to the floor. 'Keep your head down,' he rasped, 'and stay there!'

The youngster in the orange T-shirt was clutching a grenade in each hand. He coolly lifted one to his mouth, yanked out the pin with his teeth and flung it at a crowd of people that had piled up at one of the exits. Then he calmly tossed the second one at a group of screaming women who were pushing to get out behind an entrance screen in the mistaken belief that mere plywood offered some kind of shelter.

His friend in the shabby raincoat was firing measured bursts at point-blank range into a densely packed crowd at the moment the first grenade, closely followed by the second, exploded hurling bodies and parts of bodies into the air.

The German raced along the floor firing rapid bursts into the windows and large pieces of glass began to fall to the floor, showering hundreds of sharp splinters into the bodies of the stricken crowd.

Blake dived on top of Janis as a pattern of bullets ripped through the thin wood of the counter just above their heads. Another grenade exploded covering them in a thick cloud of gritty dust and an object landed just in front of their faces. Janis began to scream. It was a baby's arm, severed at the shoulder, its tiny hand still clutching its rattle. Janis thrashed out wildly in an effort to free herself, but nothing could shift her father's smothering weight. He held on, pinning her firmly to the floor.

People were running in all directions, some like phantoms through clouds of thick dust. The dead and dying littered a blood-soaked floor pitted by grenade fragments. Bright orange tracer streams crisscrossed the wide ruin of the hall. More grenades exploded adding to the hell of falling plaster.

Che Guevara was soberly pumping rapid bursts into anything that moved. He walked like someone strolling in the park on a quiet Sunday afternoon, his bullets all but cutting a wailing woman in half. A couple lurched into his line of fire, but his gun jammed and in a moment he was crushed beneath a pile of thrashing bodies intent on tearing him to pieces.

Another killer moved along the counter emptying an entire clip into some people sheltering in one of the corners. Blake materialised behind him. He only fired once, the bullet catching the killer in the back of the neck just under the base of the skull.

A woman sat on the floor staring with bewildered disbelief at one of her wrists: the hand was missing and a stream of blood spurted from the severed artery with each beat of her heart.

There was the distant sound of sirens and outside the heavy traffic had come to a standstill.

A man ran into a burst of machine-gun fire and his face disintegrated.

Someone collapsed on the body of a dying child.

Behind the counter Blake dragged Janis towards a side door leading into another room. He looked up to find himself staring into the enquiring eyes of a killer. Blake launched himself into a headlong dive and the next moment he had him on the floor. He sat on his belly, rammed the barrel of his gun into his mouth and fired. The head seemed to expand and the eyeballs popped out of their sockets and slid slowly down the little that remained of the face. Janis's screams were continuous now.

A section of the ceiling fell in, crushing some of the injured who were unable to get out of the way. Blake emerged from the dust and saw one of the killers firing into a group of people cowering along a wall. He fired and the force of his bullet whirled the man around, his finger still glued to the trigger of the stuttering gun. Already dead, the body wavered. Then Janis jumped up and dashed straight into the path of the dead man's bullets. The burst stitched a line of burning holes across her chest, the fiery tracer setting her coat on fire. Blake could not move. Unable to register what he had just seen, he just stood there. Then somehow he found the strength to go to her. He squatted beside her and gazed into her face. He heard an anguished cry and discovered that it had come from his own throat. Janis was dead. He leaped to his feet and reeled out into the hall.

The first detachment of police rushed in, split up and raced off in an effort to sort out the killers from their victims. When he saw them, one of the killers calmly dropped his gun and lifted his hands above his head. It was the Jap.

All around the hall bodies were sprawled, some in grotesque positions like discarded department store dummies, many denuded of clothing, some still alive and attempting to crawl. The room was littered with broken glass, chunks of cement and fragments of splintered furniture. There were fires burning and firemen arriving to hose them out. Soon the floor was submerged under an inch of water in some parts of the hall.

More police rushed in, some armed with machine-guns, and raced towards one of the killers who was struggling with three men and a shrieking woman. As he fell she pulled off a shoe and started to pound his face with the heel. She continued to hit him, her screams lapsing into a spasmodic stream of dull croaks. When the police finally reached them little remained of the killer but a shapeless bundle of blackened flesh.

Some policemen were dragging the German towards one of the exits and were fighting to hold back a crowd. One of the passengers, his clothing reduced to blood-soaked rags, darted in and embedded his teeth into the German's neck. The police tried to beat him off with the butts of their guns but he held on like a maddened dog. More screeching passengers arrived and soon there were too many for the police to control. Forming a tight cordon around the German, they managed to get him out of the hall.

Now the sound of the sirens was dwarfing all the other sounds and yet more police poured into the hall, followed by ambulance crews and more firemen.

A stricken mother sat cross-legged on the floor, clutching a tiny body in her arms. Her lips moved, her head bobbed up and down, she gazed glassy-eyed at the blood-soaked little bundle. Blake sprinted past and pulled up and then he saw the killer in the raincoat who was standing just behind her. He didn't see Blake because the fat man had lumbered past on the other side, heading for a group of policemen. The killer fired a burst and as the bullets hit him the fat man opened up like a tight-skinned sausage. A horrified bystander tried to scream but her vocal cords refused to respond.

Blake took off, firing on the run. The force of his bullets hurled the killer in the raincoat against a wall and he slid slowly to the floor. People gathered around and an ambulance man unbuttoned the coat and the shirt to tend the wound, revealing the firm breasts of a young woman. He gasped, 'Christ, it's a girl.'

'So what?' somebody snarled. 'They all look alike nowadays and that one's a bloody murderer!'

The ambulance man stood up and shook his head. 'It doesn't matter now – she's dead.'

Despite the police, who were arriving in great numbers now, and more firemen and ambulance crews, there were still some killers holding out in various parts of the hall.

Blake sprinted in short spurts, working his way back towards the Customs counter, hunting the killer in the orange T-shirt. He spotted him the moment the youth bit the ring out of his last grenade. Blake fired. When the bullet hit him, the grenade rolled out of the killer's hand and the resulting explosion lifted him high off the floor. He seemed to hang there, suspended in mid-air, and a shoe containing one of his feet went scudding along the floor.

Blake had become a killing machine. He darted off to find the one who had started it all back in the remote millennium when Janis had been a living entity and the joy of youth had throbbed in her trusting soul.

He leaped over bodies, hurdled shattered furniture, dodged through flames, and when he spotted him the other saw him at the same time and turned to fire. Blake stumbled as the bullets ripped into his legs, but nothing could stop him now. There was something in the way, an obstacle of some sort. Blake launched himself into the air and the man screamed at the impact of the collision which carried them crashing to the floor.

Blake brought the butt of his gun down hard on his skull and he continued to pound him long after he lay still.

III

Throughout the hall the ambulance crews scurried back and forth with stretchers, administered blood-plasma, retrieved bits of bodies and in one or more instance performed emergency operations, removing the victims to the hospitals or the morgues, a traffic which continued until well after mid-afternoon.

A young priest, pale and trembling, administered the last Rites over one of the dying and those still able to walk wandered around in a stupor until the ambulance men came to take them away. Others simply sat or sprawled, numbed by what they had seen. They gazed vacantly as their rescuers arrived, few raised their voices and when one did it only emphasised the bleak silence that had settled over the place.

There was hardly a space throughout the room that wasn't damaged and even the hard quartz of the floor was pitted by grenade fragments or armour-piercing bullets. Light fixtures dangled dangerously from what remained of the ceiling and not a plate of glass was intact. Nobody knew the full extent of the wreckage or had as yet counted the cost in human lives. That would come later when some government department which calculated such figures released them to the press.

No one knew how many terrorists had been involved or indeed had escaped, if any; but the place looked as if they could have numbered into the hundreds. No one knew who they were or where they had come from, or why they had done it, or for what cause. They might have come from anywhere, killed and maimed for just about anything, there were so many causes in the world and so many people who were willing to kill for them. They might have been IRA or Protestant extremists from Northern Ireland, Arabs from one of many terrorist groups in the Middle East, urban terrorists from the Baader-Meinhof gang, Italian revolutionaries of the Red Brigade, 'freedom' fighters from South America, Red Army fanatics from Japan – no one knew. How many really cared? To many it was just another news item in an age where the horrific was reduced to the ordinary. People had become accustomed to disaster and catastrophe, it happened so often. Only when it occurred on one's doorstep did people respond, but even then it was soon forgotten.

But someone cared, someone called Sam Blake. He was an old-fashioned man. He believed in revenge.

IV

Blake wrinkled his nose with distaste. The institutional smell was unmistakable; the mixture of surgical spirit and disinfectant would have certainly told him, had he been blind, that he was in a hospital.

There was a large window at the end of the room facing out on a grassy courtyard full of leafless trees and hedges dripping with a steady rain that had been beating down since early morning.

A heavy trolley rolled noisily down the corridor outside and he caught another unmistakable odour of hospital food. He didn't know whether it was breakfast or lunch, and didn't care. He lay there counting the little squares and circles in the ceiling. Left to right, there were a hundred and thirty-three; up and down, seventy-eight. Allowing his gaze to drift down to the foot of the bed, he saw that his legs were caged in a little tent to prevent his injured parts from coming into contact with the bedclothes.

There were no other beds in the room and some time in the morning he had wakened to the clipped cadences of the nursing sister; undeniably British and authoritarian. He wondered how long he had been there.

'Good morning, Mr Blake. How are we this morning? Do you think we might have a bite to eat… we must be famished.'

The voice and the face were lustfully horsey, the complexion unblemished and in no need of cosmetics. The eyes, the best feature, fringed with raven-black lashes, were arched over with delicately-curved brows. The head covered with a frilled starch cap of a kind only seen in British hospitals, was leaning over the side of the bed.

'No thanks, I'm not hungry.'

'But we simply *must* eat!'

'Later.'

She reminded him of someone from long ago, then he remembered: his eldest sister Agnes. This brought forth a new train of thought, something he hadn't had in years. It all came back, crystal clear, so much so that he could picture down to the smallest detail what the farm had looked like. He could see his father, driving in from his rounds in the old Chevvy, red-eyed from delivering an infant or sewing up some farmer's leg. The long hot North Dakota summers, the winter winds whistling down from the Canadian prairies, the temperatures sometimes as low as thirty degrees below zero. The one-roomed country school full of kids with Swedish and Russian names hugging up to the big pot-bellied stove, eating fresh-made bread soaked in molasses and struggling home through snow-drifts up to their waists, their faces wrapped up with heavy woollen scarves to keep out the icy winds.

And he remembered Agnes, standing on the platform at the railroad depot in Wilton the day she went off to Fargo to study nursing. Long ago. He wondered, was she still alive?

Then there had been Ernest, the eldest of three brothers, drowning in the old swimming hole on the Knife River. All the kids, uncomfortable in their stiff collars and ties, and the relatives who had driven in from places as far afield as Minneapolis for the funeral. Everyone talking in subdued whispers over the casket in the living room. Ernest had looked like a cupi-doll lying there, his cheeks two red blobs of rouge, his mouth an uneven grimace, caked with lipstick. The art of make-up hadn't yet reached the rural undertaking parlours of North Dakota in the depression years of the late Thirties.

Blake, the baby of the clan, pampered by hard-working parents and his elder sisters, particularly recalled the wooden high-chair where he had taken his meals beside the long kitchen table. The odour of freshly-baked bread, his mother, rattling away in undecipherable Russian with local farmwives, his father coming home and leaving at all hours with his little black General Practitioner's bag.

And later, when he was older, going out to pick blueberries in the swamps around Sakakawea Lake and fishing for perch with his father or elder brothers, Tom and Harry, on Long Lake and stripping bark off the birch trees to make toy Indian canoes: Tom, who had been killed on Omaha Beach in Normandy: Harry, a smiling face rashed with freckles, the only one to follow their father in the medical profession, now practising somewhere in Nebraska. It was all so long ago.

He thought of Ida Peterson who had initiated him in the breathless mysteries of sex. Not a pretty face but an inquiring one, bright eyes lit with curiosity and stick-thin legs spread so invitingly in somebody's hayloft or on the hard floor of the cloakroom at the high school when everyone else had gone home. Long winter nights, frozen fingers and Ida, even in the back seat of Tom's ancient Ford.

Then the University of Nebraska, a degree in foreign languages, a brief spell in Korea, the graduate school at Georgetown and finally the Agency. So many young smiling faces, pledges of undying love or eternal friendship, faded now to the greyness of distant remembrance. But *not* Prinny. She had been there, hovering around in his head for some days now, a face difficult to recall but surfacing with alarming clarity, waking him suddenly from a sedated sleep and bringing back the agonising pain of Janis. Prinny, long gone these past fifteen years, once a girl so like the one so irretrievably lost. He had seen little of them in those early days because the Agency had always come first. How much time did they really have together? It probably added up to less than a year, but then people working in the field in his day would have thought themselves fortunate to get that – less than a year.

Blake lay there desperately reminding himself that there had been love, enduring trust, comforting tenderness, abiding mutual respect, certainly all that and much more, but the sound of her voice, the gentle contours of her face, had been lost beyond recall until the nightmares of recent days.

Blake remembered that he had been in the field (in Prague) when they had finally managed to make contact. A routine visit to a letter-drop and there it was, the usual jumble of meaningless letters. Later in the back of his contact's farm truck he had deciphered it with the aid of an old Zippo lighter and a borrowed pencil to read: *'Wife died 3rd of September. Brain haemorrhage. Child being looked after. Fly home from nearest Air Force base. Control.'* Impersonal Agency verbiage that had driven a spoke through his brain, then limbo. Back in Washington, a visit to a grave bedecked with wilted flowers and weathered cards from people half of whom he didn't know and a small child farmed out by the Agency to one of its safe houses and the ministering hands of a succession of State Registered Nurses. Prinny? An unusual name. He had forgotten how to spell it.

They were all around him, not to be shaken, beloved faces past and recent, so young, so still. It wasn't possible. She wasn't dead, too – *not Janis?*

'Now then, Mr Blake, good morning. We must sit up, mustn't we, and greet our company. There, let me fluff up your pillows… Mr Blake?'

He must think, clear his head; he'd do that all right. But the air terminal? Not a dream. Janis was dead. They killed her. Christ almighty! They'd pay, pay with their blood as she had done... Oh, God.

'Mr Blake... our visitor is waiting.'

It was true – his Janis, like Prinny before her, was dead. *They would pay.*

'Mr Blake! Really, we must sit up.'

'What?'

'We have a visitor.'

'Go away.'

'Hello, Sam.'

It took a moment to register Monica's anxious face at the side of the bed. She attempted a smile. 'Hi.'

'I've talked to the doctor, he says you'll be out of here at the end of the week.'

He watched her forcing herself to appear casual, struggling with the things she had to say which she instinctively feared he didn't want to hear. He didn't feel disposed to help her. 'That's good,' he yawned.

'Sam?'

'Yeah?' Glancing at the table, he saw the load of things she had brought him. Books he hadn't any inclination to read and other things in ribboned Fortnum & Mason boxes. There was even a vase of flowers and a bowl of fruit. He felt oddly unappreciative.

Monica leaned forward and gently brushed her lips on his cheek. 'About the funeral...' she began hesitantly.

'You take care of it,' he said, quickly breaking in, 'you'll do it fine.'

'But—?'

Blake laughed. 'You should see my nurse, she's something out of *Alice in Wonderland*. We have Mad Hatter's tea parties with toy cups and saucers every afternoon promptly at three... she looks like Sea Biscuit the year he won the Kentucky Derby.'

'Sam, please!'

'Say, you look great. How well do I know you? Say pretty-please and you can join us for tea.'

Monica struggled to keep back the tears. Forcing herself to keep her voice steady, she said, 'It's all arranged, Sam. Just like you asked.'

'Good... you bring the muffins.'

'Oh, Sam!'

Blake broke the heavy silence that had settled over them by asking lightly, 'Did you come alone?'

'Jim Roker drove me down. He's waiting to see you.'

'Business or otherwise?'

'He didn't say, but he is a friend. You should see him.' Blake smiled. 'Why don't you ask him to come in and come back yourself in the morning... alone this time.'

V

Driving back to London, neither Jim Roker nor Monica felt much like talking. Somewhere along the way they pulled up at a service station. They saw an attractive pub next door and Roker suggested a drink and a bite of lunch. They found an empty table in a secluded corner and he ordered food and something to drink.

Jim Roker, a pleasant-faced man in his early forties and sturdily built, was a dependable type with a mild disposition and a capacity for hard work. Not one to set the world on fire, people said, but his untiring diligence and attention to detail kept the wheels turning in a department that was in sore need of such virtues and had of late found them increasingly more difficult to acquire. Contrary to popular belief, a major function of counter-intelligence work was the exhaustive cross-checking file system which required an orderly mind, endless patience and the facility to note the most trivial details relating to any subject under investigation. Roker possessed all these qualities and, in addition, was also considered a first-rate field agent. Monica had known him for some years as one of Blake's close colleagues and had grown very fond of him. It reassured her at that moment. She felt herself singularly blessed to have that rare thing – a truly platonic relationship with a man she suspected she had taken for granted too often. But he was like that, apt to fade into the background when he wasn't needed. Pretending a lightness she didn't feel, she began, 'Was it difficult?'

'Uncomfortable,' Roker replied warily. 'He never stopped talking, telling me all about his life in North Dakota when he was a kid.' He shook himself. 'Some of it was very funny.'

'Funny?'

'Amusing.' He turned to her, his honest face creased with concern. 'I've known Blake for over fifteen years and that's the first time he ever really talked about himself. Intimate things, about his family, friends and the place he grew up in. Amazing the way he remembers names and describes people. I'd have never guessed the kind of life he had. I always suspected he'd come from a big city and went to one of those Ivy League schools out East.'

Monica had some questions of her own. She asked simply, 'Did he say anything about Janis?'

Roker shook his head. 'Not a word.'

'About that ghastly business at the airport?'

Roker sighed. 'Not a word about that either.'

'About me?'

Roker reached over and took her glass. When he returned with the refills, he frowned. 'He didn't talk about anything that happened later than his senior year at college… it was weird.'

Monica put a worried hand on his arm. 'He's not like himself at all.'

'Well, it's not surprising when you think what he's just been through.'

'I don't mean that. It was something else.'

Roker looked around, but no one was paying any attention to them. The room had suddenly filled and the hum of chatter was so loud she had to lean close to be heard.

'What?' Roker lamely asked.

'I don't know,' Monica said, 'I simply don't know. It was like everything that happened to him and Janis at that airport happened to someone else.'

'What are you trying to say?'

'I don't know, but I do know Sam, or thought I did until today… he was like a stranger.'

Roker looked down at his arm and winced at the pressure of her sharp fingernails through the thickness of his heavy coat. He might have told her that in his world legends were made and Blake might well end up being one of them. Blake wasn't even his real name, that, like those of all Agency personnel, was a mere statistic in Centre's Very Top Secret file back in Washington.

When a man joined the Agency it was like a novice monk entering a religious order, he took vows of silence and obedience and the parting from his previous world was permanent once he took his final vows.

'I'm afraid of what he'll do, Jim,' Monica was saying thoughtfully.

Not for the first time Roker found himself wondering why Blake hadn't married her. She seemed so right for him and it had been obvious enough over the years how she felt about him. Roker had been tempted on occasion to ask but never did. Despite the fact that they all knew each other so well, Roker never crossed the line. People in their profession rarely did. It simply wasn't done. The less one knew of his colleagues' personal affairs the better. Even two people as close as Monica and Blake.

There were some things, particularly those touching on Agency matters, that were never discussed, not even mentioned for obvious security reasons, even among close colleagues unless they were working together on the same project, so Roker was reluctant to discuss anything that might involve the Agency, even with someone so intimately connected with Blake. He stood up, remarking lightly, 'I think it's time for another refill, don't you?'

Monica wasn't having it. She snapped impatiently, 'Look, Jim, don't you think it's about time we stopped beating about the bush? This is trouble. Please sit down and hear me out.'

'Here, in front of all these people?'

'Why not? They're all too busy talking to listen to us.'

With some show of resistance, he capitulated and dropped back into his chair.

Monica spoke rapidly, crisply stating what they both feared were Blake's true intentions. 'You're Agency, so am I on occasion,' she began. 'We both know Sam. The moment he's out of that hospital all hell's going to break loose. Shall I spell it out?'

Roker had another worried glance around the room. 'Can't it wait until we're back in the car?'

Monica sped on. 'Once he's back on his feet, once the shock wears off and his mind is clear – he'll be out for blood! Anyone even remotely connected with Janis's death – he'll run them to ground, and he won't let up until he has killed them all. God

Almighty, can you imagine what's going through his mind? And if the Agency tries to intervene, he'd go on the run, and they'll have one hell of a time finding him. Right or wrong?'

Roker knew it was no use, nothing he could say could stop her. He nodded, 'Right.'

'He'll use every trick in the trade and he's picked up a few in the years he's been with the Agency. Imagine the people he knows, tell me a part of the world where he doesn't have contacts? He'll use them all, practically every intelligence outfit worthy of the name – on both sides of the fence – diplomats, field agents, government brass, big business connections, hoodlums, fixers, even the Russians. You corner him, he's capable of anything. Blackmail, murder, torture; he'll lie, steal, cheat, even kill to reach those people.'

'The point being,' Roker interposed, now thoroughly committed to her line of thought, 'when will he begin, and where?'

'Once he can think straight he'll start getting it together.'

Roker didn't agree. 'He's already well into that. He'll be patient, you'd be surprised how patient. He'll take his time, he'll be methodical, every aspect of the problem will be studied from every conceivable angle, and when he's ready he'll move.' Roker drained his glass. 'One can almost feel sorry for them. Of all the fathers in the world they had to pick on him.'

'How much time have we got?'

'For what?'

'We've got to stop him.'

We can try, Roker thought doubtfully, *but short of killing him I don't think he can be stopped.*

'If he quits the Agency, they'll demand the routine debriefing and with his seniority, that could take months.'

'Not a chance. He'll run before he'll wear that.'

'That's why we've got to talk to him.'

'And if he runs, Centre won't hesitate – he's dead.'

'They wouldn't go that far?'

'Oh wouldn't they? Take my word for it, they will.'

Monica burst out despairingly, 'We've got to stop him!'

'Once they get wind of it they'll go to any lengths to stop him because if it ever comes out that he's one of their senior people nobody will ever believe that he wasn't acting under their instructions. Think what a meal the press will make of that when it leaks out!'

Reduced to grasping at straws, Monica pleaded, 'We might, just might be wrong.'

Roker's logical mind brought neither of them any comfort. 'No,' he concluded earnestly, 'Blake will do what he has to do and if Centre decides that the Agency's interests are threatened by his actions, they'll kill him… it's as simple as that, I'm afraid.'

CHAPTER TWO

I

RENWAY STOOD AT THE EMBASSY WINDOW SCRATCHING A closely-cropped head and looking down on the traffic moving around Grosvenor Square. The dismal sky seemed to press down on the glistening, dripping branches of the trees accentuating the dreariness of the London weather. Here it was, already the middle of August, and there hadn't been more than a dozen hot sunny days throughout the entire summer. Renway as usual was showing the strain. Although subterfuge was his business, by inclination and training he was a military man and he found it difficult to mask his feelings. Like many of his colleagues who were given cover jobs in some government department, he was assigned to the agricultural division in the Commercial Attaché's office and was granted diplomatic status as a second secretary. Jim Roker, his present visitor, had a similar cover job (third secretary) in the same department although both men were active members of the African Intelligence Agency. Renway turned to Roker who was sitting on the other side of the desk leafing through a heavy file. He asked, 'When was he discharged?'

'This morning,' Roker said.

Renway returned to his desk and sat down. 'Fit for duty?' Roker hesitated. 'Not quite... he was shot up pretty bad.' He added as an afterthought, 'But the medics gave him a clean bill.'

'No problem then.' Renway motioned for the file and Roker handed it to him. He studied it for a moment then looked up. 'When's he reporting in?'

'He didn't say.' Roker handed him an envelope. 'He asked me to give you this.'

Renway opened it and rapidly scanned its contents. Roker watched him attentively speculating on his reaction but there wasn't any. Instead Renway got up and moved to the large map of Europe that all but covered the wall behind his desk, giving no outward sign of his feelings.

'When did you get it?' he asked at last, his attention focused on the many multi-coloured pins which were placed in some profusion around the large expanse.

'This morning, in the mail,' Roker said, looking down at his hands. He wasn't in a communicative mood. Further, he had a hunch about this interview. For him it boded no good.

'Did he tell you he wanted to resign?'

'No.'

Renway fidgeted with some papers, remarking with aggravation, 'Well, that's what he's thinking of doing – he says he'll let me know in the next few days what he decides.' Roker didn't reply.

'When did you see him last?'

'Four days ago.'

'What did you talk about?'

Roker shrugged. 'Nothing important.'

'Did he mention that airport thing?'

'No.'

'…his daughter?'

'We didn't discuss any personal matters,' Roker said tightly, shaking his head.

'Then what *did* you talk about?'

'He said he was tired and wanted a long rest.'

Renway gave that some thought, then asked, 'Any sign of his cracking up?'

'I don't think so. It was a shattering experience but he'll get over it. It might take some time – she meant a lot to him.'

Renway wasn't convinced. 'We've got to be sure.' He returned to his chair, deep in thought. Then making up his mind, he said, 'Try to see him again today, if you can, and talk him out of it. Why quit now when he's so high on the list? It doesn't make sense. He could end up running Centre.'

Renway had an annoying habit of tapping his fingernails on the glass top of his desk, it made it hard to concentrate. 'Let's consider the alternatives,' he suggested, tapping away.

'I could if you'd stop that damned drumming,' Roker broke in irritably.

Renway stopped tapping.

'Well, to begin with, Centre will never wear it,' Roker said carefully.

Renway favoured him with one of his snide little chuckles. 'Then what are we talking about?' He loved to nail an ambiguity.

'Simply that I don't think that Blake cares whether it does or not,' Roker shrugged.

'And the other side?'

Roker agreed. 'Yes, he's too senior to let loose.'

Renway rummaged around in his top drawer until he found what he was looking for, one of those mint pills people take who suffer from indigestion. The drawer was full of every conceivable brand. 'Far too senior,' he said, sucking on the pill.

'…and vulnerable.'

'That too.'

'And that's dangerous for everyone concerned.' Roker continued. 'What do we do about all that Top Secret material he carries around in his head? He knows as well as we do that he wouldn't last a week outside on his own. On the other hand I don't know… if it was anyone but Blake…?'

Renway cut in dryly, 'Of course he's quite within his rights if he goes ahead with it, we can't stop him.' He pursed the thinnest pair of lips in the Agency, '…officially, that is.'

Roker looked up with surprise.

'You with me, Jim?'

'Not all the way, no.'

'He can leave any time he pleases so long as he's willing to submit to the debriefing procedure. After all, why should he be exempt?'

Roker shook his head. 'Not a chance, at least not at the moment. It would take too long.'

'What, six months? Then he's free of it… it's the ideal solution if he insists on leaving.'

Roker looked doubtful. 'I can tell you now – I don't think he'll wear it.'

'Why not?'

'I don't think he has the time.'

Renway shot off his chair. 'Time for what? What did he say to you?'

Roker stubbornly held his ground. 'He didn't say anything, not in so many words – it was just an impression I got.'

Renway stood there eyeing him suspiciously. 'Are you sure you've told me everything? By God, Roker, if you're holding something back you're going to be in trouble.'

Roker bluntly rasped it out. 'I'm not holding anything back! And I can tell you this, if you force him in his present condition to submit to a prolonged debriefing, he's liable to do anything, even leak it to the press. How would the Agency look if some congressman got wind of it? Right now he's a hero – taking on a gang of terrorists almost single-handed, seeing his daughter murdered. Suppose Centre gets involved in one of those public TV exposures, they'd run a mile. And this brings up another problem – what happens about his status? Don't forget, he's field and you're only admin; he outranks you and everyone else in Europe. Centre has given him a roving brief, you can't touch him. He knows too many people in the top echelon, has lots of muscle in the most sensitive areas. A lot of people owe him favours, you'd never make it stick, but then how can you? Over here he's top dog, Control... your hands are tied.'

'I suppose so,' Renway reflected with some bitterness. 'But what the hell does he think he's playing at? Some of the things he's been up to lately, like that caper in Hungary. What the hell did he think he was doing? Was that a job for Control...?' Renway suddenly realised he was shouting, stood there, his mouth open, staring at Roker. When he continued his voice had regained its customary rasping tone like a defective saw cutting through ground glass, '...when there were at least six field hands in that sector capable of doing that job? It doesn't make sense!'

Roker shook his head. 'On the contrary, he was keeping his hand in. It doesn't pay to get rusty in the field, even when you're Control.' He didn't add that Renway wouldn't know much about that because he had never been anything but administration. The Agency was no different than any other government department in that respect: there was little love lost between the two branches of the service.

Renway impatiently brushed the comment aside like someone swatting a particularly bothersome fly. 'All right. Why not extended leave then, five or six months on medical grounds? After that he might see things differently.'

Roker let it drop gently. 'You haven't told me everything, have you?'

Even an old hand like Renway was caught off guard. He sat there, fiddling with his short stubby fingers.

'Centre ordered you to deal with it, is that it?'

'Yes.'

'Nothing in writing, of course?'

'Is there ever on a thing like this?'

'If anything goes wrong, you carry the can?'

'That's about it.'

'But they're only speculating? Nobody knows what's on Blake's mind but himself. All anybody knows right now is that he's thinking of resigning. What he does after that is anyone's guess.'

Renway held up a restraining hand. 'You know as well as I do, Roker, that half this business is digging through files and the other half is speculation. Contingency, remember? We've got to be prepared to deal with whichever way the cat jumps. The way it's shaping, we've got three problems here. One – if he resigns, Centre will insist on debriefing. Two – if he runs before that happens and the other side get their mitts on him, they could blow our entire European operation… it doesn't bear thinking about.'

'And three?' Roker asked sitting up.

'Speculation again. If what you say is true why *doesn't* he have the time to be debriefed? What's he up to? What would nine out of ten of us do if we had his track record and we saw one of our kids gunned down by a gang of butchers? Come on, Roker, if you were Blake what would you do?'

'I'd squash everyone I could get my hands on.'

'Agency or no Agency?'

'That's right.'

'Which brings us right back to where we began half an hour ago. We can't let that happen. If he quits, he's got to be debriefed.

39

It's as simple as that.' With that Renway started on another impulsive hike around the room.

'Forcibly?'

'If that's the only way we can do it, yes.'

'Here or in the States?'

Renway looked strained. 'There, of course.'

Roker sat there, convinced that in his present state of mind Blake would never agree to it. It was also possible that he wouldn't be capable. Debriefing was an exhausting process, particularly when the interrogators were dealing with a senior operative. It required one hundred per cent cooperation and a mind utterly free of personal problems to get through it. It was like writing one's memoirs, leaving out nothing, not even seemingly trivial details. With a man of Blake's seniority it would require what amounted to total recall regarding everyone he had met and worked with in an official capacity, including personnel on both sides engaged in espionage and counter-espionage for the entire period of his active service. Nothing less would suffice and every operative he had had personal dealings with who was still active on the Agency's books would have to be recalled and transferred to other duties in the event that he (in this case Blake) defected to the other side. The very nature of counter-espionage was a continuous process of horse-trading with the enemy; by definition an effective counter-espionage agent was a double-agent otherwise he didn't get results. To be creditable his information had to be reliable. If he was dealing with military secrets it often transpired that he had to give away valuable information which his superiors either knew the enemy already possessed or would be obsolete before it could be used operationally. During a final debriefing all dealings of this sort had to be reported in detail although full transcripts had been filed at Centre prior to the exchanges which could have taken place years earlier. It was a never-ending process of duplication, aside from the obvious danger of a defector betraying valuable operatives still in the field, in the event he escaped debriefing before his defection and there wasn't time to remove them to safety. This was why the debriefing process took so long.

Roker waited attentively, watching him. 'That's final then?'

'Yes.'

'And if he refuses to cooperate?'

'Then he goes on ice until he does,' Renway said flatly. 'Centre prefers to call it "protective custody".'

'He's the best we ever had. Nobody I ever knew could run agents like him, or for that matter mainline operations with backups that went wrong. If we're not careful we'll lose him for good.'

Renway had gravitated to the window as if it was a sort of refuge. 'It's up to you to see that we don't. He'd better listen to you.' It sounded more like a plea than a threat. 'He never does anything on the spur of the moment, it all has to be thought out first, and that should give us time. If you think he needs a little rope, give it to him. Hell come around in the end.'

Roker climbed to his feet. Everything that had needed saying had been said. 'I'll do what I can,' he sighed.

Renway stiffened. 'Who are the minders? There better be somebody.'

'Same two we assigned when he went into the hospital.' Sensitive to the unseasonal weather, Roker climbed into a topcoat. 'One thing we didn't mention. Even someone with Blake's record could defect. We're all human and by that definition security risks.'

Renway's smile was strained. 'That's why I want legmen on him until we know otherwise, understood?'

At the door Roker suddenly remembered. 'He's talking about buying a small farm up in New Hampshire somewhere and settling down for good.'

'When?'

'He didn't say.'

Renway waved him away. 'After he's debriefed he can settle wherever he wants – in an igloo in the Arctic for all I care.' Roker turned to leave.

'One last thing, Jim. Centre would rather he served out his full time, he's a valuable man to lose… be careful.'

II

The hearse turned slowly through the gates and moved down a narrow road flanked on either side by long rows of gravestones. It finally eased to a stop beside a freshly-dug grave that was roofed over with a canvas tarpaulin to keep out the steady drizzle. There were two gravediggers in rubber boots leaning placidly on their shovels, standing by to finish the job once the brief burial service was read and the funeral party had departed. They removed their caps and waited with a propriety born of long practice as the mortician and the four pallbearers moved around to the back of the hearse to shoulder the flower-bedecked coffin.

At that moment another car, hired for the occasion, arrived and Jim Roker, Sam Blake and Monica Riley stepped out. A young clergyman appeared and together they took their places behind the small procession. It moved slowly, the pallbearers stepping gingerly over the sodden ground. The leaden sky, the steady drizzle, the absence of relatives and family friends was somehow appropriate to the occasion, accentuating the inconsolable finality of it all, the premature end of a young life so full of promise and shortened so wantonly being buried among strangers in a foreign land so far removed from everything that in life it held so familiar.

For Blake, the solitary loved one left behind, the day, the place and the event fittingly symbolised the unbearable emptiness of his soul. He stood like a sleepwalker throughout the ancient ritual, deaf to the age-old words enunciated with such finality as the coffin sank slowly into the earth. And only then, at the sight of his dead hopes sinking so inexorably away from him, did he wake to the excruciating agony of it all, unleashing the full flood of his despair. This sudden release stirred other things, memories of that fatal day, the screams of the dying, an infant's chubby little hand clutching a blood-spattered rattle, and the moment that would remain with him to the end of his days, when the bullets had ripped into his daughter's chest and set her clothing on fire and that final glimpse of the life leaving her face. Blake broke down and wept.

There were two others present at the funeral, standing at a

discreet distance from the small group gathered around the grave. They were young men soberly mindful of the occasion but nonetheless aware of the reason for their presence. Hats in hand, they stood there, their eyes never still, missing nothing. They both saw the car parked out on the highway at the same time and shared a knowing glance. 'Right on time,' one said softly.

'Just letting us know they're there,' the other whispered.

And Blake saw them. Even in the depths of his heartbreak reflexes forged in the relentless school of his trade functioned unimpaired. It didn't occur to him to question the ethics of an act that denied him even the elementary right of privacy at a time like this. On the contrary, had they not been there this might have occasioned some alarm, but as it was, it was simply routine.

The gravediggers were shovelling large lumps of damp clay down into the grave as he reeled back and Monica took a firm hold on his arm, gently helping him out to the road. When they reached the car she opened the door and helped Blake into the back seat. Roker climbed in the front beside the driver.

As they drove off, Blake never once looked back.

III

Roker went with him down to Southampton because he had decided to make the crossing by boat. Roker had come straight to the point. 'You've made up your mind then?' he stated bluntly.

'That's right.'

Roker glanced into the rear-view mirror. 'We're leading quite a parade.'

Blake looked bored. 'How do they manage to keep from tripping over each other's feet?'

'I guess you really do mean it,' Roker said returning to the point.

'I mean it all right.'

'Nothing will change your mind?'

Blake looked at him. 'You never were one to take no for an answer.'

'What about Renway?'

'He's out of his depth. This is field, he's an administrator, he should stick to what he knows.'

Roker kept his eyes on the road. Like Blake he had no interest in the ridiculous procession that was following behind. 'He's under orders from Centre, Sam,' he suggested evenly.

Blake's laugh was bitter. 'I should have thought that Centre had better judgement in these matters.'

'I don't believe you, you know… about any of this.'

'I know you don't.'

'Even you can't buck the system, ours or theirs. You won't last long out there on your own.'

'Watch me.'

Roker persisted. 'One way or the other one of them will get what they want out of you in the end.'

All of a sudden, Blake looked tired. 'Like bidders at an auction,' he said.

'You said it, not me.'

It was a beautiful day. Blake looked out at the green hills. 'They'll insist on the debriefing, you can't avoid it. You know as well as I do that there are no exceptions.'

Blake grinned. He was beginning to enjoy himself. 'They can go to hell.'

'And the others?'

'They're already there… don't you ever read Solzhenitsyn?'

'It's not something to joke about,' Roker said irritably. Blake's indifference to his position was beginning to annoy him.

'The Russians know something about death,' Blake went on, warming to his subject. 'They ought to, they do enough dying. We try to kid ourselves that it doesn't exist, every coffin a Cadillac with all mod cons. Death is no longer fashionable.'

Roker refused to be sidetracked; he stuck doggedly to the real subject of the discussion and although he didn't reply directly there was a hard edge to his voice when he did. 'They also know something about counter-espionage and they have the resources to carry it out. All right, so you want that farm in New Hampshire, have it; you can be debriefed there as well as anywhere else.'

Blake flushed angrily. 'And have them turn my place into a

goddamned prison crawling with interrogators and armed guards – the hell with that. I thought you were a friend of mine?'

Roker gave himself time to formulate a sensible reply. 'What do you expect them to do, particularly with someone from the higher echelon who has had access to the most highly-classified material; and until that knowledge is superseded, dispositions changed and new personnel assigned to sensitive areas, you are going to be debriefed. Why are you so against it?'

Blake said simply, 'I don't have the six months.'

'Why not?'

'I've got things to do.'

'Nothing's *that* important, Sam!' Roker exclaimed losing his patience. 'Don't try to kid me.'

Blake's mood darkened again and he was back to where he had been for so long now, the poison gnawing away obsessively, demanding admittance. 'Somewhere along the line,' he said softly, 'we lost our balls.' Then sensing his friend's anxiety, he turned to him. 'Renway saddled you with this, didn't he?'

'He had no choice.'

'Then why are you letting me go?'

'I'm not,' Roker said unhappily.

'I see.' Outside, the sun went behind a cloud; in the car the temperature plummeted to below zero but it had nothing to do with the weather. Blake's face was a tight, bloodless mask. 'Then we're not going to the boat?'

Roker flushed. 'Oh, for God's sake!'

'Where are the scalp-hunters? In that ludicrous parade back there?' Blake glanced through the back window. 'Or waiting to pounce at the pier when I step on the gangway?'

'There aren't any goddamn scalp-hunters – and nobody's going to try to stop you boarding that goddamn boat!' Roker shouted.

Waiting a moment for him to cool down, Blake enquired, 'Your idea, or Renway's?'

'Christ! The man's only doing his job.'

'You haven't answered my question.'

Roker threw him a swift pleading look and plunged: 'I gave him my solemn word that you would turn yourself in for debriefing once you got stateside and had a day or two to sort yourself out.'

'Did you now? Did he believe you?'

'Of course not.'

'Did you?'

'You're damned right I did.'

Blake reflected that poor old Jim was having his problems. It must have been a strain to sit there, to try and drive, and reason with someone who hated the world and just about everybody in it, but the feeling passed. Blake didn't trust him and hadn't done since the moment he had reluctantly stepped into the car back in London. It was rather like a man walking knowingly into a trap because he was curious to discover why it had been set for him. 'I believe you did, Jim,' he said at last in the same soft voice. 'Meaning that I'll have plenty of company on the boat.'

His smile was gentle and Roker felt like a demolition expert who had just defused a bomb but suspected there was another one he might have missed. He got out the words with some effort: 'Both sides will be aboard in numbers – you're hot property.'

For the first time in many long weeks Blake gave way to helpless laughter.

IV

It was a Dutch ship, the *Batavia*, and Blake was in a high good humour when he stepped into his cabin. A quarter of an hour aboard had been all he needed to know that the ship was crawling with security agents, both NATO and otherwise.

It was a nice cabin, up on the boat deck in first class with two portholes giving him an unobstructed view of the sea and furnished like a comfortable sitting room in an expensive apartment. He wasted no time, it took him less than five minutes to find the bugging devices, one of which was of Czech manufacture, the other probably made in Belgium. It was comforting to know that they were taking their work so seriously.

There was a knock on the door and Blake threw it open to a short horse-faced man in a white jacket. Blake stepped aside with a jaunty wave. 'Come in, come in, whoever you are... what can you do for me?'

His visitor hesitantly stepped inside and fixed him with a sad stare. He was holding a long cellophane bag and was somewhat startled by the prompt answer to his knock. Recovering himself he managed lugubriously, 'Your trousers, sir, you wanted them pressed in a hurry... I'm the valet, sir.'

'Really? I didn't know I'd sent any.'

The valet was confused. He stepped back to the door to check the number, then became overly apologetic. 'I'm so sorry, sir. I've come to the wrong cabin, very sorry.' He turned to leave but Blake had slipped ahead of him and stood in front of the door.

'So, what is it,' he snapped, losing his affable smile, 'and don't waste my time. What do you want?'

The valet gaped, startled by the sudden transformation. 'I don't understand... sir,' he stammered looking more like a horse than ever.

'What do you want?' Blake snarled.

The other winced.

Blake lounged against the door and pulled the bugging devices out of his pocket. He made a big thing about examining them for the valet's benefit. 'What's your name... Pete, Hans, Dimitri? It'd be cosier if we're on first name terms.'

The other swallowed with some effort. 'Joseph, sir.' Blake pointed to a chair. 'All right, Joseph. You better sit down and say your piece, you don't have long.'

Joseph wavered slightly but he managed to reach the chair. When he settled he perched on the very edge of it like an old-fashioned servant, embarrassed to be sitting in the presence of his betters. He kept glancing behind his back as if he expected someone to leap out of the bathroom.

'Right, Joseph, first we establish who you're working for, okay?'

The eyes were large, very dark and apprehensive. He said, 'I'm the valet for this deck, sir...'

Blake cut in impatiently, 'Who do you work for Joseph, the *Abteilung*, the Czechs, Centre, KGB? You wanted to see me, well here I am, let's have your pitch.'

Joseph looked nervously around the room.

'Of course, how forgetful of me… I might have forgotten one of these little beauties,' he said lifting one of the bugging devices, 'and you don't want your priceless prose going over the airwaves. Good, why not join me out in my office?'

Blake opened the door and stepped out into the passage. Joseph followed as if he had a lynching mob on his tail. Blake beckoned him to follow and turned through a door leading out to the boat deck. It was very windy, but they had the place to themselves.

'I hardly think they've bugged this place,' he said. 'Lousy reception with all this wind.' He turned to him and waited expectantly. 'Right, where were we?'

Joseph thought it over and revealed a set of resplendent stainless-steel teeth.

Blake laughed outright. The only country in the world where the dentists fitted their patients with that kind of bridgework was the Soviet Union, it was a dead giveaway. 'No need to tell me, Joseph, I know your dentist. You'll want everything, of course… the complete debriefing?'

Joseph nodded. 'Of course.'

'Where?' It was interesting to note how one agent spoke to another once they got over the preliminaries. Like the oldest profession in the world, it took one to know one.

'Some neutral place,' Joseph offered guardedly, all signs of subservience having departed.

'Like Switzerland, maybe?'

'Yes, that would do.'

'When?'

'As soon as it can be arranged.'

'Don't you want to know my price?' Blake went on expansively.

Joseph shrugged as if it was a trivial matter, inferring that money had no importance in the workers' paradise. He favoured Blake with his bright steel smile again. 'We will pay whatever you want,' he smirked.

'I'll think about it for a while, then let you know,' Blake said briskly turning towards the door. 'But not on the ship, it'll have to wait until we get to New York.'

Joseph said helplessly, 'But how will we find you?'

Blake turned back to him. 'You won't, I'll find you.'

It was working better than he had expected. The Russians were speculating, of course; waiting to see which way he might jump. In their books anything was possible in the light of what had happened to him. But then like his own bunch they were professionals. They had nothing to lose. Put out a feeler then wait and see. The Agency was obviously thinking along similar lines. And what of himself? It was all there in the rough but there remained much to be done before he would be prepared to plunge. There was no room for imponderables even if there were some good pluses. Quite a few people could be prevailed upon to help for one reason or another. If need be they might do so whether they wanted to or not; for past favours or, if pressed very hard, to avoid blackmail. Some were in influential positions, even in Moscow. He wouldn't lack allies, willing or otherwise. It was dangerous, betrayal was always a possibility, then again somebody might panic and he could end up with a bullet in his head. But then nobody knew but himself that he would welcome it.

As it worked out, the crossing by ship was a fortunate choice of transport. Aside from the minor irritant of being under constant surveillance and one or two further offers, one surprisingly from the South Africans (Blake enjoyed it all), the six days gave him time to think.

Now that he had come to a decision to avenge himself on Janis's killers, he began to consider the problem, as he would have done a hazardous assignment for the Agency. Out of this came three major decisions. First, it was imperative that he work alone and take as few people as possible into his confidence; no one but himself must know the entire plan. To survive in the intelligence world you put your trust in no one but yourself, and then only if you didn't talk in your sleep. Second, due to the scope of the project it was imperative that he find a good coordinator, preferably an old Agency hand with influential connections outside the government networks. He knew the man, the only possible candidate. Blake had started out in the Agency with him. It was a question of availability. Somehow Blake had to talk him into it. Linderman was a first-rate administrator and during his long service with the Agency had become a superb field agent as well – which made him a rare bird indeed. Having left the Agency some time back to go into his own business, he had in the short space of seven years firmly established himself as one of the most reliable operators in the little-known field of industrial counter-espionage.

Widely respected among a tight circle of large multi-national firms who numbered among his clients, Linderman had purposefully remained small. Better still, he had remained mobile. In essence, he ran his business like a miniature intelligence network with few people on his permanent payroll. But despite this, never using more than twenty key ex-intelligence agents (from a dozen different countries) working on a casual basis, his success ratio was close to eighty percent, which in that field was considered phenomenal.

Linderman had contacts everywhere: in the underworld of many countries, in Interpol, with agents active in the intelligence network of many governments, including some behind the Iron Curtain. He had sources of finance in Swiss banking circles, his own letter-drop service, safe houses scattered around Europe, South Africa and the Middle East, and all paid for by corporate clients, including oil companies.

Linderman was the man to put solid flesh on the bare bones of Blake's maturing plans. Besides, he was an old and trusted friend. But then, Blake would be asking a lot, possibly too much. It was also possible that he might not have the time. Blake decided to cross that bridge when he came to it.

Third, although the Agency's reaction was predictable it deserved, for no other reason than his own survival, careful consideration. An agent never left the service until he was debriefed; that was policy. And in Blake's instance, it was unthinkable to do otherwise; he knew too much about current operations and many still in the pipeline. Were he to defect or otherwise fall into the hands of an enemy service, the damage to operations could be incalculable, not to mention the loss of highly-trained agents throughout the network as happened when the British agent, Kim Philby, defected to the Soviet Union in the early 1950s. For its own well-being, the Agency could never risk a repetition of that notorious episode.

Yet Blake could not spare the time to be debriefed. He had no alternative, he had to go to ground and remain there until either he accomplished what he was setting out to do or the Agency or someone else caught up with him.

How it would end was anyone's guess. At the worst most likely a bullet in the head from a hit-team dispatched by the Agency itself or someone else. It didn't matter. Blake was committed and willing to accept the consequences if he failed. Once it was established by the Agency's enemies (both foreign and domestic) that one of its own senior agents had embarked on a murderous vendetta, it followed that they could claim that he was acting under its orders and it would be next to impossible to disprove.

Yet Blake was willing to risk all that, and as the plan took root and gradually developed, it took on an added dimension. It was no longer just a matter of simple revenge, of him personally killing the terrorists who had murdered Janis. Now it was one man's declaration against terrorism in general. The free nations of the West had shown themselves powerless to cope with the phenomenon. Laws formulated by high moral principles to protect the freedom of the individual were cynically abused by anarchists whose avowed object was to overthrow the system of government which had passed these laws. Trials deteriorated into obscene charades and in many instances when punishment was decreed (in most Western countries capital punishment having been abolished) the accused only served short prison sentences because other groups of terrorists kidnapped hostages, or hijacked airliners, demanding their release in return for the lives of innocent people.

So it went on. No one in power had come up with a solution to what had become the Great Dilemma throughout the West.

Blake felt he had the answer. The one way to deal with terrorists was to become a terrorist, to dispense with civilised methods, with courts of law, with prisons, to deal with them as they dealt with their victims – to show no mercy. In effect he decided to become a one-man pest control agency, his sole object being to weed out vermin and exterminate them.

He didn't consider the implications of his actions to what was called civilised behaviour in an enlightened society; he ignored the dictum that only the enemies of the free world benefit when a private individual takes the law into his own hands, that the vigilante – that harbinger of Fascism – appears when the forces of law and order in a free country are unable to cope with the madness of anarchism, where freedom is interpreted as licence and responsibility to the majority a decadent tool in the hands of the privileged establishment.

Blake was a hard man with a nature forged in the merciless fires of a furtive world, where murder was routine, torture a common practice, degradation a mere statistic. Those who were part of it spared themselves the luxury of words like freedom, justice, fair play, law, order, of-by-and-for the people. These were platitudes indulged in by citizens who in the day-to-day living of their ordinary lives managed in one degree or another to bestow value on them. For them, sages of the ancient world still retained validity. In the desert of the furtive world they and their message was incomprehensible.

Fate had decreed that one day at a London airport the two worlds would collide. There was one basic difference – one was motivated by the idealistic belief that any crime was justified if it destroyed a 'repressive' system, the other by a knowledge that despite its faults, it was within this system that man – its weakest link – was capable of evolving for the best and, as such, it deserved his support.

The former was impulsively amateur in approach, the latter clinically professional.

Terrorism had more than met its match in Blake.

V

On the afternoon of the fifth day of the crossing, when most sensible people were sleeping off their seven-course lunches, Blake led a pair of hapless minders on his version of a Cook's tour of the ship. They went everywhere on the double, covering just about every nook and cranny, pausing but once in the nauseous cupboard where the garbage was ground into swill before being piped overboard. At this stage Blake's leg-weary escorts were, as the saying goes, 'hanging on the ropes'. But there was worse to come deep in the bowels of the hull. Wedged in a maze of steaming pipes and forced to get down on all fours to make their way along the tunnel housing the twin propeller shafts, the intrepid threesome, covered in engine oil and sliding precariously on greasy deck-plates, reached what appeared to be a dead end. Deafened by clanging machinery, gasping for breath and hopelessly lost, the minders peered through the steam and found themselves alone.

A few minutes later, Blake materialised in the Purser's office and shoved a blackened envelope into a startled clerk's hand.

Blake's smile was cherubic. 'Forgive my appearance but I fell into a coalhole. Far-sighted, you see. Can't see a thing without my glasses.'

The clerk, a wholesome nineteen-year-old from Rotterdam, showed her teeth. 'Yes, sir.'

He pointed to the envelope. 'That contains a telex. How soon can you send it?'

'Right now, sir,' she giggled. 'You look funny, sir.'

'Don't worry about all those numbers. Business code... trade secrets, got it?'

The girl knitted an attractive brow. 'Oh, yes, sir. We've been sending a lot of those on this trip.'

Blake's smile widened. 'Have you, indeed?'

'Is there something else, sir?'

He handed her a ten-dollar bill. 'I'm up on A deck. Stateroom five. When it's sent, bring me both copies... can you do that?'

'I'd be delighted, sir.'

'Good girl.'

Back in his stateroom, Blake glanced at his watch on the way to the shower. Linderman's telex machine would already be recording the message. With any luck, he should recognise the old code at first glance as no one used it anymore but Blake.

The problem was would he be on hand to receive it, and, if so, would he be able to organise Blake's unseen departure from the ship? If not, it might prove awkward.

VI

Early in the morning on the final day, there was some difficulty off Sandy Hook in picking up the pilot due to fog, but they finally managed it. At five a.m. Blake opened his door to a brief knock.

He was fully dressed and his one piece of luggage stood beside him.

'Ready to go?'

'Where?' Blake took him in at a glance. Thirties, dressed in warm tugman's clothes, sturdy, matter-of-fact. A strong face which took a while getting around to the password.

'Bye-bye,' the other remembered, reading his thoughts.

Blake relaxed. 'Thought you'd get around to it.' He cheered up considerably. 'That was good. Your boss has picked up a sense of humour – how is he?'

'Busy as usual. That all you're carrying?' he asked, stepping past him and picking up his bag.

'That's it.'

The other stepped out into the passageway. 'Follow me.'

The pilot boat was pitching in a rough swell as Blake climbed down a ladder. Dense fog made it even more difficult as he waited to time his jump, but finally he made it. Two hours later a taxi was on hand as he stepped ashore, and thirty minutes after that he was tucked away in one of Linderman's safe houses on 14th Street. As usual when that old pro was involved, things had gone off without a hitch.

The house mother, a gay version of William Bendix the actor, replete with the same broken nose, was a colourful addition to Linderman's team. He said to call him Eddie.

'All the comforts of home, doll,' he lisped, 'no bugs, shower, sheets, towel, and three squares a day – cash in advance.' He held out five plump fingers covered with rings.

Blake looked around.

'Don't worry, doll… you're safe as houses. Two exits with accompanying gorillas, and one on the roof. Mafiosi soldiers. You savvy Italian you'll get along fine; if not, Brooklyn will do.'

The bejewelled fingers were still outstretched.

Blake coughed. 'How much?'

'You got a good appetite?'

'If the chow's good.'

'Twenty bucks a day and cheap at the price. A week in advance, 'kay?'

Blake paid up. ''Kay.' He knew better than to ask for

Linderman. That worthy would show when he was good and ready. Meanwhile Blake would have to cool his heels.

'Where am I?'

Eddie pointed up a gloomy narrow stairway. 'Top floor. Business is good. All I had left was the attic rear.' He sniffed.

'Not much of a view.'

Blake headed up the stairs. 'When do I get out?'

'You don't, doll… that's what you're paying for. Rules of the house, no fresh air till the boss says so, 'kay?'

''Kay.'

'When you get bored there's the telly in the parlour.' Blake paused on the first landing lit by a single naked light bulb. 'No floor show?'

Eddie tittered. 'Dawn till dusk. Here, doll, I top the bill – wait till you see me in drag, you'll bust a gut.'

'All the comforts of home,' Blake offered from the second landing.

'Supper's at six… I'll knock on the pipe.'

'Much obliged, doll,' Blake said.

He waited for three days then was bundled out the back door, shoved into a car by a burly Italian and driven to the nearby dock area adjacent to the Holland Tunnel. Blake noted the time on his watch. It was just after three in the morning.

VII

Blake entered the bar, all plastic and neon, with artificial leather seat covers on the barstools and a lonely bartender with sleeves rolled up to his biceps, revealing an exotic array of faded tattoos. Blake ordered a beer and took it over to one of the booths. As he sat down, he saw Big Tony saunter in and sprawl on one of the bar stools. Little Tony materialised from the back and dropped into a chair beside the jukebox. There was nothing to distinguish them other than size. Little Tony was a dead ringer for Tony Calento, a one-time heavyweight contender, Big Tony a George Raft gone to blubber. Other than those two and Eddie, Blake hadn't seen another soul for three days until he entered the bar.

He never did see the minder on the roof of Linderman's safe house.

The place was sprinkled with longshoremen and an overweight redhead who gave him a tentative once-over then decided he wasn't a likely customer. Blake was thirsty, he emptied half the glass in a single swallow. When he lowered it, Linderman was sitting opposite looking as he usually did, like an overworked bloodhound that hadn't had a decent night's sleep for a week.

'Why this joint?' Blake wanted to know. 'You seem to go in for the seedy side of life… what's wrong with a little comfort?'

Linderman favoured him with one of his dyspeptic scowls.

'The barkeep's a friend of mine and it's got a back door.'

Blake waited for him to get down to business.

Linderman sat there fingering the catch on his briefcase. He said finally, 'It's a sellers' market and you surfaced at just the right time. I could get you twenty deals. They're losing money hand over fist. In a word they can't wait.'

'Who are *they*?' Blake asked, amused at Linderman's monosyllabic delivery. Linderman never wasted words on unnecessary preliminaries; he said what needed saying and nothing else.

'Every oil company in the business. They're strapped. It's open house for every nutcase who thinks he has a cause and nobody out there has the guts to do anything about it. If it goes on much longer they'll all wind up broke.'

Blake reached over and tapped him on the shoulder. 'How are you, Linderman? You're looking fine.' He didn't offer him a drink because Linderman didn't drink. He didn't smoke either. He was a fastidious man.

Linderman ignored the salutation. 'I narrowed it down to two companies,' he went on as if there had been no interruption. 'They're getting aggravation where it hurts, in their pipelines running down to the tanker ports along the Persian Gulf. Terrorist sabotage. It's costing them plenty and they want to do a deal.' Linderman sat back. It was obvious that he had more to say but he had an orderly mind so he thought it over carefully before continuing. At last he said, 'Both these companies are heavily financed by the Arabs who are squealing as loud as anyone else in private. In public they back the terrorists.'

'What did you tell them?'

Linderman's lower lip drooped. He was also a sensitive man. 'What you said to tell them, nothing more. They know what you do and who you do it for. They also know where you stand in the league tables.' He glared. 'All right?'

'It's liable to get pretty rough. Are they willing to go all the way?'

'One might not,' Linderman calculated carefully. 'But I'm pretty sure the other will. I made two appointments, in each case with their lawyers. One uptown tomorrow morning, the other off Wall Street in the afternoon.' He pulled a loose-leaf notebook out of a pocket, tore out a page and handed it to Blake. 'Names, addresses and time of appointments. Not that you'll need them because we deliver and return you to the house ourselves.'

Blake studied the page.

Linderman anticipated the question. 'Lipscomb, White and Skolnik, they're representing the hundred percenters... on second thoughts, forget the other one. Lipscomb etcetera will make a deal.'

'That was neat, that trick on the boat... getting men on the pilot's launch. Must have cost some bread.' Blake reached over and patted him on the head. 'You always were good, but you're getting better. I didn't give you much time to set it up. And that telex bothered me a bit. For all I knew, you might have forgotten how to decode it, or not be on hand to receive it – nice work.'

Linderman blinked. Having conditioned himself over the years to think of only one thing at a time, digressions annoyed him. 'Oh that,' he grumbled. 'They're professionals, I pay top-dollar, and they deliver – is that so surprising? As for that code; well, the less said about that the better – a nine-year-old could have cracked that. Anyway, I've got a new one worked out. I'll give it to you before you leave... now, where were we?'

Feeling properly rebuked for his levity, Blake told him: 'With Messrs Lipscomb, White and Skolnik, professor.'

'Forget White. He's a windbag, window-dressing to impress the sheiks. And Skolnik's a silent partner, if he exists. I've never met him. Lipscomb's the one who cuts ice in that office... he's the boss man, the senior partner – and the brains. What he says goes, all right?'

Blake nodded. 'Did you mention money?'

Linderman beseeched the ceiling with affronted dignity.

'Of course. Two hundred and fifty thousand dollars up front and if you need more, contact me, stipulate why, and Lipscomb will send it through the agreed channels.'

Blake whistled. 'That's a lot of money.'

'You'll be paying off a lot of people. None of them work for nothing, not counting your other expenses'

Blake was genuinely surprised. 'He didn't bargain?'

'This isn't government money. Unlike the Agency, he's used to paying market prices... It'll be cash on the line where you want it. They will deliver by courier, anywhere, any time... or if you prefer it, by cashier's cheque drawn on the Union Bank Swiss, Zurich. Either one will do.'

Blake lifted an admonitory finger. '*If* I don't disappoint them too much on first acquaintance.'

Tact wasn't one of Linderman's virtues, he nodded readily. 'Play it straight. Lipscomb's sharp as they come, but his clients are desperate. He'll play ball if you don't get greedy.'

The point was Linderman was a genius. An ageless cherubic face, a myopic stare and a mind like a computer. Blake had unearthed him in the Agency's accounts office back in the year dot when he had first gone into the field and had been reaping the rewards ever since. In army parlance, Linderman was what was termed a *dogsbody* but one who could wheel-deal in the very top echelon, a Mr Fixit supreme, one of the few real indispensable people he had ever come across in the Agency. It was said that everyone was expendable – Linderman in his opinion was the sole exception.

Blake could feel his body loosen. He hadn't realised what a strain he had been under. 'That's it then.'

Linderman got up to leave.

Blake smiled. 'Always said you're the best legman in the business.'

Linderman ignored the compliment. 'If you run into any roadblocks, you know where to reach me, same letter-drops I always use – you remember them?' he asked dryly.

'You've expanded a bit since we last worked together... I might not remember them all.'

Never one to be caught unprepared, Linderman delved into his briefcase and produced a letter-box list. 'Memorise it then burn it,' he cautioned warily, 'I don't want that floating around.'

Blake folded it carefully and placed it in the inside pocket of his sports coat. 'Yes, Daddy.'

Linderman was impatient to leave. 'Anything else?'

'Since when do you hire hoods? And that queen – isn't she something!'

Linderman sniffed, 'They're disciplined and good at their jobs... in some instances Syndicate people are more useful than ex-Agency hands in certain kinds of work. As for Eddie, don't let appearances fool you. He's the best house mother I've ever had and I've had a few.'

'You, too, buddy? Christ, what's the world coming to?'

The *double entendre* was lost on Linderman. He had other, more pressing, matters on his mind. When Blake stopped laughing he was gone.

Blake departed soon after by the back door, escorted fore and aft by the two Tonys.

VIII

Blake was impatient to keep his appointment on time, but he wasn't prepared for the kind of transport Linderman had laid on. As it turned out he didn't even have to step out of Eddie's safe house to reach it. Instead, flanked by Big and Little Tony, the Brooklyn hoods, he was taken to the basement, a steel culvert lid was lifted, and he found himself descending down metal rungs sunk into the cement wall of a circular tunnel plunging vertically deep into the ground. They seemed endless.

'Where the hell are you taking me?' he exclaimed.

Little Tony was leading. He said, 'To the subway.'

'Christ, don't tell me Linderman runs his own trains?'

Big Tony, whose shoes were landing dangerously close to Blake's fingers up above, was full of high spirits, 'Haven't you ever *hoid* of the Post Office Subway, boss? We just plug into it, like, when we don't *want'a* be seen, *gottit*?'

Blake got it. It was so simple it was brilliant. For years the New York Post Office had been transporting mail from one outlet to another on its own miniature subway system. One could travel practically the length and breadth of Manhattan without having to surface once. 'My appointment's in Rockefeller Center on Fifth Avenue… what's the nearest station on this thing?'

'Right there, boss. They got a big post office there, ain't they, Tony?'

'*Thoid* stop.'

Blake roared with laughter. 'Do tell!'

'Da mobs used to use it all the time,' Little Tony wheezed. 'Den it got kind'a crowded.'

'I'll bet,' Blake choked. He was doing a little wheezing himself. 'We get much deeper we'll need pressure suits.'

'Real comic we got, hey, Tony.'

'Cle…ver.'

At last they reached a small tunnel platform and Big Tony glanced at his watch.

'Train late?' Blake asked dryly.

'We're early,' he was corrected.

'May I smoke?'

All three lit up. Blake was impressed. This was total security. 'Why did you leave the mob to work for Linderman?' he asked blandly.

'Pay's better,' both agreed.

'Didn't the Godfather get a little annoyed: or did Linderman make him an offer he couldn't refuse?'

Both grinned. 'Hey, Tony,' they chorused, 'boss has seen the pitchur, too.'

'Seriously.' Blake admonished. 'Thought there was only one way to leave the mobs, feet first.'

Both citizens of Brooklyn roared with laughter. 'It ain't like that no more, boss. Families move wid da times.'

The other agreed. 'Now dey send the young soldiers to Princeton, toin them into accountants… they loin to rumble wid computers. Gone legit, see. More like the old days wid Linderman.'

'Like he uses more muscle.'

'Amen,' Blake intoned as the tiny mail train moved noiselessly into the station. All three climbed aboard one of the miniature gondolas. 'Like ore cars,' Blake remembered.

They piled out at the third stop and this time there was a lift which brought them to the main floor of the sorting office. Hardly a clerk along the sorting tables gave them a glance as they passed through a side door leading into the central foyer of the Rockefeller Center.

The Tonys insisted on accompanying him into the elevator and took up stations along the hallway leading up to Lipscomb, White and Skolnik's office suite.

'You're not going to wait out here?'

Both Tonys nodded. 'Until you come out, boss. Den we take you back da way we came, right?'

Blake gulped, 'All right, fellas.'

IX

Blake didn't like the feel of it. He didn't like the richly-furnished room, nor its occupants. They were too self-satisfied and well-heeled to be associated with what he had in mind. But then, Lindeman was good at his job, ideal for this kind of an operation, so he had no option but to go along with it.

William White Jr. was a type he loathed: a wordsmith, every inch the pre-war Yale man when that place catered to rich men's sons, early sixties, born with a silver spoon in his mouth and a stuffed shirt on his back. One of those who would condone practically anything just so long as he himself was never actually involved or seen to be connected with it. He had sat there, pompously aware of his own self-importance, and never once had committed himself.

But he wasn't so sure about the other one. Clement Lipscomb, the senior partner, hadn't opened his mouth throughout the meeting, had simply sat there listening, contributing nothing. It was a face utterly devoid of expression, easy to forget. The kind that fits a good intelligence agent.

While Blake was speaking, he concentrated his attention on a spot just above the elder White's elegant hairline. 'The object is to stop the terrorists, to root out their leaders and the people who back them financially. I can do that, my contacts are reliable and world wide.'

White digested this with distaste and glanced at Lipscomb who sat there perched on the edge of his chair like a watchful barn owl.

Blake ploughed on. 'The problem is to penetrate their security screens, find their safe houses, prove to their followers that they can be killed.'

White suppressed a disdainful shudder and looked out of a window on the twin spires of St Patrick's Cathedral some fifty floors below.

'…and I know people on both sides of the Iron Curtain who can be prevailed upon to help me do just that,' Blake concluded quietly, though he was seething inside.

'I see,' White frowned petulantly. Lipscomb said nothing.

Blake stood up. 'No, I'm afraid you don't. Your kind never does.' He spun around and took off for the exit. The hell with it. Linderman would have to find him another backer, he'd had enough.

White called out, 'Am I right in assuming there is some kind of official sanction behind what you propose, Mr Blake?'

'No,' Blake said reaching the door.

'But you do belong to one of the intelligence agencies?'

'Not any more. They have nothing to do with this.'

White hadn't bothered to get up from his chair. 'Yet you propose to threaten certain people who allegedly provide finance for terrorists, is that correct?'

It was painful but Blake managed to control his temper. 'No, I propose to publish a list of the three top terrorist leaders, stating that they shall be killed *one by one* until it stops. And when the others see *how* they are killed, you can take my word for it – *it will stop!*'

White had shed some of his superior manner. Lipscomb merely stared. Blake still had his undivided attention.

Blake added, 'That's very important… how they are killed. I know some good killers. It won't be nice.'

White shot to his feet. 'This is disgusting!' he exclaimed.

Blake solemnly agreed. 'Very,' he said. 'The first two will die painfully and slowly, one will be humiliated as well. Humiliation can be a vital factor with some kinds of men, particularly if it outrages their religion. But then, you wouldn't know about that sort of thing, it just isn't done in your circles.'

White was bewildered, he couldn't quite believe his ears. He shook his head with some hesitation, whereas Lipscomb could have been asleep, but his eyes were open and, as ever, fixed on Blake.

'There'll be a lot of notoriety of course,' Blake went on. He was beginning to enjoy it. It wasn't every day he had the chance to puncture a smug balloon. 'Newspapers love that sort of thing, it increases their circulation, particularly if it's illustrated with on-the-spot photographs, which naturally I will supply. Readers like to be horrified as long as it happens to others. When it happens to them they run.'

White had paled under his rich Bermuda tan. 'That's enough, Mr Blake, now if you…?'

'And our friends *will* run,' Blake cut in, overriding him. 'Far and fast, and those pipelines will start pumping again.'

White was having difficulty with his breathing. 'You expect us to become parties to that?' he shouted. 'To sink to the level of the very people we are trying to stop… there must be another way!'

'There isn't,' Blake said. 'Fear is the one thing they understand.' He turned and walked out.

Out in the hall Lipscomb materialised at his shoulder as he pushed the elevator button. 'Where are you staying?' he asked softly. Like the face the voice had no expression. He ignored the two Tonys, who took up stations on either side of them.

Blake turned with surprise. 'Well, well, so you do have vocal cords after all.'

Lipscomb's unblinking eyes simply stared and the rest of him waited patiently for a reply.

Blake obliged. Glancing at his minders, he said, 'Can't say.'

Lipscomb's eyes might have been made of glass. 'We must go into this more thoroughly, preferably with Mr Linderman present. My clients will want more details before they commit themselves… surely that isn't too much to ask. How do I reach you?'

63

'You don't. Linderman will arrange things – I'll ask him to call you.'

'Very well.'

The elevator arrived and the door slid open. It was empty as it was now well past office hours and required no operator. Lipscomb leaned in and held the door open, adding by way of an afterthought as Blake and the Tonys stepped inside, 'Our clients' representatives will want to meet you.'

Blake faced him squarely. 'Now I've got a question or two... to begin with, who are they?'

Lipscomb replied evenly, 'Friends of ours from one of our older banking houses who represent an international consortium of businessmen...'

Blake was beginning to like him. 'You mean they'd prefer to remain anonymous?'

'They've been authorised to give you what you need, within reasonable limits, of course,' Lipscomb concluded, looking more like a barn owl than ever.

'I'll need some of it straight away in cash.'

'That has been anticipated. An adequate sum will be advanced to you at the termination of that meeting, if we are all agreed.'

'Until the meeting, then.'

Lipscomb held the door open. 'Oh, by the way. You didn't mention how you intend to dispose of the third on your list?'

'I haven't decided yet,' Blake said. 'But then I've got plenty of time to give it some thought.'

Lipscomb's gaze never wavered. 'How soon can you get started?'

'I've already begun.'

'If you can, ask Linderman to contact me this evening. I'll be here, working late.'

'You had your mind made up before I came here.'

Lipscomb became almost expansive. 'Not quite, Mr Blake. Although you've been thoroughly investigated, and my clients are satisfied that you will accomplish your end of the business, I wanted to meet and have a chat with you first. Until our meeting then.' He turned and moved down the hall as the elevator began to descend.

X

Linderman was frying himself some eggs when Blake found him in the kitchen. Eddie was making the toast. Blake looked around appreciatively. 'Behold the high and mighty come to pig it with the peasants. Aren't we comfy... mind if I join you? That subterranean jaunt has given me an appetite.'

Linderman glanced at Eddie who promptly swished out, closing the door softly behind him.

Linderman buttered his toast and grunted between mouthfuls. He neglected to ask how the business had gone with Lipscomb, but then Linderman never did ask questions unless he was directly involved.

'Lipscomb wants to arrange a meeting, and asked me to have you phone him.'

'I already have. He's coming along this evening with some other people.'

'Here?'

'I don't risk exposure. You don't step out of this house until you leave, understood?'

'You're the boss.' Blake watched him resume his meal with interest. For a large man Linderman had abnormally small hands. The nails were meticulously cut and spotlessly clean. Blake was at a loss to know what this indicated about the man's character but it certainly didn't fit in with his baggy unpressed clothes and frayed linen. 'When is that likely to be? This place is a bit claustrophobic.'

Linderman blinked behind his thick bifocals and continued to chew, adding noisy toast for an encore. 'Soon.'

Blake sighed. 'You run a mighty tight ship, Lindy old boy... I'm not likely to tell anybody, as if there was anybody to tell.'

'They're turning this town upside down looking for you.'

'Who?'

Linderman grimaced; his chubby cheeks bulging with un-swallowed toast. 'Just about everybody. Centre and the Russians head the list. You're a popular fella.'

'You're a great jailer.'

Linderman sniffed. 'Merely home-ground advantage. Let's keep it that way.'

Blake grimaced. 'You've got revolting table manners.'

Linderman went on chewing, spraying the table with bits of toast. 'Rene Duscharne will be meeting your plane in Nice.'

'When?'

'Couple of days.'

Visibly relieved, Blake reached over and took the last slice of toast off Linderman's plate. 'Rene's an old friend, besides he still owes me a favour or two. Did he squeal much?'

'Have you ever met a Frenchman who doesn't when you're asking for his blood?'

'You don't like it?'

Linderman's shrugs were always impressive. This one denoted disapproval, at the same time indicating that he had no serious objections. Then he changed the subject yet again. 'About that meeting tonight. It's merely a formality. You sold Lipscomb this afternoon. The bankers just want a look at you. I'll have them out of here in half an hour…'

'How are they coming – same route, courtesy of the New York Post Office Department?'

'Of course.'

'I love you.' Blake got up and drifted to the door. 'When are they arriving?'

'Couple of hours.'

'Think I'll have a kip.'

'You do that. When they leave, we have one final briefing on the entire operation and that'll be that. Once you step out of this house we don't meet again until it's all over. You reach me by letter-drop or in emergencies by coded telex, understood?'

Blake yawned. 'Don't know what I'd ever do without you, Lindy,' he reflected affectionately.

XI

The weather in Nice was unseasonably chilly for September as he stepped out of the airport terminal, aware that his watcher (fresh out of some Ivy League college by the look of him) was making a hash of the whole thing by the taxi stand. Blake had been expecting him. They were bound to locate him sooner or later, it was blanket coverage. At this stage he calculated it wouldn't be any more drastic than that. They'd shadow him until they found out what he was up to. As usual, Centre was going by the book. For a moment he considered going over to comfort the kid, but then he saw Rene waiting in the old Citroen. He climbed into the front seat beside him and Rene headed for the main highway into town. Blake was amused at the look of marked disgust on the Frenchman's face and promptly forgot the young African back at the terminal. Rene invariably had that effect on him. 'Aren't you going to ask me how I enjoyed the flight, old buddy?'

Rene grimaced, 'Hate aeroplanes,' then treated him to a well-remembered self-pitying look up at the roof. 'Judas!'

Blake played up. 'Fine way to greet an old friend.'

'Go to hell!'

'I'll forgive you this time,' Blake sighed.

Rene sniffed disapprovingly. 'That infant back at the airport, your people must be hard up. The word's out, they've blanketed the whole of Europe and probably everywhere else, looking for you.'

'It's good to know they care.'

Rene was a good driver and the car moved effortlessly through the heavy traffic along the Corniche. 'His name is Abdul Khalifa,' he began resentfully like someone arguing with his wife, more from habit than irritation. 'A Syrian from Damascus who used to operate out of Beirut and now bases himself in Cannes. As you Americans say – a very big wheel indeed. He's well in with the oil sheikdoms in the Trucial States, including Saudi Arabia, and is one of the main sources of income for most of the more extreme terrorist groups based in Syria, Iraq and Libya. The oil sheiks privately condemn these people, stay publicly noncommittal and pay millions to keep them off their backs. Abdul Khalifa manages to have the confidence of both groups and acts as a middleman when they negotiate for funds.'

Blake asked casually, 'Does he do anything else?'

Rene grunted, 'Plenty. There's substantial evidence linking him with the actual organisation and, in at least two instances, personally conducting terrorist operational raids – abortive hijacking of an Israeli airliner in Frankfurt 1972 and that shootout at De Gaulle Airport in Paris a few years back. Nobody knows how much cash he syphons off for himself in these go-between deals but he lives like a millionaire in Cannes.'

Blake cut in, 'Background?'

Rene shrugged, 'The usual, middle-class Muslim. Father was a doctor. Bright in school, got a B.Sc. degree from the American University in Beirut, scholarship to the Sorbonne where he studied law, became legal adviser to one of the Gulf States in early negotiations with British and American oil companies…'

'Anything else?'

'A playboy in off hours, gambles to excess – not that he can't afford it – lusts after plump blondes, and why the hell come to me when any mediocre field-hand could have found that out?' Rene was disillusioned with life that morning.

'You're getting fat.'

Rene glared at him. 'You're getting thin.'

'I've stopped eating.'

'A fate worse than death.' The thought of food cheered him up a little. He actually smiled.

'Where's he staying?'

'The Carlton, Cannes, where else?'

'Where's your nice French accent gone?'

'I study at Berlitz like every other damned fool in Europe.'

'Next thing you'll be munching hamburgers instead of escargots.'

Rene exclaimed bitterly, 'Escargots. What are those?'

'Bodyguards?'

'Of course. No respectable Arab would enter a *pissoir* over here without at least four. This one's got 'em working in shifts around the clock.' The Fernandel face broke into a joyful grin and, leaning out of the window, he gave the taxi the two-finger sign as it sped past with the young American in the back.

'Amateurs!' he shouted, reminding Blake that only a Frenchman could get such colourful mileage out of a single word.

'And the farm?'

Rene's India-rubber face dissolved into helpless sorrow. 'Why did it have to be pigs?'

'An idiosyncrasy of mine, I'm a sucker for symbols.'

'Rented for three weeks, money in advance,' Rene said sticking out a greedy hand.

Blake found an envelope in his pocket and passed it to him. Rene promptly tore it open and ran an expert finger over the enclosed banknotes.

Blake chided, 'Never count and drive, Rene; you might go bang.'

Rene pocketed the envelope. 'Anything else?'

'The girl.'

'Name's Erika, she's one of the best.'

Rene pulled over to the kerb and Blake got his bag out of the back seat and stepped out. They both noticed the taxi slip past them again. Neither made any comment.

Blake bent down and stuck his head through the window.

'Can I use Claude?'

'He's driving you.'

'You think of everything.'

Rene suddenly turned thoughtful. 'Remember, no bodies, not on my ground, *mon ami*. That I won't tolerate.'

'Promise.' Rene once again had proved himself a friend. Blake shook his hand.

When Rene pulled through the gate at the *Gendarmerie* a few minutes later the two uniformed police guards snapped to attention and saluted. When he reached the front entrance another hurried down the steps to open the door. '*Bonjour,* Commandant,' he said.

At the same moment in London, Roker was ringing off on a phone in Renway's office. 'He's just arrived in Nice,' he said.

Renway sniffed. 'Maybe he went down there for the sun.' Roker looked pained. 'I don't like it, he's twice as vulnerable once he gets on the other side of the channel. They wouldn't hesitate to drug him and chuck him in a plane if they got the chance... the Russians have done it before to people.'

'They didn't do very well in New York.'

'Neither did we.'

'Linderman again,' Renway moaned. 'Damned fixit merchant – there must be some way to stop him.'

'How are you going to stop him? Even we use him, Centre

says hands off,' Roker objected, waving both hands as if he was fighting off a sudden invasion of mosquitoes. This was out of character but understandable in the present circumstances, both men having been under considerable strain since Blake's disappearance from that Dutch ship off New York. Centre had been exerting what amounted to intolerable pressure and neither had been out of that small office for more than a few hours at a stretch for two weeks.

'We don't *know* that. That's just speculation,' Roker flared. 'Centre's got to find a scapegoat, and as of now you, Linderman and me are the chief candidates!'

'Stop shouting!' Renway shouted. 'You want the whole goddamn embassy to know what we're talking about – Christ, could I do with a shower.' With that he took off on one of his habitual jogs around the office. Roker sat there watching him with ill-concealed annoyance.

'What the hell *did* happen to him?' Renway asked, stopping in mid-stride. 'How can a man simply vanish into thin air with a boatful of security men dogging his heels? That required organisation. Now he blithely turns up in the south of France and Centre, for reasons known only to itself, decides against grabbing him because some desk-bound idiot says he might lead us to something – *you tell me what he's supposed to lead us to.*'

Roker replied with a hopeless shrug.

'Who else could it have been *but* Linderman? They used to work together, they're friends of a sort, and Linderman's the only one I know who has the kind of organisation that could mount an operation like that. Centre covered the entire Eastern Seaboard looking for Blake, and I don't know how many KGB operatives were assigned to the same job, not to mention all the others. And what did they get – not a smell.'

Roker moved to Renway's favourite window overlooking Grosvenor Square and watched a pair of squabbling pigeons disputing territorial rights on President Roosevelt's bronze head. 'It would require well-trained men, safe houses and plenty of know-how. Blake must have been kept holed up in one place, never allowed on the streets... Linderman's a possibility all right,' he grudgingly agreed.

Renway scratched an itchy unshaven chin. 'Thanks for that anyway.'

'And if he was behind it, it's a possibility that he's going all the way. Look at the set-up he's got in Europe, industrial espionage is big business. He's got all that multi-national finance to hire the best and he's got the pick of Europe to choose from, including KGB defectors. If it is Linderman, we're in for one hell of a merry chase. Running him to ground would be like trying to find the invisible man.'

Renway nodded gloomy agreement. 'And without Centre's say-so we can't touch either one of them.' He started to fidget. 'How well does Blake know Rene Duscharne?'

'They're old friends.'

'Nobody from the Agency should get that chummy with French intelligence.'

'You forget, Blake's no longer with us.'

'Who's on it?'

'Young Page.'

'Christ! With Blake of all people, you should have known better. Page is still in swaddling clothes.'

'It was Centre, not me.'

'That figures.' Renway started to roam again. It was a major feat of dexterity in that cluttered office. 'I wish Centre would stop interfering.' He gravitated to his favourite spot at the window and elbowed Roker out of the way. 'How well do you know Duscharne?'

'We worked together a couple of times, he's one of the shrewdest I've ever come across.'

'What the hell is Blake playing at?'

Renway looked down at the trees, some of which were already beginning to shed their leaves. 'Why Duscharne and why now?'

'To know that we would have to know what he wants.'

'What the hell is he up to?' Renway was in one of his niggling moods. When Roker looked up he was back behind his desk. 'How does that Frenchman come into this?'

'…he's one of the SDECE's leading experts on Middle Eastern affairs,' Roker remembered, thinking back to what he had read in his file, but that had been some time back when they told him

71

that he might be working with him. 'The majority of his foreign assignments usually centred around the Lebanon, Cairo, those places. Counter-intelligence mostly, particularly after the Soviet involvement when the French were trying to get a foothold around the Suez Canal. He's something of an Arabest, so I've been told.'

'Why's he helping Blake?'

'We don't know that he is yet,' Roker was quick to point out. 'I know they're old friends and I think I know why: a pretty strong rumour went the rounds some years ago that Blake saved his life during an abortive French operation against the Syrians. Blake was said to have wangled him out of it somehow by pressurising their foreign office. That was the educated guess at the time. He's pretty basic, Blake; you know, keep 'em owing you.'

Renway exhaled with his customary gusto. 'That's a beginning anyway.'

'It's the only one we've got.'

'It could be a blind.'

'We have no choice, we must follow it up.'

'Why did they let him go? Why didn't they pick him up? Why wasn't he debriefed? Why do we have to pussyfoot now? What the hell is Centre playing at?'

Roker sat there thinking of Blake's wild laughter that day in the car when he had driven him to Southampton. He had been so sure of himself, so obviously indifferent to what Centre might or might not do. 'Suppose it has been Centre all the time, I mean after the massacre at the airport? They might have put him on a special assignment.'

'Without telling us?' Renway shook his head. 'They've never done it before.'

'It's possible.'

Renway couldn't hide it, he was appalled.

For that matter, so was Roker.

CHAPTER THREE

I

THE FULL ORANGE DISC OF THE RISING HARVEST MOON LIT A fiery trail on the autumnal sea as the two limousines containing His Excellency, Abdul Khalifa, and his retinue of youthful bodyguards rounded the flower beds and pulled up at the main entrance of the floodlit Monte Carlo Casino.

People hardly gave them a second look. The sight had become so repetitious since the *Yom Kippur* War and the Arab oil embargo had transformed Western Europe into a shopping centre-cum-playground for a people who in a single, breathtaking stride had come in from the desert and casually exchanged their goat herds and Bedouin tents for Cadillacs and air-conditioned suites in luxury hotels.

As Khalifa stepped out of the limousine, he was immediately surrounded by his restless-eyed young men and as he made his way up the steps he might have been a prisoner being led to a place of execution rather than a rich Arab out for an evening's relaxation at the Casino's famed gaming tables.

Inside, the procession moved directly to the main salon, a spacious *fin-de-siècle* room with a high ceiling, enclosed on all sides by wide windows and liberally sprinkled with widely-spaced gambling tables. An archaic atmosphere pervaded a place that had been built to cater to a different age; it was out of its time and place, a relic of a plutocratic past that somehow had survived to serve a less hidebound and discriminating public.

The procession continued on to the big table where Khalifa settled himself into the one remaining empty chair, undoubtedly reserved for his personal use. His alert young men discreetly withdrew a pace or two as the croupier passed the Chemmy shoe to one of the players, who proceeded to push out the cards.

73

Khalifa hardly followed the action of the play, his eyes having strayed to the young woman sitting directly opposite. He barely blinked so intense was his gaze, and the object of this scrutiny, Erika Bannerman, startlingly pretty, almond-eyed and blondely Nordic, looked precisely what she wasn't – a generously endowed film actress or good-time girl kept by a well-heeled boyfriend. For her part, she ignored him and, coolly detached, focused her full attention on the game. Rene Duscharne had given Blake a good one for the job at hand.

Khalifa lifted a hand and one of his young men materialised at his side. A few moments' whispered conversation and he was gone again. If Erika noticed the sudden flurry of activity across the table she gave no sign of it.

Indistinguishable from the legion of dolly-birds that migrated seasonally to the Riviera in search of men to pay the bills, she was somewhat older than she looked. Clear of complexion and well-fed, there was nothing in her face to betray the hard times of her past. Although she travelled on a Swedish passport she had been born in Krakow to a Polish lawyer and his Silesian wife who had long since departed to a Siberian labour camp never to be heard of again. So all alone in the world at the tender age of sixteen the practical child had studied herself in the mirror and decided to capitalise on her assets. The road hadn't been easy but an innate caution had kept her out of the potholes on her slow but sure journey to the West. There had been a few lean months in Dresden where professional prostitutes were frowned upon by Party officialdom, until she received a helping hand from one of its major functionaries. This gentleman, apart from gratifying his personal appetites, promptly appreciated her other gifts – a quick mind and a total lack of conscience – and put her to work to learn at the *Abteilung* Academy for junior operatives. Diligent and hard-working, Erika quickly proved that she had talents other than those she had so liberally displayed in bed; consequently her paramour marked her for quick advancement. Matriculating near the top of her class she was then dispatched to an exclusive brothel in Bonn which catered to influential West German businessmen and highly-placed government officials. Rising gradually in the apparatus, she was soon dispatched to foreign postings and in Paris had the good fortune to be blown by Rene Duscharne himself on behalf of French counter-intelligence. Rene, like the man before him, quickly saw her potential and Erika had no compunction in switching her allegiance to the West.

In a matter of moments Khalifa's emissary found Monsieur La Favre, the Casino director, and shortly thereafter this elegant dignitary presented himself at Erika's shapely elbow.

'Good evening, Mam'selle Bannerman, I'm having a few people around to my *bureau* between shoes and would be delighted if you would attend.'

Erika's smile was cool. 'That would be nice.'

'One of the staff will show you the way, Mam'selle.' Erika lifted her eyes to find that His Excellency's attention was now firmly focused on the cards.

The croupier announced, '*C'est le dernier coup.*'

A player called, '*Banco.*'

The dealer dealt four cards from the shoe, turned over his two and announced, '*Huit a la banque.*'

As the croupier passed him his winnings on the paddle the others began to rise from the table.

II

Monsieur La Favre's rooms were an elegant blend of the past and present; spacious, comfortable and furnished with exquisite taste.

The host, an urbane Monagasque in his early fifties, hurried forward extending his hand as Erika was brought in. 'Ah, Mam'selle, how good of you to come.'

A waiter appeared with a tray laden with brimming champagne glasses. Monsieur La Favre handed her one and led her to a nearby group of chattering guests. One by one they stopped talking as they got an eyeful of her gown: sheath-tight black taffeta that hugged her ample figure like a second skin. It was guaranteed to engender instant hatred or captivation depending on the sex of the beholder.

Monsieur La Favre led her around the silent circle. 'Monsieur and Madame Lukesh, Lady Crawford, Signore Puntavelli and His Excellency, Abdul Khalifa, Vice Consul for the Trucial States in Monaco… Mam'selle Erika Bannerman from Stockholm…'

Erika moved gracefully along the line acknowledging the introductions, impervious to either admiration or hostility.

For a large man, Abdul Khalifa's movements were agile and swift. In no time at all he had whisked her to a quiet corner. 'Now that we have been properly introduced,' he began grandly, his bulbous eyes riveted firmly on her cleavage, 'I would be delighted if you would accompany me to dinner.'

Erika regarded him with a cool stare.

Caught unawares by what he had thought to be just another *belle de nuit* – albeit a very pretty one – Khalifa faltered, 'I haven't seen you here before, Miss Bannerman, do you come often?'

'No, I prefer San Tropez.'

His Excellency was at a momentary loss for words. Women of this type were usually more forthcoming with a man of his wealth and importance. He finally managed, 'A younger crowd?'

She looked him straight in the eyes. 'You arranged all this, didn't you?' She noticed that even here he had brought his guards. At the moment two of them were trying to look unobtrusive behind a nearby table lamp.

Khalifa reddened, more mystified than ever. 'Forgive me, Mam'selle… it seemed more polite to make your acquaintance that way.'

Erika shrugged. 'They'll be starting in a minute, would you care to see me back to my table?'

Reduced to grasping at straws, His Excellency offered her a grateful arm and led her out of the room.

III

Blake had found a room in a small backstreet hotel that catered to tourists on all-in tours. After a nap, shower and shave, he set out for a small seafood restaurant where the cooking was good and the prices comparatively cheap. In no hurry, he stopped at a news-stand on the *Croisette*, strolled along the seafront for a while then turned into a narrow side street. His watcher was the same Ivy League kid he had spotted earlier that day at the airport. Blake slowed his pace to a window-shopping crawl. He felt a little sorry for the kid, but then there was only one way to learn this job, the hard way, and the sooner the better, so why not now?

Blake continued the pace, stopping to watch a baker pulling hot loaves out of an oven and a shapely clerk in a chemist's shop dispensing laxative to a struggling six-year-old, his mother shrieking south of France argot with the speed of a computer. Then he ambled over to the other side of the street and strolled past another couple of shops.

Suddenly Blake was running. He vanished around a corner, leaving his young tail standing flat-footed in the middle of the road.

He huddled in a dark doorway waiting for Junior, who eventually showed up out of breath, his well-shod feet clicking along the cobblestones. The kid slowly approached, unaware of the old Renault that was inching along behind him. Suddenly the rear door flew open, hands reached out and scooped him into the back seat. Blake jumped in front with Claud and the old bus accelerated down the street like a racing car. Junior didn't even have time to open his mouth.

Nobody spoke for a while. Blake glanced at Claud and grinned. The little Frenchman was typecast for those French gangster films which invariably were set in Marseilles. Minuscule, a rat-faced forty, the inevitable cigarette butt tucked in a corner of his mouth, shifty-eyed and dour. Claud rarely smiled, but this time he made an exception. Blake was pleased to see him again.

A bit later out on the highway, Claud reached back and asked, 'Got your passport?'

The American, fresh-faced, neat and bewildered, blurted anxiously, 'Where are you taking me?' He glanced apprehensively at the two burly Frenchmen who were flanking him on the back seat. Claud nodded to one of them who promptly emptied the American's pockets and handed the stuff over.

The youngster was on the verge of tears. 'You have no right to do this,' he protested.

Blake asked, 'What's your name, kid?'

'Page, sir.'

'You're pretty far from home.'

'Yes, sir. I was assigned here, sir.'

'Forget the sir.'

'Yes, sir... I mean... oh, hell, I don't know what I mean.'

Claud made another exception. Laughter didn't fit his face. He rapidly checked the stuff and tossed everything back but three passports. One was American, the other two Mexican and British. Claud pocketed the latter two and handed the other one back together with a small envelope. 'Your return ticket back to London, *mon enfant*, fair exchange.'

A few minutes later they pulled up in front of the Nice airport terminal and Claud nodded, 'Get his bag.'

One of the bruisers climbed out and went around to the luggage compartment to fetch it.

Claud turned to the young American, 'You checked out of your hotel, paid the bill.'

Page replied with a tight smile, 'Did I get a receipt? Our bookkeepers like to be tidy – otherwise I don't get an expense refund.'

Claud grunted, rummaged in his pockets until he found it then passed it over.

'Thanks.'

Claud favoured him with a Jean Gabin shrug as the other bruiser helped him out of the back seat.

Page looked at Blake. 'Next time I'll avoid narrow streets,' he said bitterly as the Frenchman came around with his bag and handed it to him.

Blake said kindly, 'Don't feel too bad about it. Next time you won't be so easy. And something else, always wear rubber soles and heels, you won't announce yourself so early.' He nodded and the two Frenchmen escorted the youngster into the terminal.

Settling back as Claud drove out of the airport compound, Blake wondered why the Agency hadn't brought out the big guns. Apparently they were going to let him run loose for a while. It would have been interesting to hear what Linderman would have thought, but he was back in Manhattan. It was an odd feeling. Blake and the Agency were now on opposite sides of the fence.

IV

Claud drove around for a time then parked the car a short distance along the street from Erika's apartment building. He didn't seem disposed to talk, neither did Blake, so they sat in silence. Claud sat there, occasionally dragging deep on the wet end of his cigarette, his shifty little eyes missing nothing. They knew each other too well for small talk, that had all been said years ago. Claud was good, entirely dependable. Blake had no reservations regarding his ability, nor for that matter did he question that of any of the other men Rene had given him. The little Corsican had been born in Bastia and like so many of his kind had as a matter of course drifted as a kid into petty crime; drug trafficking, managing sleazy waterfront brothels and bars for the *Union Corse,* until he found himself working for Rene Duscharne and French Intelligence.

Blake broke the silence, saying, 'Sorry to keep you up so late, Claud.'

Claud rolled his window down, spat out the butt, lit another. 'For what they pay us, it isn't worth it,' he frowned keeping his eyes fixed on the road. 'Sometimes I think I should have stayed with the old crowd.'

'Why didn't you?'

Claud treated him to one of those full Gallic shrugs which denote the Frenchman's fatalistic view of the world. 'You've never been in a French jail?'

'No.'

'Had you been, you wouldn't have asked such a question.'

'Occupational hazard.'

Even Claud was unable to suppress the shudder that convulsed his sparrow-like shoulders. '*Beaumettes* is not a pleasant place.'

Blake looked at him with new interest. 'They sent you there?'

'It's no place for choirboys. I was twenty-two when they sent me up. I was lucky, it was a short stretch, five to seven years. When I got out I was twenty-eight. I looked forty-eight.'

'So you went to work for Rene.'

'Nobody crosses him. We work good. If he stops trusting us, it's back to *Beaumettes* and the smell of urine.'

Blake sensed that he didn't like to talk about it so they just sat there in silence and Claud smoked.

Back at the Casino the floodlighting had been switched off and there were few people about as Erika hurried down the steps, followed by a protesting Khalifa, his faithful retinue close at his heels. Erika hailed a waiting taxi, which promptly drove up. Khalifa was pleading, 'Please, Mam'selle, I'd be delighted to drive you home.'

'Some other night,' Erika said firmly, climbing into the taxi. She had to shut the door fast or he would have jumped in beside her.

The unhappy Khalifa bowed to the inevitable. 'May I see you tomorrow?'

'I might be on the beach in the morning, say about eleven at Eden Rock – bye!'

Her smile was radiant as the taxi moved off. Khalifa's young men hurriedly hemmed him in.

Back in front of Erika's apartment building, Blake and Claud hadn't moved. They still sat in the old car. Blake said, breaking another silence, 'I didn't know your instructions also included keeping an eye on me,' adding just enough acid to his voice to indicate his annoyance.

Claud shrugged. 'That's standard procedure. We never trust anybody.' He didn't add that Blake, of all people, should certainly accept that.

'Not even an old friend?'

Claud's look said it all. One had to make some sort of conversation during these tiresome waits. Then too, he knew Blake of old, how fond he was of stirring it up, picking the scab, particularly around the more tender areas. 'We know our business, n' est-a-pas?'

Blake was not amused. 'Makes one feel at home,' he quipped archly.

Their eyes moved to the windshield as the taxi drew up in front of the apartment building and Erika got out and hurried up the steps.

'A bit on the plump side?'

'He likes them fat and round,' Claud observed with a note of admiration in his voice. Like most Frenchmen, he considered himself an expert on women.

V

The mountain road was full of sharp hairpin turns, and being a clear day, Blake could see far below the distant suburban sprawl that disfigured the landscape for miles in both directions along the coast road from Nice until it faded into the blue haze of the Mediterranean.

Turning off the highway, he moved up a narrow dirt road past lines of ancient olive trees which ended in the clearing that contained the farm itself.

It was an old property and the house and outbuildings were in a bad state of repair. As Blake drove up an elderly *Provençal* appeared and ambled over to the car. Blake got out and they shook hands. An old peasant woman carrying a suitcase stepped out of the house and climbed heavily into a rusty farm truck. Blake and the farmer moved towards one of the pens. The Frenchman handed him a string of keys. 'For the house and all the other buildings, Monsieur,' he explained slowly. The face was weatherworn and full of deep wrinkles.

He seemed worried about something. 'But who's going to look after my stock?' he protested.

Blake replied pleasantly, 'Me.'

The old farmer studied him doubtfully. 'You ever lived on a farm, Monsieur?'

'I was born on one,' Blake answered truthfully. 'Don't worry about your pigs, they'll be well fed.'

The farmer seemed relieved. 'That is good, Monsieur. *Merci.*'

Blake stepped up expectantly on the bottom rung of the high rustic fence surrounding the pen as a young farmhand (probably the farmer's son) appeared with two buckets of swill, emptied them into an already brimming trough then hightailed it for safety as an enormous boar roared into the pen with his ravenous harem.

Blake climbed up and perched on the top rung of the fence to watch the show. It had been some years since he had watched pigs being fed so he wasn't prepared for the deafening hubbub.

They grunted, they squealed, they fought for a place at the trough, they wolfed down the swill. Then the boar went on a rampage, butting the others out of the way with his vicious tusks.

'He's a bad one,' Blake observed quietly, somewhat subdued by the brute savagery of the scene.

The old *Provençal* nodded proudly. 'But an excellent breeder, Monsieur. He will eat anything as long as there is plenty of it… you will feed him well, please?'

Blake sat there, mesmerised by the spectacle, nodded absently, 'Very well.'

Reassured somewhat the old farmer thanked him gravely and concluded, 'If you will come with me, Monsieur, I will show you the inside of the house.'

Blake reluctantly jumped down from the fence and followed him into the house. Everything he required had been arranged ready on the shelves in the kitchen larder and closet. The old farmer pointed out the light switches and showed him how to start the stove. Blake wasn't interested in the rest of the house; he produced a large wad of francs and proceeded to settle the bill.

There is nothing in this world as pleasing to a French peasant as the sight of hard cash, particularly if the bills are of large denomination and destined for said Frenchman's own pocket. He all but drooled as Blake counted them out, placed them one by one into his outstretched palm, then added a five hundred franc note by way of a tip to the pile.

The old farmer's hand closed vicelike over the money and he all but tore his pocket in his rush to offer them sanctuary in the event of the American changing his mind. 'God bless you, Monsieur! *Merci! Merci!*' he cried, hurrying to the door.

Blake followed him out into the yard and as the truck rattled off, he turned back towards the pen to have another look at the feeding animals.

VI

Erika was seated at a table for two in front of a large picture-window overlooking the sea, watching His Excellency Abdul Khalifa wolf down his food. Immediately adjacent the rest of the party was likewise occupied over large plates of couscous. Some were using knives and forks but most had settled for their fingers and all of it was being washed down with large glasses of Coca-cola. No one spoke, everyone chewed.

Khalifa delicately dabbed the grease off his chin with a napkin and observed politely, 'Yon speak very good English, Mam'selle.'

Erika nodded. 'Most Swedes of my age group do… we learn it in school.' Erika never took anyone lightly, nor did she underrate them. This man, for instance. He was quick and, despite his overdeveloped libido, suspicious. She decided that it was safer to play it straight. 'I'm expensive,' she said boldly. 'Are you willing to pay my price? If not, it has only cost you lunch.'

A shrewd businessman from a part of the world where bargaining was as natural as the imbibing of one's mother's milk, Khalifa was pleased. She had struck precisely the right note by putting their relationship on a strict financial basis. Encounters across gambling tables were a risky way to scrape up an acquaintance unless the lady was a good-time girl. Had she claimed to he anything else his security people would have certainly had her investigated.

Khalifa couldn't suppress it. Too many generations of oriental blood flowed in his veins – he leered. 'Money is no problem, my dear. If you please me I can be generous.' His throat muscles constricted thus giving the words the consistency of thick syrup.

'I'd rather settle the price now,' Erika insisted.

Khalifa's eyes gleamed with pleasure. 'Very well. As you wish… how much do you want?'

'Three thousand francs for the night.'

Khalifa showed his even white teeth. 'But isn't that too much?'

Erika gave her curls a pretty shake. 'Never. I have my pride – take it or leave it.'

Khalifa nodded. 'You're a good business woman. In francs or American dollars?'

Erika shrugged. 'Money's money. Either will do.'

Khalifa's smile revealed his back molars. 'Now or later?'

'Later will do, thank you.'

You're expensive,' he concluded, meaning it as a compliment. His bulbous eyes fastened on her breasts. A man of imagination, he could see her on his bed, himself removing the last tantalising vestige of her clothing, parting her thighs, reaching out for the heavenly tufted triangle. He fidgeted on the verge of orgasm.

She knew all the signs, stood up mumbling something about the ladies' room and moved off feeling his eyes on her buttocks. But then she was a professional in more ways than one. It was all in a day's work. She didn't feel the slightest embarrassment.

In the ladies' room, she rummaged in her purse, found a *jetton* and dialled a number. Blake picked up the phone on the other end. She confided, 'It'll be tonight... two o'clock,' and hung up.

CHAPTER FOUR

I

ABDUL KHALIFA WAS BUBBLING WITH GOOD WILL. LIFE WAS good. The girl he wanted was willing and, better, all it would cost was money, and he had plenty of that. Yes, life was good. A nice cheque would solve everything. The sheiks frowned on their people, particularly married men with families, getting involved with European girls, and further, they could be extremely strait-laced when it came to scandal. It was all relative, even people in his position couldn't afford to offend them, therefore he decided against bringing her to his hotel suite, it was too public, so he suggested her place.

Erika had done her homework and readily fell in with the suggestion. Further, now that it was settled it was better to let him make the decisions. The bodyguards, of course, presented a problem, there was no way of getting rid of them. She was also aware that Kalifa was finding it difficult to contain his impatience. As the evening progressed, he had been holding his breath, so to speak, counting the minutes until they could be alone, and as a consequence his Chemmy losses were considerable.

Erika had paid particular attention to her dress. No one would have dreamed of criticising the garment, it was in perfect good taste. Nothing blatant, she was amply covered from shoulder to ankle. Knowing her man she had left it to his imagination, which was inclined to be volatile. It was what he couldn't see that tantalised him. She had rightly concluded that for him it all boiled down to the pleasure of anticipation. So close yet so far.

Not for Khalifa the 'Bang, bang, thank you, Ma'am,' in the back seat of a chilly automobile, nor a stolen grope on a crowded dance floor. He required comfort and time to indulge his erotic fancies of sight, sound and touch. Like a long dinner at *Maxime's,* he wanted to savour every swallow.

As all things, good or bad, come to an end sooner or later, the moment finally arrived when he was escorting her down the Casino steps into the back seat of the limousine. As usual, his entourage piled into the other car and he pulled away into the empty streets of Monte Carlo. Khalifa leaned over and politely pecked her cheek, secure in the knowledge that it wouldn't be long now. He thrilled to the feel of a gown that he would shortly be removing.

'Soon, we'll be alone together,' he whispered softly, caressing the little curls at the nape of her neck.

She lifted a cigarette and he promptly lit it for her. The point was, he didn't sit too close. The agony had become a challenge, he had the urge to prolong it a little longer.

Blake and Claud were on hand in the old Renault as the limousines appeared and slid up to the main entrance of Erika's apartment block. Neither spoke as Khalifa's young men spilled out and took up positions around the front door. Others were promptly deployed, presumably around to the back, and two moved promptly into the building.

'I'm impressed,' Blake observed.

Claud grunted. He wasn't.

'At least they're well rehearsed,' Blake insisted.

Claud flicked on a small walkie-talkie, spoke rapidly, 'Two men coming around to the back to cover the service stairs.'

Erika and Khalifa stepped out on the street and moved languidly up the steps. Upstairs, one of his men was standing beside her door. She unlocked it and both men followed her inside.

The apartment was large, luxuriously furnished and several floors up from the street. Erika removed her wrap and nodded to a tray on the coffee table containing a bottle of champagne. Neither paid any attention to the guard as he hurriedly checked the rooms and the terrace. As the man nodded the all clear to his employer, Erika said sweetly, 'Poor man, having to wait outside. Maybe he would like some, too?'

'No alcohol,' Khalifa smiled. 'A Coke, perhaps, if you have it.'

She was back from the kitchen in a moment with the Coke. She added some ice, the man murmured his thanks and scooted back into the hall, closing the door softly behind him.

Khalifa uncorked the bottle with a flourish and filled two glasses which had different coloured stems, one pink, one green. Khalifa handed her the latter. She settled gracefully on the settee and Khalifa sat beside her. Now that they were alone the bird was his. He could afford to take his time.

He gently gathered her into his arms and lightly nibbled the lobe of an ear. Tilting her chin, he studied her face and kissed her lightly on the mouth. Privy to the game, she didn't open her lips, that would come later.

He rose and refilled their glasses.

She softly suggested. 'Would you like me to slip into something more comfortable?'

He shook his head. Any slipping to be done would be done by him. 'Later,' he whispered, 'much later.'

What happened over the next few minutes would have prompted cynical laughter from someone more opinionated than Erika. A natural-born student of human behaviour, she revelled in it, and as was her habit, she learned something as well. He didn't touch her, he brushed her, etching his strokes with the delicacy of a Titian lighting the face of a shadowed Madonna. She enjoyed every moment of it, even regretted the knowledge that it was all destined to be so short.

II

As the elevator doors slid open, Claud had a quick furtive look down the hallway then stepped out followed by one of his men, an ex-middleweight boxer. Both were wearing white overall coats over their clothes. Each pulled an empty wicker laundry basket down the hall to the man sitting cross-legged beside Erika's front door. Claud bent down, lifted his eyelids, muttered, 'That stuff she uses is potent, he's out cold.'

They opened one of the baskets, lifted him in and secured the lid. Then Claud took a key out of his pocket and opened the door. They dragged in the hampers and moved into the lounge. Finding it unoccupied they continued on into the bedroom with the empty hamper. Erika had already changed into a tweed suit for the street. Khalifa was lying fully dressed on the bed and snoring heavily.

Erika glanced at her watch. 'What took you so long? You're two minutes late.'

Claud scowled, 'We allowed for five minutes. Drugs work faster on some than on others… you can go now.'

She cleared the last of her toiletries off the table and placed them carefully into an expensive crocodile case, checked her make-up and, looking the picture of the fresh-faced outdoor girl, moved to the door.

There were two suitcases standing at the end of the bed. 'We'll take those,' Claud said. 'You'll find them in the luggage room at the airport.'

Erika nodded and slipped out without so much as a glance at her latest victim.

The boxer watched her go with something like approval.

'Rene picked a good one – hard as nails.'

Claud hunched his narrow shoulders. 'She'll do. How's the time?'

'We're dead on schedule.'

Claud lifted the lid of the hamper and the ex-pug moved to lift Khalifa. He half managed it then dropped him. '*Merde*, is he fat! I'll need some help with this walrus.'

Claud gave him a hand and even then it was a struggle, but they managed it.

Down below in the foyer, Khalifa's guards were wide awake. The one near the elevator checked his watch, got up and pressed the button. Nothing happened. Evidently someone on one of the upper floors had left the door open. He crossed to the staircase and started up the steps. At the same moment Claud was struggling to get one of the hampers into the elevator.

He grunted irritably, '*Idiot!* I'm not Samson, give me a hand with this.'

When the hampers were safely stowed in the elevator, Claud closed the doors and pressed the button. As they started to descend the guard from the foyer reached the top of the steps and, hurrying down the hall, checked the apartment numbers until he reached Erika's flat. Bewildered, he wondered what had happened to the man who had been posted there. Finding the door firmly locked, he hesitated, then moved reluctantly back along the hall.

Down in the basement, men were on hand to help Claud and his mate lift the hampers out of the elevator and carry them out to the laundry van which was parked in the alley at the service entrance. As the hampers were lifted into the van, Claud glanced with satisfaction at the two young Arabs who lay in a corner blindfolded, firmly trussed up and gagged. All but Claud piled into the back. He stayed behind, secured the door, then moved around to the cab and drove off.

As he turned out into the street it was just beginning to lighten and a few early-risers were moving sleepily towards the bus stops.

He drove carefully, heading north for the foothills of the *Alpes Maritimes* that fringed the entire coast from Cannes to the Italian frontier at *Ventimiglia* and beyond. There was a gradual rise and as he progressed, the turns became sharper. Giving no thought to pursuit, he didn't hurry. As it was he should arrive on time.

Back in Monte Carlo, Khalifa's frantic guards had summoned the *gendarmes* and got the protesting caretaker out of bed. He found his master keys and together they all trooped up to Mam'selle Bannerman's flat. After a thorough search and much chatter in French and Arabic, it was ascertained that there was no sign of human habitation. The bed had been neatly stripped of its linen which lay in its appointed place in the bathroom laundry basket. All shelves, surfaces and drawers had been emptied of all personal belongings, the cupboards, closets and tables were empty, even the ashtrays had been washed. Moreover, there were no fingerprints. It looked what it was: furnished, unoccupied premises.

Furthermore, under the intense questioning of the officer in charge, the caretaker was unable to shed any light on the recent events.

'But what do you expect?' he maintained staunchly. 'It is true that this apartment was occupied by a Mam'selle Bannerman, a young lady from Sweden. It is also true that she paid to the end of the week, and it isn't unusual for temporary tenants to leave a few days early or to ask for small extensions, it is done all the time. She paid in cash,' he said, producing the rent ledger for all to see. 'And, further, may I add, Monsieur, that few tenants leave their apartments in such excellent condition,' he concluded, unable to restrain, even under the eagle eye of the law, his satisfaction regarding the saving of expense in having it available on such short notice.

For the officer in charge, it was an alarming business. The disappearance of so important a personage on Monagasque soil, involving as it would hostile diplomatic and consular officials from states whose nationals had of late been spending large amounts of money there, wasn't pleasant. Everyone would suffer. The golden flood of Arab cash would suddenly cease. The jewellers, the clothiers, the restaurants and hotels, the Casino, what of them? One day knee-deep in cash, the next with nary a sou in the cash registers. Monte Carlo, the recent refuge of the sons of Allah, the mistress of the Mediterranean, once again relegated to the modest expenditure of German industrialists and Italian car-makers, the mad bonanza a fond memory of things past. The stolid officer winced at the thought of the next Council meeting, shopkeeper and banker alike thirsting for his blood. He shuddered at the thought of the repercussions, and worse, the bitter recriminations that would be showered on his head.

To be cursed in Arabic, the peer of all tongues when it comes to profanity and dire threats of revenge, is not pleasant, particularly when you grew up in Algiers, understand the language and are on the receiving end. Everyone was shouting at once. People whined, they wheezed, they wept. Allah was prevailed upon to strike him dead. Under such circumstances it was difficult to uphold the dignity of the law. So it went on, all that day, all that night and all the next day.

The peace of the tiny principality was shattered. The wound was critical. It had struck where it hurt most – in the bank balance and pocketbook, and for that the people mourned.

III

Claud pulled up into the farmyard and hurried around to the back to let the men out. Next he checked the hampers. Gingerly lifting one of the lids he had a quick look inside and closed it again. 'Lift this out and carry it around to the kitchen.' Squatting on the other one, he grinned, 'This one will wake up *au naturel* on the beach at *Juan Les Pins* with a hell of a headache.' When the men returned they all piled into the back again.

One of them glanced at the two prisoners, still huddled in their corner. 'What do we do with them?'

'Dump 'em in the same place,' Claud said, closing the door. He hadn't shown the slightest interest in what was going on in the house, nor did his eyes stray to the pigpen which at that moment was densely populated. Its inhabitants, accustomed to regular meals, hadn't been fed for two days and were vociferously protesting their torment. Claud didn't hear them, he climbed into the van and drove off.

Blake entered the kitchen through an inner door. It was a large room which had the appearance of being inhabited by simple country people of modest means. The plumbing was up-to-date, there was an old-fashioned wood-burning iron stove, a heavy rectangular wooden table that could seat a dozen people and a sprinkling of rustic dressers, sideboards and chairs. The floor was stone and an electric lamp was suspended from the ceiling over the table. A homely place, traditionally the most lived-in room in the house.

Blake moved directly to the hamper that had been left in the middle of the room. He pulled out the bar and as he lifted the lid Abdul Khalifa leaped out like something jet-propelled, his momentum rolling both himself and Blake along the floor. Khalifa struck out blindly, hitting, kicking, scratching, biting. He fought like a cornered cat. Blake stared at the crazed face an inch above his own, felt the numbing pressure of the thumbs on his windpipe, waited for them to tighten. The clatter in his head told him that unless he did something fast this was the end of his life.

He finally managed to gather up his feet and desperately heaved, hurling the enormous weight off his chest. There was a dull thud as the Arab's head smashed into one of the table legs, which splintered then broke away. The full weight of the table came crashing down. Khalifa screamed, thrashed about for a moment like an insect pinned to a board, then lay still.

Blake was stretched out on the floor gasping for breath, his lungs afire, his pulse booming in his ears, his mind a throbbing mass of confused impulses. He had lost his equilibrium. The shock of the sudden attack, the vicious struggle, had left him bereft of everything other than the instinct to survive. Khalifa's fingernails had carved deep rents in his face, blood from a gash on his head was flowing down into his eyes, where he didn't ache it was numb. He couldn't think. He lay there waiting for Khalifa, but Khalifa didn't come, then he found himself on his knees crawling to find him.

Khalifa lay crushed beneath the table, his eyes wide open, staring up at the ceiling. He was dead. Blake suddenly felt very tired. He settled slowly to the floor and was asleep before his cheek touched the cold stone.

IV

Blake looked out of the window and saw that the sun was still high above the hills. He had cleaned the cuts on his face, there was a Bandaid or two and other than some stiffness in his joints and a couple of bruises, he felt good. Crossing to one of the dressers, he loaded a film roll into his camera and screwed it into its tripod. Then there was the flash. When this was attached, he moved out of the house, crossed to the pen and wired the tripod to the top railing of the fence. The mere sight of a human started a stampede of famished pigs. They threshed about in the mud, fighting for a place near the fence, and when no food materialised the maddened animals turned on themselves, the boar butting the sows, weaving his ugly tusks like knives. Blake returned to the house.

Back in the kitchen, he stoked up the stove with an armful of logs, found a sharp knife and moved to the table. This was back in its place, supported by a pile of books in the corner where the leg had been broken, and Khalifa's body lay stretched out on its surface. Blake placed the blade of the knife under a trouser cuff and slit it up to the waist. When he was finished, the body was stripped and the clothing (including the shoes) was burning in the stove.

Blake put another log on the fire then lifted the body over his shoulder. It was dead weight and it took some time to manoeuvre it into the right position, then he carried it out to the pen. It was more difficult to lift it to the top of the railing. When this was done, he adjusted the focus on the camera, checked the flash-apparatus, lifted the legs of the corpse and let it drop into the pen.

The hungry herd had wandered off and were restlessly milling around the empty swill-trough. The king boar was the first to sense the presence of the corpse. Perhaps it was its sense of smell heightened by ravenous hunger, but whatever it was, the huge beast knew it was there. It lifted its head, pawed the ground like an angry bull, whirled and with a deep menacing grunt – charged.

Blake straddled the fence, rapidly snapping its progress as it closed on the body in the mud, the rest of the herd squealing in its wake.

Blake aimed the camera down on the body as it vanished under the writhing welter and he sat there coolly clicking away until the last splintering bone and fragment of flesh was consumed.

For a Muslim it was a lamentable burial.

CHAPTER FIVE

I

ONCE AGAIN THE CLAMOUR OF HEAVY TRAFFIC RESOUNDED on the roads and the crowds flowed through the sun-baked streets of the ruined city; for although it was the first of October, summer weather still blazed down on the empty tourist beaches.

The shelves in the shops were glutted with goods and the market stalls bulged with fruit and vegetables, the shopkeepers and hawkers, many in badly-damaged premises, were doing a roaring trade, but the ravages of the intermittent civil war were apparent everywhere. Hardly a street had escaped the shelling, almost every large building had sustained serious damage, and some of Beirut's most modern office blocks and hotels had been reduced to burnt-out shells. But everywhere there was evidence of rapid rubble-clearance and rebuilding. The remains of badly-shelled buildings were being levelled altogether and new ones were being built on their foundations, and as a consequence, firms engaged in the demolition and building trades were doing unprecedented business.

The troops of the Arab peacekeeping force, ironically the majority of them Syrian regulars who at one stage had helped the Maronite Christians subdue the Palestinians, and at another had reversed the order and supported the Palestinians against the Maronites, patrolled the streets to forestall outbreaks of fighting which could erupt at any time and escalate into full-scale war.

Soviet and American interference in the area, subsequent arms deliveries from both to the factions they favoured to keep the place in an uproar. The arch enemy Israel periodically launching punitive expeditions over her frontiers to protect her forward border settlements. Vociferous left-wing Palestinian groups fighting to keep a foothold in a land that didn't want them. Right-wing Christian Lebanese fighting like the Jordanians a few years earlier to kick them out. A negligible UN gesture (as usual, too little too late) in a futile attempt to keep the factions apart. Lack of logic (or power to put it into practice), mindless passion, wayward hatred degenerating into armed conflict. It was happening all over the world and the emergence of the oil-rich states of the Persian Gulf who, apart from their strategic proximity to the Suez Canal, provided what the industrial West could not do without: fuel for their machines. Behind the scenes nothing had changed. The bitter hostility that had already cost over fifteen thousand lives, the hatred between the native Lebanese and their unwelcome guests still festered like a running sore, but despite all this, this industrious trading race was in the process of restoring the country to its former prosperity. The 'Switzerland of the Middle East' was back in business, and if another war knocked it all down, they would build it all over again. Thus, who on that particular day would have guessed that the carefree young postman cavorting through the traffic on his new motor-scooter had in his possession something so explosive that in a matter of hours its repercussions would ring around the world.

There would be some strange turnabouts. Unlikely people would voice their opinions and add fuel to the controversy. Pundits would pronounce their verdicts, the doom-merchants their forecasts, the stock markets would tremble, governments would close ranks to the threat of another world war.

Happily unaware, the young postman skidded into a kerb on the *Boulevard Khalil El-Khuri*, skirted a freshly paved shell-crater and shot into the offices of the *Pan-Arab News*, a militant Arab publication temporarily housed in the patched-up remains of a supermarket. The package was addressed to the editor, Asaf Barakat, who was hard at work on the next day's editorial page when it landed in his in-basket.

Barakat, a conservative by nature and a political dissenter by conviction, was a good newspaper man. Later that morning as he sifted through his mail he opened the package and emptied its contents out on his desk. Lifting one of the enclosed photographs, he gave it a brief glance, moved to discard it, then looked again. His eyes widened, he paled, it seemed to burn his fingers. He dropped it and picked up one of the other pictures depicting the remains of a human arm being devoured by a huge tusked boar. Barakat lunged for the wastepaper basket and vomited.

Later that day he hightailed it to a Palestinian enclave up in the hills on the outskirts of Beirut, a place bristling with weapons and trigger-happy sentries. The meeting was held in the underground headquarters of Habib Yasli, the leader of one of the more extreme terrorist groups which had broken away from the less militant Palestine Liberation Organisation headed by Yasser Arafat. Other than Barakat there were three others present: Yasli himself, a German national of many aliases who currently called himself Hans Reichter, and a Muslim banker named Mahmoud Farak, a diminutive Lebanese who had been pressured by Yasli into contributing large amounts of money to the movement.

Yasli sat behind a small table examining a short typewritten list containing three names that had been enclosed with Blake's photographs presently being circulated around the room. He lifted his head and said quietly, 'This list contains three familiar names, mine and Mr Reichter's here. Khalira I didn't know personally... only by reputation,' he concluded wrinkling up his nose with marked distaste.

Reichter, a thin-lipped ex-lawyer with thus far unproven connections with the Baader-Meinhof terrorists, was neatly dressed and nondescript; indistinguishable from the legion of civil servants that inhabit the government departments of northern Europe. He scratched a bluish chin, acknowledged the introduction with a slight inclination of his head and promptly returned to his careful perusal of the photographs.

Habib Yasli continued, 'They seem to have singled out the three most successful leaders presently involved in the liberation struggle.' He spoke not from conceit but conviction.

Reichter sat stiffly. Little beads of sweat had broken out on his forehead. He passed the photos on to Farak, who seemed reluctant to touch them.

Yasli stood up, his sharp scholarly features at odds with his ill-fitting dungarees. 'I wouldn't take it too seriously. To find us they shall have to discover our true identity, these names mean nothing...'

Reichter cut in softly, 'They identified Khalifa.'

Farak moaned. He had risked a glance at the photos after all. He stumbled over the floor and flung them on the table. 'It's horrible!' he cried, 'Obscene. They not only kill, they desecrate – it's barbaric!'

Yasli ignored the outburst. 'Does that surprise you?' he asked turning to the German. 'Khalifa I understand was an extrovert, liked to attract attention to himself.'

Farak sat fervently muttering over a string of amber worry beads. 'They'll kill us all in the end,' he sighed. 'Merciful Allah, what do you expect of us?'

Like a schoolmaster chastising a miscreant, Yasli turned to him contemptuously, 'Your name isn't on the list. Spare us the histrionics.' He turned back to Reichter. 'Ask yourself – who are they working for? It's obvious enough. American Intelligence... it was a professional killing. Now they think they can frighten us into giving up our cherished objectives with this preposterous ultimatum.'

Barakat hadn't spoken for some time. 'It could have been an Israeli execution squad,' he suggested uneasily.

Yasli was becoming impatient. 'Jews wouldn't feed a man to pigs any more than we would,' he snapped pettishly. 'It's perfectly simple. What the Americans can't do publicly they're doing secretly. Who else could it be? They'll deny it, of course, but it won't do them any good. This time they've bitten off more than they can chew. Must I remind you that we have powerful friends and the capability to strike back?'

He moved around to his desk and said, dismissing them, 'We have intelligence sources ourselves and I can inform you that they will soon be in the process of tracing the source of this threat and the murderers of our brother in the south of France. We shall track them down. Only a large organisation would have the financial means and the trained personnel to attempt such a thing. This alone tells me who they are,' Yasli said grimly. 'Well, we shall see. We have funds as well, and the men, we shall deal with them.' He stood up, terminating the meeting with a peremptory wave of a hand.

The others got up and there was a hard edge to Reichter's voice when he observed, 'You can do what you like, we take our own precautions. Also allow me to remind you,' he added coldly, resenting what he took to be Yasli's arrogant dismissal, 'that although we have been generous with our donations and at times, at no little risk to ourselves, helpful on some of your more dangerous operations, we might not be so forthcoming in the future. Furthermore, I might also enquire why you failed to mention the footnote added to that list,' he went on, rising stiffly to his feet. 'Although they weren't specifically mentioned by name, it states that all survivors responsible for the executions at London Airport last July will be... I believe the word used was "*exterminated*". To conclude, I believe that these people, whoever they are, have shown themselves to be capable of carrying out their threats. It remains to be seen what you can do to stop them.' Before the terrorist leader could reply, Reichter stalked out.

Barakat had a lot to do. The story had already been released to the wire services and he had his own edition to get out. He hurriedly followed, mumbling an apology from the door.

The little banker, unaware of the exodus, still sat there mumbling over his worry beads.

Yasli shrugged indifferently and picked up the phone. He was an active man. After all, murder was his business, threats the source of his daily bread and death lists, either his own or anyone else's, were merely routine.

II

Hunched over like a sprinter on his starting blocks, Renway took off as Roker stepped into the office. 'Don't tell me. Duscharne was polite but knew nothing.'

Roker looked tired. 'He was also touchingly apologetic. Anything we require in the way of assistance we only need ask. French Intelligence is anxious to cooperate.'

'Blake couldn't have moved an inch without his help.'

'That's right.'

'But why? What's in it for Duscharne?'

'Who knows? Maybe Blake's paying good money or Rene owes him, most people do.'

Renway observed hopefully, 'We could be wrong, it might not have been Blake after all.'

Roker was doubtful. 'His trademark is all over it. The planning, the way it was done, the place, the aftermath. That town was wiped clean, they found nothing, not even a cigarette butt. That took organisation and men. It was Duscharne all right... seen this?'

Roker spread the morning edition of a London daily out on the desk. A banner headline covered the entire front page,. Block letters an inch high proclaimed:

ARAB BUSINESS MAN MURDERED IN NICE!

Renway turned to the leader on page two for more of the same:

Victim's reputed links with terrorist gangs. Three names on death list in worldwide vendetta against terrorist groups. IRA, Jap Red Army, Argentine Tupamaros, Baader-Meinhof among those mentioned. USA and Israel accused in UN General Assembly.

Late last night at a hastily-called press conference in Beirut, the editor of the influential Pan-Arab News, *Asaf Barakat, tearfully announced what he called 'the barbaric murder' of Abdul Khalifa, a millionaire prominent in Middle-Eastern political affairs and Vice-Consul in Monaco for the oil-rich Trucial States of the Persian Gulf. Barely able to control his emotions, Mr Barakat revealed to the hastily-assembled press corps that he had received a batch of 'horrifying' photographs through the post showing the dismembered parts of a human body purporting to belong to Khalifa being fed to pigs. These were distributed to the pressmen, all of whom said they were sickened by the inhuman sights these revealed.*

Mr Barakat then distributed copies of a death list containing the names of three revolutionaries claimed to be either actively involved in recent terrorist acts themselves or accused of providing financial aid to those responsible. The editor then produced a letter from the unknown assassins – an ultimatum – bluntly stating that the killing of Abdul Khalifa was only the beginning, that the other two persons named on the list would suffer a similar fate, or far worse, until terrorism was outlawed throughout the world and its perpetrators promptly exterminated by order of all member governments represented in the United Nations General Assembly.

Early today a French Police spokesman in Nice announced the sudden disappearance of the alleged victim, adding that a large-scale hunt has been mounted by the authorities which will continue until he is found. When questioned regarding the Lebanese editor's allegations, he replied that there would be no comment until the French Police had an opportunity to examine Mr Barakat's evidence. He also stated that there would be no further announcements regarding Abdul Khalifa's disappearance until his present whereabouts are established.

One Arab diplomat in London, declining to give his name, announced after hearing a late-night radio broadcast from Beirut, that if Mr Barakat's allegations are true such a death will result in widespread unrest throughout the Muslim world until the killers are found and brought to justice.

An informed source in Beirut also reported that the death list contained a reference to last summer's massacre at Heathrow Airport and stated that all surviving terrorists who took part would be killed.

Renway grunted and pushed the paper aside, exclaiming, 'They're all the same this morning, so much for British understatement.' He sat there for a moment collecting his thoughts, then asked, 'Where could Blake raise the kind of money it takes to finance an operation like that?'

'Who knows? But it's odds on that Linderman arranged it. His trademark is all over it. At a rough guess I'd say one of the big oil outfits. They're taking a beating from terrorist shakedowns, particularly in places like Libya and Iraq, and don't forget the Sauclis and the other Gulf States are hurting along with them. But then, it could be anybody – Linderman has a lot of high-powered connections, that's his bag, isn't it?'

Renway stood there, musing on Roker's remarks. He kept at it like a surfeited dog pawing a bone, gravitating to his favourite window. 'Arabs finance the murder of one of their own people? Can't see that. Particularly now. Things are pretty delicate out there, why rock the boat?'

Roker pressed his point, even if he was shooting in the dark. 'Like a lot of people out there they're fed up with extremists. Look what the Syrians did to the Palestinians.'

'Centre's interrogation report doesn't substantiate that. Lipscomb and White don't deny meeting Blake but they both claim nothing came of it... they would, of course. Linderman would steer him to the right people.'

Roker stood up. 'Anyway, what are we talking about? There are no hard facts, we're simply speculating. Centre will decide what has to be done.'

'I'm afraid they already have,' Renway said, reluctantly returning to his chair. He opened a drawer, drew forth a neatly-folded piece of paper and handed it to Roker. 'That came in from the code room just before you arrived.'

The two men's eyes met and held. Roker hadn't opened it, but raw intuition and the uncomfortable expression on the other's face gave him a pretty good idea what it contained. He slowly unfolded it. The directive, like all such documents from Centre, was brutally brief and to the point, this one contained one word – *Eliminate*.

Roker stared at the paper. He had been with the Agency too long to be caught unawares and had expected something of the kind. But to see it written like that, in black and white, an actual order for the execution of a trusted friend, and more – one of that same Agency's most valuable men – was more than he could absorb. It required great effort to articulate the question. 'Who are you assigning to this?' he asked, lifting his eyes.

Renway's voice was strained. 'You, Jim. Right now there's no one else.'

Roker wadded up the paper, dropped it gently into the wastepaper basket, and moved to the door. He found the knob and with slow deliberation turned it. He didn't raise his voice, he simply said, 'Centre can go to hell. Like the Mafia they send a friend to kill a friend... because no one else could get that close. As of now, I quit. And something else; they can start their debriefing any time they like – I'm at their disposal.' As he stepped out, Renway shot out into the hall after him. He was a determined man.

III

The ordnance supply clerk down in the basement, one of many experts in that department, probably knew as much about the art of killing as his counterpart in the Lubianka compound in

Moscow. Of indeterminate age, he was wearing a tracksuit, reminding Roker that it was the weekend.

'I have anything you want,' he was reciting knowledgeably, 'depending on the nature of the assignment and, of course, individual preference.' He lifted a tube of toothpaste. 'This, for instance, perfectly simple. You pop it into his luggage or bathroom cabinet, we issue them in kits containing all the popular brands. He scrubs his teeth and a minute or so later he's dead. The beauty of it is it gives him time to rinse his mouth before he drops. Difficult to trace, even in a lab.'

Roker thought it was an ordinary face, but the eyes betrayed it. Large, soulful, brown, those of a bloodhound gazing mournfully towards the kennel after a kill.

'Then there's this. Fairly new, this one.' He lifted an instrument roughly the size of a hypodermic syringe but containing a flat round surface in place of the needle. 'You can't see them but this is perforated with microscopic holes. Principle is beautifully simple. You place it against any naked surface, cheek, neck, hand, then push the plunger, forcing the poison through the pores. Nothing other than a more compact replica of the instrument they use to inoculate people nowadays.'

Roker had a sudden urge to bring something hard down on that grinning head, but too late, the expert was on his feet, opening a long drawer in one of the many cabinets cluttering the room. He lifted out a long leather case smelling of Cosmoline oil and zipped it open with loving care, revealing the parts of a high-powered sniper's rifle complete with telescope. Each piece lay snuggling in its velvet compartment. Roker turned away. Somehow more than anything – perhaps because it was so familiar – this symbolised the horrible nature of the assignment. He fled.

Upstairs, Renway was waiting, and like everyone else in the building he was anxious to get away. He had promised to drive the kids out to Surrey for a nature walk. Roker didn't bother to knock. He went in slamming the door behind him. 'I must be out of my mind to let you talk me into this!' he shouted. 'But not now – I'm through. Jesus Christ, what do you take me for?'

'A good Agency man,' Renway said, hiding his impatience.

Then more sympathetically, he added, 'Sit down, Jim, we'll get nowhere like this.'

Roker was on the verge of going over the top, but sensing that the other really was sympathetic, he cooled down and settled into a chair.

'Look at it this way,' Renway began gently, 'if you were Centre and Blake was running wild, what would you do? Somebody's got to do something. You've read the papers, watched television, listened to the radio, no need to tell you how bad it is. Even without proof, they're blaming us for everything, including the Recession, and if it ever comes out that one of our own men is actually responsible, people are going to believe them. If you can tell me how Blake can be stopped short of killing him, I'm willing to listen.'

'What you're really saying is,' Roker protested, jumping up out of his seat, 'we're willing to kill a man on mere speculation to appease Arab public opinion, and we both know why – we need their goddamn oil!'

Renway reluctantly agreed, 'That's part of it, yes.'

Roker stood there, struggling with his temper, 'That's *all* of it!'

'Look Jim…' Renway began helplessly, but Roker cut him short.

'They run in packs like mad dogs, shooting up airports, machine-gunning innocent people, and its hands-off because we mustn't hurt their feelings – Arab public opinion, bullshit! Arab oil! What a pack of hypocrites.'

Renway raised placating hands, 'Calm down. We've got to get out of this somehow. Why do you think I picked you? He might listen. Blake's a lot of things but he's not stupid. He knows the position we're in… an oil embargo could bring the whole country to a standstill: he'd be playing right into the hands of the Russians.'

'It's worth a try,' Roker admitted doubtfully.

Renway brightened, 'You do that, Jim. You might even talk him out of it.'

Roker despaired again, 'But why me?'

'You know why. Better than I, better than Centre. I'll say it again – because no one else could get near him.'

Roker stood there, his head bent, his eyes tightly shut. 'He'll know the moment he sees me.' He looked up, his eyes blazing angrily again. 'It's so obvious.'

Renway didn't answer directly, aware that this was precisely what Blake would do. He'd know. Roker was right, it was a chance in a thousand. 'I agree, except for one thing – it'll have to be done deliberately. If you can convince him that you agree with what he's doing…'

Roker laughed bitterly. 'Oh, come on! You know damned well I agree. So do you, so does everyone else in the Agency. We're sick and tired of wiping the ass of every simpering crackpot who takes it into his head that he's got a cause worth killing for. And who gets hurt? Always some poor bastard who happens to get in the way. Blake's got a lot going for him and everybody knows it.'

Renway set off on another voyage around the windows. 'Plenty,' he admitted. 'Ten, twenty years ago, I'd have agreed with you, but times have changed. The stargazers are running the show right now and they're everywhere, even in the President's oval office. Let 'em do what they want, run hog wild, even kill people, and the "progressives" will come up with an excuse. We're breeding a race of illiterate yahoos and we call it the Permissive Society.'

Roker hadn't moved, he still stood there, his head down, his eyes closed.

Renway went on, 'We can't change it, not yet anyway. It'll have to get a lot worse before somebody gets up and says, "That's enough." Then what do you get – Fascism. The ice is that thin. How do we deal with people like the ones who killed Blake's daughter and still live in a free country? Vigilante action is out. We give in to that and the Birch Society will have us marching in jackboots. We're in this for keeps, Jim. It's too late to ask why, but not late enough to do what Blake has done.' Renway moved back to his desk. 'It's quite simple really. We're professionals. We do what has to be done. The plain fact is that Blake, like the terrorists, has taken the law into his own hands and put his country into a very dangerous position. If we don't find him before they do, our enemies will have a field day… you with me, Jim?'

'You haven't given me much choice.' Roker sighed. His intuition had been right: he was the patsy after all.

'You know the rest, we won't accept any more oil embargoes and that could lead to something very nasty at a time of unprecedented Soviet military expansion.'

Roker sat up, the strain of the last few days having etched deep circles under his eyes. Renway didn't know it all. Blake was only part of it. He had personal problems as well. 'When it rains, it pours,' he groaned.

But he was wrong. It was Renway's job (and he was good at it) to know what went on in his men's personal lives. Little escaped his notice. 'Give my best to Edith,' he said.

IV

Edith Roker was a beautiful woman. Unlike many of her kind she exuded a warm charm and a natural friendliness that people found captivating; even on short acquaintance they realised that this was genuine, consequently she never lost a friend. She was a rare phenomenon in an age that bred aggressive, dominating females. Gentle, delicately feminine, a keeper of confidences, unbitchy, there was but one flaw: she had married the wrong man.

For his part Jim Roker loved her dearly, as she loved him, but somehow they weren't suited to each other. They had little in common. Edith liked people, enjoyed their company, delighted in seeing old friends. She liked to entertain, adored the theatre and the ballet, was an avid reader of the better authors and the heavy Sunday reviews and regularly went to painting exhibitions. The arts were a vital part of her life.

Jim Roker on the other hand was a solitary, an introvert, who valued the friendship of a few trusted friends but liked nothing better than to slip off alone somewhere for a few days fishing. People in numbers made him uncomfortable, he mistrusted intellectuals and others who 'went on' about art. In his younger days, he had won letters in three sports both in high school and university and even in England, where there was no American football, he had become a Rugby Union fan. He wasn't much of a reader and other than the occasional movie or detective series on television, which helped pass the time, he suffered in silence when Edith dragged him off to a concert or a play.

Oddly enough it had never occurred to either of them to get a divorce, but time had taken its toll. There was nothing dramatic, simply a gradual parting of the ways, until they reached the stage where they didn't have much to say to each other.

Edith had no idea what her husband actually did in the government service other than he was something of an agricultural expert who in recent years had done a lot of work in collaboration with the Unesco food organisation in under-developed countries. During his frequent absences she missed him, but then too – although the thought had never actually occurred to her – she felt less guilty when he was away and freer to pursue her interests.

This being the situation between Jim Roker and his wife it is surprising how dramatic the realisation was when it finally came. Both were desolate. There were no villains in the piece, no 'other' man or woman. They had simply come to the end of the line. There was nothing to hold them together, not even children. After eighteen years of marriage they were strangers.

That was the position when Roker received orders from Renway to kill Blake. Leaving the embassy and walking through Grosvenor Square, he found that the day was unnaturally bright. Things took on an unreal definition, even something so trivial as a pedestrian walking down the street. Roker remembered exactly what he looked like, even the colour of the socks he was wearing; and the silences, right there in the midst of the roaring traffic, were unnerving. He was like a man with rubber plugs in his ears. And Edith was waiting with the ritual martini (very dry with two olives) when he walked into the living room.

He pecked her cheek and slumped into the sofa, utterly drained. 'God, I'm beat!'

Edith Roker settled into the armchair opposite. Her dress was simple but as with all her clothes it suited her perfectly. He found it a pleasure to simply sit back and look at her.

'Rough day, darling?' she asked gently. Of late they had been that way with each other; not that they ever spoke sharply, throughout their marriage there had never been one serious quarrel about anything. But now more than ever, like skaters on thin ice, they moved warily.

Roker sipped his martini and announced lightly, 'I'm off again on one of those damned trips.' It was a lightness he didn't feel.

She nodded. 'I'll help you pack.'

'Edith?'

'Umm?'

'I love you.'

'I know.'

Words. Pathetic probings by two lost people. Why was it so hard to say? Why, whatever was said, would it be so inadequate if either summoned the courage? How did one articulate the ending of all those thousands of days and nights of genuine affection and loving tenderness? People didn't. They stumbled in the dark, telling themselves that somehow it would all come out right in the end.

'Jane Renway phoned this afternoon,' she said. 'She wants me to stay with them for two weeks. They've rented a cottage in Cornwall. It's five minutes from one of those lovely coves.' She emptied the shaker into his glass.

'Going?'

She nodded. 'It'll be good to get out of town for a while. Come, I've made you something nice for dinner.'

Words? But that was not what they said.

'This is goodbye,' they said, 'and I won't be here when you return. You know it, I know it. There is no one else. We love but we part. Together we are only partly alive. It is no one's fault. We've done our best. If we remain together we will die.'

That was what they said.

V

Edith drove him to Heathrow as she had done all the other times and when he passed through into the departure lounge, she went up to the platform on the roof where she might have one last look at him as he walked on the plane or entered the bus that would take him out to it. She had always done this, that last brief glimpse was important to them both. He knew exactly where to find her, she always stood in the same spot.

It was insane. Here he was, his life falling apart, waving a last goodbye to the woman he loved, then flying out to kill his best friend.

He stopped at the bottom of the steps leading up into the plane and turned to see her waving frantically on the distant roof.

He wondered if he would ever see her again.

CHAPTER SIX

I

IT WAS CLOSE ON TWO A.M. WHEN BLAKE PAID OFF THE TAXI and started to walk along a desolate stretch of road well up in the hills behind Nice. After ten minutes he found Duscharne's car parked off a side road, its lights switched off and well hidden behind some trees at the agreed rendezvous. Blake climbed into the front seat beside Rene and found him in a sullen mood. 'I've got better things to do,' the Frenchman growled, 'than meet you in the middle of the night in the middle of nowhere.'

Blake didn't reply. Instead he produced a bottle of Calvados, unscrewed the cap and passed it over. 'Drink it while it's hot, too much fresh air takes the wallop out of it.'

Rene exploded. '*Salaud!* I welcome you, I bend over backwards to give you what you say you need, I even ask a fair price for the use of my men, and you shit all over my back yard!'

'If you don't need it, I do,' Blake said, snatching the bottle and tilting it up to his mouth.

'*Canaille!*' Rene yelled, snatching back the bottle. 'You agreed. No bodies. Liar!'

'*Bonne chance, mon ami,*' Blake declared as Rene gulped down the raw liquor. He was in a jovial mood. He suddenly remembered. 'What bodies? or to be more precise – what *body*?'

The Frenchman writhed in his seat just managing to contain his anger.

'Those photographs, that's what body. Right now they're on the front page of every paper in France. Already I've been summoned to Paris. What then? How am I to explain that? You tell me, you traitor!'

Blake threw a fond arm over his friend's shoulder. 'Perfectly simple. You say, yes, there are photographs, but is there a sign written over the pigpen stating that it belongs to a farm in the *Alpes Maritimes*, or for that matter even in France itself? You also mention that there were three bodyguards, one of whom saw nothing but his late boss and a girl called Erika before he fell asleep. The other two saw nothing after they left Khalifa and the girl at the front door of the apartment block. They woke up hours later blindfolded, gagged, firmly trussed up and didn't even know where they were until somebody dumped them out of a truck on a beach somewhere. And by the time one of them had the presence of mind to rip off his blindfold, the truck was lost in traffic. To sum up, none of them saw anything, so *voilá*,' Blake concluded snapping his fingers, 'where did it happen – Spain, Italy, Switzerland, even Britain? Nobody knows.'

But Rene wasn't mollified. 'What about those headlines in the papers, that news editor in Beirut and his death list, the threatening letter, how am I going to explain that?'

'With one of your better shrugs. All that anybody knows is that somebody snatched Khalifa out of his girlfriend's apartment, and even she has disappeared. You did the only thing you could do, you blanketed the area with search parties and had the Monaco police question the bodyguards. It's only a few miles from Monte Carlo to the Italian frontier, it's anyone's guess where Khalifa wound up – and the photographs, well, no one yet has managed to identify the victim in those. So cheer up, old buddy, and say *Adieu.*'

'Where to this time?' Rene enquired grudgingly, still engrossed in what Blake had said.

'Ever been to India?'

'Once was enough. I like cows but not when they wander around the streets.' Rene felt much better now. Paris HQ didn't have a leg to stand on, they could only suspect, but then in his trade suspicion was a permanent adjunct of the job.

'I might spend a day or two in Bombay, then go up to Agra and have a look at the Taj Mahal.'

Rene didn't hide his relief. 'Who's the poor fool meeting your plane this time?'

'Another old pal,' Blake mused. 'Don't think you know him.'

Rene gave his large head an emphatic shake. 'Don't want to either.' He kicked the starter and began to back out into the road.

II

Yuri Yarabin was a fastidious man. Of meticulous temperament, he took great pains with his appearance. His superbly-cut clothes were made by a tailor in London's Savile Row, his linen in Rome and Gucci of Florence provided his shoes. Born out of his time, he would have felt more at home in the days of the Czars living the leisured life of a nineteenth-century aristocrat. Something of a hedonist he secretly regretted the more puritanical aspects of life in Soviet Russia.

But as is often the case with people, there was another side to his character. Paradoxically, Yarabin was one of the faithful, a true believer in the Marxist ethic, a pragmatist. Ostensibly the Soviet Consul-General in Bombay, he was in fact Blake's counterpart in the intelligence secretariat of the Department of Internal Security (KGB), a Lieutenant-General and supreme head of its activities on the Indian subcontinent.

Having just risen from a good meal, he was in excellent spirits as he stepped out of the old Victorian mansion that housed the consulate and into the spacious back seat of the embassy limousine. Not long afterwards, as the vehicle pulled up for a traffic-light, the door suddenly opened and Blake jumped in beside the astonished Russian. 'You're looking fine, Yuri,' he grinned, 'curry evidently agrees with you.'

Yarabin hurriedly leaned forward and closed the window which divided the back seat from the driver. Settling back on the cushions, he stormed, 'Are you mad? Out in the open like this? Suppose I'm seen with you!'

Blake was enjoying himself. 'Oh, we've been seen all right, old buddy, that driver of yours isn't exactly blind.'

Yarabin flinched like someone trying to avoid a blow. 'He isn't exactly deaf either so keep your voice down. There are such things as letter-drops, or haven't you heard of them?' he concluded wearily.

Blake followed Yarabin's eyeline and found himself staring into the large burly back of the driver. His high spirits overflowed. 'Who is he, Yuri? Brezhnev in disguise or someone equally important – don't tell me he outranks you. Still, it wouldn't be the first time.' He dug his unwilling host in the ribs with an elbow. 'Your watcher, is he? Who does he report to, you?'

Yarabin raised an outraged hand. Even in anger he had style. 'Enough! And the answer to whatever you want is no.'

'Now that's too bad, Yuri. I always had a high regard for you, even though we are on opposite sides of the fence, as the saying goes. Maybe I just wanted to see you, you're a sight for sore eyes. Why forego the pleasure with a letter-drop?'

'It's safer,' Yarabin cautioned, his eyes straying back to the driver's beefy back.

Blake clicked an admonitory tongue. 'Yuri, how *could* you? That sort of thing went out with high-button shoes.'

Yarabin's smile was tightly contemptuous. 'Don't teach your grandfather how to suck eggs.'

Blake admitted defeat. 'Sorry, I forgot. You're senior.'

'By fifteen years, and don't you forget it.' Yarabin was regaining some of his good humour.

The limousine had reached Ocean Drive, a wide boulevard with palm trees in the middle which skirted the sea. Luxury apartment buildings began to appear with an occasional Victorian mansion set back in its own grounds.

'The Indians call it the Queen's necklace... reminds me of the Bay of Naples,' the Russian remarked reminiscently, gazing out over the water. He offered Blake a cigar which was refused. Yuri sighed, reminding Blake of someone out of the British Raj when the dominant colour on the map of the world was red. Yarabin was one of his favourite people.

Yuri went on. 'Last time I saw you was on Capri. That hotel on the top of the hill... the name escapes me?'

'The Vesuvio,' Blake drawled, this prompting thoughts of Monica and a few stolen days years back, her joy a wonder to behold when he had acted as her guide on a tour of Axel Munthe's villa.

'The Vesuvio,' echoed Yarabin, 'how stupid of me. I was thinking of its view of the Bay of Naples, one of the loveliest sights in the world.'

Slowing at a crossroads, the car started up the gradual rise leading to the Hill of Silence, a sacred place encompassed by a high stone wall. Here the Parsees, one of many religious sects in India, disposed of their dead.

There were no tombs or mausoleums, no graveyard, because the Parsees didn't bury them. There were some high towers resembling medieval battlements which were roofed over with iron-grills. When someone died, his body was borne to the top, stripped of its shroud, covered with flowers and laid out on the grill. It was an ancient ritual, also a practical one, because the vultures – those great winged sanitary machines – soon gathered and when the bones were picked clean they simply dropped through the grill.

Both Blake and Yarabin knew India and were familiar with the custom. 'An appropriate place to do our little business,' Blake quipped. 'How about a breath of air?'

Yarabin was not amused. He ordered his man to pull up at the gate and wait, then stepped out with Blake. Once inside, except for a funeral party of two, they had the place to themselves. When they reached the top of the hill, Yarabin stopped to wipe a damp forehead with a silk handkerchief smelling of *eau de cologne*.

'All right, Sam, what do you want?' he demanded grimly.

'A favour.'

'God, what insolence! You have the effrontery to jump into my car on a crowded street where half Bombay can see you and now you want a favour – God help you because I certainly won't.'

He turned to leave but Blake restrained him. 'Watch it, lovey, that's the second time you mentioned that gent's name. If you're not careful, they'll haul you up before the Atheist tribunal in the dear old Lubianka.'

Quivering with rage, the Russian lost his temper again.

'I could have you shot!'

They were standing beside a bench. Blake sat down. 'Undoubtedly. You could also put me to sleep, tuck me into a stretcher and fly me to Moscow, never to be heard of again. If you weren't already a Hero of the Soviet Union, you'd certainly make it then.' Blake looked bored.

Yarabin readily agreed. 'Don't think I haven't thought of it.'

Curiosity compelled him to settle beside Blake on the bench.

'You're a bit late, old friend. I'm already considering one of your firm's bids and finding it awfully hard to refuse...'

Yarabin looked away in disgust. Blake thought it was a refined face, although hardened by years in the field and a long spell of solitary confinement in one of Stalin's jails for having the temerity to survive the Spanish Civil War. Yarabin hadn't been alone. Even an exalted personage like Julius Kadar, the present Prime Minister of Hungary, had suffered the same fate. After personally ordering men to fight in Spain the little Marshal had condemned them on their return for the crime of 'having exposed themselves to decadent Western materialism'.

'Wouldn't it be nice if I wasn't around any more,' Blake resumed. 'Me out of your hair for good, you in the lovely dulcet clear – a pleasant thought.'

Yarabin was beginning to feel sorry for himself. 'Some of us do have feelings, sometimes we can even remember past little favours.'

'Sometimes… but this isn't one of them, eh, Yuri?' Blake wasn't smiling.

'It might be,' Yarabin managed with great reluctance. Committing oneself in their line of work was a dangerous luxury that few could afford.

'Come on, Yuri, spit it out, it won't kill you.'

Yarabin held up a well-manicured hand. 'For heaven's sake, will you kindly be quiet and let me think!'

Blake looked suitably contrite. 'Sorry.'

The Russian sat there lost in thought. He took a turn around the bench then resumed his seat. 'It goes something like this, doesn't it?' he began. 'If I don't do as you ask, there is a letter, is there not, addressed to someone in the ministry back in Moscow, acquainting him with certain unauthorised bank deposits in Switzerland? Correct me if I'm wrong.'

Blake obliged. 'Numbered accounts, to be specific,' he reminded him.

'Your work has been thorough as usual,' Yarabin sighed. 'One thing leads to another and I find myself in front of a Department Thirteen firing squad.'

Yarabin had seemed to age ten years in as many minutes. His ruddy complexion fading to a rather unhealthy grey like someone afflicted with a terminal disease. Blake decided to be sympathetic. 'You've got a choice, it doesn't have to end that way.'

Yarabin shook his head with a certain sadness. 'There you're mistaken. I don't have to make one. I made up my mind when I read of your daughter's death in the newspapers that if you ever came to me for help, I would give it. Not, of course, that I ever thought you would... but what I'm saying is who can help you now? You're a leper. Every intelligence agency in the world is after your scalp, including your own. You've committed the unpardonable sin, you've upset the applecart. They're not going to let you get away with that, and who can blame them.'

The Russian was on his feet and the two men stood confronting each other like opponents in a grudge-fight. The pallor had left Yarabin's face, he was no longer the tired old man. The words rattled out of his mouth like live sparks, his grin so wide the gums glowed above his bridgework. 'That was a nasty business in France, Blake, feeding a devout Muslim to the pigs. They won't forget that in a hurry.'

Yarabin's outburst had fallen on barren ground. Blake wasn't interested. He didn't even bother to deny it. 'But you *will* help,' he insisted. 'Don't worry about the letter, I'll destroy it in front of one of your own witnesses. You have my word on that.'

Yarabin made an impatient gesture with both hands. 'I already said I'd help!'

'That was good, damned good!' Blake reached out and shook his hand. 'In a theatre you'd have had them in the aisles, you're a great actor. For a moment there you almost had me believing it.'

'You blackmailing son of a bitch!' Yarabin stood there spluttering with anger again.

Blake put a friendly arm around his shoulder. 'Pithy and to the point. Your English is improving. First thing you know you'll be making love in it.'

Yarabin spun away and started to move down the hill.

Blake stayed with him. 'One last thing, Yuri,' he warned, 'if anything happens to me that letter will be posted. In your own interests I'd advise you to make sure nothing does. It might even be prudent to lay on a couple of your computerised gorillas to see I don't fall into any manholes... now about that little favour?'

A tight-lipped Yuri pulled up in his tracks, muttering, 'All right, what is it? What do you want?'

'Who do you know around here in the gold trade?'

'The top men, of course.'

'Naturally. You wouldn't waste your valuable time on the small fry.'

Yarabin doggedly stuck to the subject, ignoring the pleasantries. 'Why?'

'I'm looking for somebody. I understand he's into gold-smuggling big.' Blake chuckled. 'Don't look so worried, old son. Not here in your garden, back in Europe – he'd have a contact out here.'

'This person's name?'

'That's what I want to find out. This contact might be acquainted with him.'

Yarabin favoured him with a mirthless smile. 'Don't tell me I'm getting off that light. You'd come all the way out here just for that? What else do you want short of an arm and leg?'

Blake spread his hands as if it was too trivial to mention. 'A passport or two, some forged credentials. Top quality stuff that only you Russians know how to make.'

Yarabin sneered. 'Your people are pretty good at it themselves.'

'But I'm here, they're there. And as you so forcefully reminded me – at the moment I'm *persona non grate* with my former colleagues.'

Yarabin was considering it. 'Nothing else?'

'Cross my heart.'

Yarabin grimaced. 'That piece of stone?' He nodded. 'Very well. And for that you'll burn the letter?'

'I will.'

Yarabin decided. 'There's an Indian named Dilip Patel who obliges us with little services from time to time.'

'Trustworthy?'

Yarabin's shrug was expressive. 'He has been known to render similar services to our opposite numbers in other embassies around town.'

'A double-agent?'

Yuri was contemptuous. 'He's not a professional.'

'And we detest amateurs.'

'Sometimes they are useful.'

Blake found himself becoming interested. 'What's his pitch?'

Yuri made a face. 'A finger in every pie.'

Blake laughed. 'A capitalist! No wonder you dislike him.'

'He has reliable connections throughout Europe and the Middle East. I can't think of anyone better placed at the moment to help you with what you have in mind.'

The brightness suddenly went out of Blake's morning. 'And what do I have in mind, Yuri? I wasn't aware that I mentioned it.'

Yuri chuckled. 'My dear chap, come now, I do read the papers like everyone else. You've been front page news just about everywhere for the past week, although they haven't identified you yet. I also study our agents' reports – would we be likely to lose track of you?'

Blake made up his mind. 'Dilip Patel, you said?'

'You'll find him listed in the phone book. I'll let him know that you will be getting in touch with him…' The Russian hesitated, then continued. 'On second thoughts, you'd better be briefed before you do. I'll send one of my bright young men around to your hotel.'

Amused, Blake enquired, 'And where am I staying, Yuri?'

Yarabin ignored the witticism. 'Have you checked in anywhere yet?'

Blake shook his head. 'Didn't have time. I wanted to see you first.'

'Good, I know just the place. You'll be well looked after there.'

Blake's spirits were fully restored, the morning once more wore a cheerful smile. 'By the KGB's catering and housekeeping department, you mean.'

Both men resumed their descent down the hill, ignoring the big birds that were settling on top of one of the Parsee burial towers.

III

Like all such places east of Suez the street was teeming with people. Hawkers, artisans and thieves were pursuing their ancient crafts, all dedicated to finding a bargain or making a profit and unanimous in the eternal worship of the great god Mamon.

Urchins fluttered along the fringes like sparrows, Mary Magdalens brazenly flaunted their wares, buyer and seller haggled, grey-beards cluttered around coffee tables, hags cackled obscene epithets at one another. It was a familiar scene re-enacted daily from the souks of North Africa to the banks of the Euphrates and beyond.

Such a place was the bazaar in Bombay and Blake revelled in it. He liked crowds for the same reason that watchers hated them. It was too easy to lose a man on a crowded street.

Luigi's Trattoria was passing through that fashionable phase that kept the cash registers jingling and its proprietor's name in the gossip columns. Since independence even the sternest critics of the Old British Regime had become loud in their praise of London manners and etiquette, thus the English-language *Bombay Times* was widely read, particularly among the rich and influential. Once again it was fashionable to be British and nowhere was this more apparent than in the society pages. People liked to keep up with the Joneses every bit as much in Bombay as they used to did in Cheltenham before Britain's socialist revolution. The city's elite flocked to see and be seen and the usual queue of hopefuls clamoured for tables eager to pay extortionate prices for indifferent food, inferior wine and the chance to gape at their favourite movie star in the latest innovation, the foreign restaurant.

Blake threaded his way through the crowded tables behind the fawning headwaiter, noting the absence of local colour. There were no photographs of the Taj Mahal and aside from a few ladies in saris nothing else to remind him that he was in India. The headwaiter led him into the exclusive confines of the VIP room, escorted him to a spacious booth in one of the corners and departed.

'Ah, Mr Blake, how good of you to come. I'm Dilip Patel... do sit down.'

The voice was English public school, the face rotund, the handshake flabby and wet. Blake settled into the seat opposite the Indian.

'Prompt, too. One of your Christian virtues we Hindus find so hard to adopt.' He flicked his fingers and a waiter materialised at his elbow with a menu the size of a large poster. 'I recommend the roast lamb, a Neapolitan speciality, I believe. But first a drink.'

Blake decided he didn't like him. Self-satisfaction could be dangerous as it was so often coupled with the tendency to talk too much.

Patel, radiating good-will and conspiracy, leaned forward. 'Our Russian friend,' he whispered, 'was explicit. I'm to give you all the help I can.'

'Tell me about the gold route,' Blake asked, getting straight down to business.

Needing no further encouragement, Patel licked his lips and plunged. 'It's an ancient trade, probably started by the Phoenicians,' he began, 'and little has changed since.'

An anxious waiter arrived with their drinks and as promptly vanished again. Blake didn't touch his glass. True to his word, Yarabin had sent around one of his young men, whose brief had been thorough and boiled down to the fact that Patel was the right man. He was a bastard, hadn't scrupled to have people killed who stood in his way, and starting from nothing had in ten years become top man, controlling everything from prostitution to the Bombay waterfront, something of a one-man Mafia he ran the roost, had prominent politicians on his payroll and monopolised the smuggling rackets, including the lucrative gold trade. Nothing moved without his say-so. Patel was king rat.

'Nowadays,' he was saying, 'gold is exported legally from Switzerland to Dubhai in the Persian Gulf and taken from there by *dhow*, operating along the Oman coast from ports like Muscat and Ras al Had, then on across the Arabian Sea to our western coastline. These *dhows* are propelled by powerful engines that can easily outrun our latest naval patrol boats, so it isn't difficult to reach our ports. From there on it's relatively simple.' Spreading expansive hands, be added, 'The cargo is loaded on the usual transport and when it arrives here in Bombay it's sold on the open market.'

When the meal arrived, Blake picked a bit then let it alone. Patel ate like an Englishman, masticated slowly, kept his mouth closed. The manners were impeccable.

'Fascinating,' Blake nodded. 'Do you ever meet any of these

people personally? Those who control these operations from the European end, I mean?'

The Indian's eyes, like black mirrors, were fixed on his guest. He even stopped eating. 'From time to time, but rarely the top people... in the main they leave the details to middlemen, mostly Arabs.'

Blake sat back and looked out over the room. 'That's too bad,' he reflected after a spell of silence. 'I'm trying to locate one of these men, discover his true identity, how he deals, and where from.'

Never once taking his eyes from Blake, Patel carefully wiped his lips with his napkin. 'There are several who fall into that category. A Portuguese who formerly worked out of Goa, but I doubt he's your man, having been confined to a nursing home for some two years or more.'

'The man I'm looking for is very active. He runs a large international organisation and channels a lot of his funds out of Europe via the gold route, or so I've been given to understand.'

After a furtive glance at the nearby tables, Patel leaned forward. Lowering his voice, he confided, 'There is someone who answers to that description. A certain influential German, a man of considerable means, whom I understand can be ruthless where his enemies are concerned. You will forgive me if I don't wish to become one of them. Needless to say, he is extremely difficult to approach...'

'You're speaking from experience, of course?'

'Of course.'

'You've met him personally?' Blake asked endeavouring to keep the sudden eagerness out of his voice.

Patel shook his head. 'I've never had the pleasure. What business we've done has always been conducted through intermediaries.'

'I see,' Blake replied, thinking back to his briefing on Patel by that whiz-kid Yuri had dispatched so promptly to his hotel room, trying to recall what had been said; then he remembered his own comments regarding the Baader-Meinhof gang. That had to be it. Russian logic. It follows that they would conclude that he was only interested in the top man. But no one, neither the Russians nor Patel, could possibly know why. Nobody knew that but himself. Relieved, he relaxed a bit, even spared a few moments to enjoy the local talent that was encompassing them on all sides of the room.

'Very attractive, don't you think?'

'What?'

The expression was familiar, that worn on the face of every pimp he had ever run across. 'The ladies,' Patel smirked.

'Oh, those?'

'Anyone you particularly like? I could introduce you.'

Blake recalled a Maltese brothel keeper he'd once met in Valetta. The approach was identical. 'Some other time, when I'm in the mood,' he replied unsmiling. 'Right now I've got other things on my mind.'

Over a rich dessert (Blake didn't indulge) the Indian returned to the subject. 'To learn how to approach this man and – far more difficult – to ascertain his whereabouts and actually make his acquaintance... that shall require certain bonafides.'

'Why not save time and simply tell me where he is yourself?' Blake asked innocently.

'My dear chap, I can assure you that if some of his closest colleagues saw him on the street they wouldn't recognise him. He's a voice on the telephone, his letters are signed by accountants, even his cheques, which come from places as far afield as San Francisco and Hong Kong. I've never met him and to date I know no one who has. He might not exist at all, he may be several people.' Patel shrugged. 'He's a hard one to pin down.'

Blake had travelled halfway around the world to meet this Indian who might lead him to a man who could be hiding out back where he had started from. It required a special kind of patience to run people to earth, like sitting for days in a parked car or sheltering in a doorway in bad weather waiting for someone to come out of a house. 'But it can be done,' Blake maintained stolidly.

The waiter brought a large jug of coffee and brandy glasses. Blake broke his fast. Patel gleefully exclaimed, 'Best coffee you ever tasted and the brandy is superb, from my own stock.'

'You mentioned bonafides?'

'Credentials, my dear fellow, that can be promptly verified, like a letter of credit amounting to some impressive sum, say, two and a half million American dollars. Even Hans Reichter wouldn't sniff at that.'

'Hans Reichter?'

Patel's smile was condescending. 'The man you're looking for. The name means nothing. He obviously uses several and as many passports. No one knows his real name.'

Like most people Blake resented being patronised, most of all by a provincial racketeer, but he managed to keep his voice level and his face devoid of expression. Reichter was a shadowy figure. Never having been arrested or even held on suspicion, the authorities up to the present hadn't been able to identify him; more disappointing, the Agency had no file on him. Through odd bits of unsubstantiated rumour and hearsay it was suspected that he had a legal background, was heavily involved with international terrorism, was a man of considerable financial means, had negotiated sugar and tobacco agreements with European importers on behalf of the Castro regime, had financed extremist political groups in the Middle East and, lastly, was the financial brain behind the Baader-Meinhof terrorists. It was also rumoured that this man invested large sums of this group's money, accumulated through a long series of successful bank robberies and kidnappings of rich men, on the Bombay gold market where profits were enormous. Blake had no choice. Thus far he had nothing better to go on. Rumour and hearsay had brought him out to India because that was where large-scale gold dealing was done. Time alone would tell whether or not this Hans Reichter was the right man. But Blake was accustomed to chasing up slender leads. On many past occasions he had started out with little more than a hunch; this time at least he had a name, even if it was an alias.

'And what is more, this letter of credit must be issued by a reputable banking house together with a personal letter from myself,' Patel was saying importantly, 'which can be checked by telex or telephone, introducing you as my personal representative on a transaction involving one of my companies and Mr Reichter. The letter I give you now, together with a passport. You will find them in the briefcase.'

'Briefcase?'

'It's sitting beside you on your seat. You have it and its contents with my compliments.' Patel actually winked.

Blake regarded him steadily, imagining Linderman's misgivings had he been present to witness it. Patel had evidently seen too many spy movies. 'Thank you,' he said, 'and the letter of credit?'

Patel could barely contain himself. 'That I presume will be given to you by one of our friend's associates when you arrive in Geneva.'

Blake decided to get a little of his own back, the Indian had patronised him long enough. 'I see. You must mean Yarabin – from the Russian Consulate,' he announced in a loud voice resulting in a head or two being turned in their direction.

Patel's chin began to quiver with alarm. 'Please, no names! It's more than our lives are worth!' Like the kid caught with his hand in the cookie jar he glanced apprehensively at the nearest table. 'You know the Russians!'

Blake's nod was solemn. 'I know them very well.'

Patel squirmed. 'Please! Not so loud. A man in your position...'

'A secret agent, you mean?'

Patel all but put his hands to his ears. 'Please, remember where we are!'

'In the most popular restaurant in Bombay. You couldn't have chosen a more public place for a top secret conversation,' Blake went on, gravely favouring him with one of his gentle smiles. This faded somewhat too rapidly from his face. Patel lost all interest in his fine coffee and vintage brandy. 'That letter of credit will have to be genuine if it's going to do any good,' Blake concluded dryly. He looked out over the room. As he suspected the other diners were too involved in their own small talk to pay much attention to them.

Patel burst out angrily, 'It will be unless you or one of Herr Reichter's staff attempt to cash it. You may rest assured that (here he lowered his voice to a tremulous whisper) the Russians will give their bank suitable instructions to forestall anything like that happening.'

Torn between anger and fear, the Indian sat fidgeting in his seat like someone whose bladder was about to burst.

'Of course. Ivan always takes logical precautions,' Blake confided. 'But then, I have no interest in the money, the object being to convince Herr Reichter, or whoever he is, that I'm the genuine article, right?'

Patel managed a sickly nod.

Blake glowed with good fellowship. 'Good. Now that passport, who's it made out to?'

Patel fell back into his seat, 'Suddenly it's very hot in here,' he groaned. 'The passport? Ah, yes. It's made out in the name of Philip Barnes. He works for me in Dubhai and shall vanish for a bit until your business is concluded.'

'British?'

'American, which should suit you perfectly. The passport itself is an exact duplicate of the original.'

'No need to ask where that came from. Ivan is good, he can counterfeit anything,' Blake replied raising his voice again.

Patel shuddered. 'Please!'

'Now where were we? I keep forgetting. Ah yes, we're past Ivan, mind filling me in about this man Barnes? How old is he?'

'Roughly your age,' Patel sighed, regaining some of his composure.

'How old is that?'

'Early fifties, I should think.'

'Thanks. I'm a little older than that, but it doesn't matter. He's travelled to Europe on business for you before?'

Patel shook his head. 'No, never.'

Blake pressed on. 'Would Reichter or any of his associates be likely to recognise him?'

'Would I be likely to suggest you impersonating him if they would?' Patel asked tightly. He was beginning to regret that he had ever met this troublesome American. 'None of those people ever visit Dubhai. Their part of the transaction is complete once the gold is shipped out of Europe.'

'Have you got a photograph of Barnes?'

'Of course,' the Indian gloated. 'Would I forget something like that? I've stuck it in the passport, together with a brief rundown on his family background, education and what have you – is that satisfactory?'

'I won't know until I've read it. I've got to know everything about this man: what he eats, his sex habits, where he was born, brought up, went to school, who his parents were, does he have a wife, kids, is it a happy marriage? In plain English, if I'm going to successfully pass myself off as Philip Barnes to a man as astute and ruthless as you say Reichter is I've got to crawl right into his skin. I've got to know it all – does your "brief rundown" contain all that?'

Patel shifted uncomfortably in his seat.

'I see, it doesn't. Right, so you go home right now and write one that does.'

The Indian faltered, 'I'll do my best.'

'You'll do better than that. If you can't, better say so now.'

'Oh, but I can.'

'Okay, do it then. Get it over to my hotel first thing in the morning.' Blake sat there, studying him like a laboratory specimen under a glass. 'What's your price for all this?'

The struggle between fear, anger and greed on that rubicund face, fierce though it was, was mercifully brief. It was an intriguing transformation. Patel announced warily, 'My services aren't cheap, Mr Blake.'

'How much?'

'My expenses will be considerable. Mr Barnes will have to be compensated while he goes to ground, the other arrangements.'

'*How much?*'

Patel threw up his hands. 'Please! Do keep your voice down. Fifty thousand dollars, cash,' he whimpered.

Blake shook his head. 'Twenty. I've got a budget, I can't go any higher than that.'

Patel began to protest, then seeing the expression on Blake's face, decided against it.

'Which will cover your expenses and more than adequately compensate you for your services, right?' Blake leaned over close, lowering his voice, 'Besides, our friend Ivan can be very persuasive, and need I say it – mighty helpful on occasion, *if* you play ball.'

Patel's eyes glinted like a couple of newly-minted dimes. 'I said *cash*,' he stuttered hoarsely.

'That's right,' Blake nodded, picking up the briefcase Patel had placed beside him on the seat and sliding out of the booth.

Patel gasped, 'Cash *now!*'

Once more exuding sweetness and light, Blake replied innocently, 'I know. It's sitting beside you on your seat – a neat little bundle of thousand dollar bills, twenty to be exact.'

Patel looked down and his eyes all but popped out of his head when he spotted it. He hurriedly stuffed it into a pocket and when he looked up, Blake was gone.

IV

Linderman's Bombay letter-drop was situated in a large jewellery firm located at the beginning of Ocean Drive. Blake reached the place well after closing time, hurried down an alley to the trade-entrance and rang the bell. The minuscule Hindu, Saranjit Singh, who eventually padded up to admit him was a placid little soul who spoke in a high piping voice and kept his hands clasped in an attitude of permanent prayer.

Blake muttered the current password and followed him into the lavishly furnished room that was used to receive important visitors. Bowing ceremoniously, Saranjit enquired, 'Your pleasure, sir?'

'How soon can you get a message through to New York?'

'If it's urgent – tonight, sir.'

Blake handed him a brief coded message requesting information on Hans Reichter. 'It's urgent. When can I expect a reply?'

Little Saranjit's smile was gentle. 'If what you request is readily available,' he advised in his birdlike falsetto, 'and allowing for the time difference, sometime in the morning, sir. If it is not, several days perhaps. They are well organised, but crosschecking takes time, particularly if it entails foreign channels of information.'

The little Indian bowed once again and, indicating that the meeting was over, bade Blake to follow him back to the side door.

V

The Rubicon Hotel, a ramshackle, two-storey affair, was situated opposite the station and catered mainly to half-caste Anglo-Indian railway workers. When Blake entered, he crossed an empty hall and slipped up the stairway. Everyone had gone to bed, including the desk clerk.

Upstairs, he moved along a dark hallway and bent to unlock the door to his room. He wheeled as the light was switched on and he found himself facing his old colleague Roker. It was a revealing still-life. Roker stood facing him from the other end of the hall with a levelled rifle in his hands. Behind Roker stood the burly figure of Yuri Yarabin's driver. Then two other figures, one armed with a machine-pistol, stepped out of the shadows.

As Roker lowered his rifle, Blake saw the pistol pressed to the back of his head. He crossed to him, took the rifle and slid back the bolt. It was empty.

'Well, Jim, no bullets, funny way to go hunting, isn't it?' His glance moved to Yarabin's driver. 'That was good,' he nodded. He glanced at the other two, their ill-fitting clothes betokening the KGB supply shop, Moscow. He added, 'Very good. Any more around?'

'Just one or two others,' one of them shrugged.

'Mind if I invite this one in for a while?'

Yarabin's driver took possession of the rifle and gave Roker a quick professional frisk. 'Don't keep him too long. They tend to get nervous when their people overstay their absence,' he said with unexpected humour.

Roker rather sheepishly followed Blake into the room and closed the door. 'I just wanted to talk. The gun was just window-dressing in case you didn't want to listen. Where did they come from?'

Blake flung himself down on the bed. 'I don't know.'

Roker settled on the edge. 'Yarabin's taking no chances. Want me to guess?'

'Go ahead,' Blake said tiredly. He was still holding Patel's briefcase. He tossed it on a nearby chair.

'Whatever it is you've got on him, your death won't get him

out from under it. You play it rough, I sympathise with him.'
Roker sat there considering it, then added, 'He's got no option.
He's got to keep you alive.'

Blake fluffed up a pillow, propped it against one of the old-
fashioned brass tubes on the bedhead and settled back. 'Centre
wants me eliminated, Renway's detailed you for the job and
you've chickened out. When that gets back, you're washed up. All
that hard graft and no pension at the end of it. All of a sudden
you're a fool, how come?'

'I told you, I wanted to talk.'

Blake sat up lazily. 'Nothing's going to change my mind, you
know that. You're only wasting time.'

'Let me have my say, then I'll get out.'

Blake made a weary gesture for him to continue. 'It's your
nickel.'

'It's not Janis any more, Sam. That's done with. Nothing you
can do can bring her back, but now it's too late to stop. You've got
to prove it to yourself that where everyone else has failed, you
won't.'

Blake agreed. 'Garbage disposal – I'm good at it.'

'There's nothing else?'

'That's it.'

'Even if we come out losers?'

Blake had no need to control his feelings, long ago these had
dried up. 'Why complicate what is perfectly simple?' he asked
mildly. 'I flush shit down the toilet and everybody starts thinking
how it's going to affect them. They're all so afraid I'll puncture
the pumpkin. Revenge is like killing a guy who rapes your wife or
robs your home, it's no longer fashionable.'

Roker got up and moved to the window. Down on the street a
couple of men were huddling beneath a dim streetlamp but they
were too far away to distinguish whether they belonged to him or
Yarabin. He turned back to Blake. 'Depends which way you look
at it, Sam. To some poor bastard, sitting on a dirt floor living on
Unesco handouts, those people are heroes. You can kill all three
on that list of yours and it will solve nothing. All that will happen
is that you will hurt the very people you're trying to help.'

Blake laughed. 'That's right,' he drawled, 'for a few weeks the

Reds will replay all their old records in the UNO talking shop and nobody's going to *do* anything but me! Everything else is bullshit.'

Roker knew it was useless, but he wasn't finished yet. 'You don't care whether it kills you or not, do you?'

The rims of his old colleague's eyes were red from lack of sleep and he had lost a lot of weight. Already the cost was clearly visible.

'Nope,' Blake said.

'You're no different than those you're trying to kill.'

Blake blurted out bitterly, 'I don't kill innocent college girls.'

'You would if they got in the way of one of your victims.'

Blake shot off the bed. 'Get the hell out of here!'

Roker didn't budge. 'Would you or wouldn't you?'

If there had been a weapon handy at that moment, Roker knew that Blake would have killed him. He had driven him to the very edge and oddly he didn't care. He was that desperate.

Blake slumped as the anger left him and returned to the bed.

Roker resumed, 'Maybe you wouldn't, maybe you'd abort and try it some other way.'

'Thanks for that, anyway.'

'Next time we meet it'll be for real.'

'I know.'

'I'm still with the Agency, Sam.'

'Yeah.'

'Like everyone else, I've got my orders.'

'Sure.'

'I've said what I had to say.' It was more of a plea than a factual statement.

Blake nodded. Never since that moment at the airport when his only child had died in his arms had he felt so alone.

Roker reached the door and slowly opened it. 'That's it then,' be concluded wearily.

Blake had to say something, anything, to keep him there. He needed his old friend's company for a while. 'Jim?'

Roker turned hopefully away from the door. 'Change your mind?'

'How's Edith?'

'Now that's a funny question in the middle of the night in a fleapit hotel room in Bombay. Last time I saw her she was fine – why?'

'I heard somewhere that you were splitting up,' Blake offered sympathetically. 'I liked her, everybody did.'

Roker regarded him with sudden suspicion. 'Why are you trying to keep me here, Sam – stalling for time?'

Blake reddened. 'Don't be a damn fool!'

Realising that Blake simply wanted to talk, Roker softened his tone. 'Don't tell me that you're lonely?' he scoffed more in amazement than derision. 'Not you, not Blake?'

'You still haven't answered my question.' Blake pressed.

'Odd time to discuss my personal life,' Roker thought aloud, 'but then you always were unpredictable.' He exhaled deeply and resumed his seat at the foot of Blake's bed. 'What's there to say? We've come to the parting of me ways, that's all.'

'You still love her?'

Roker suddenly found it difficult to speak. He nodded.

'And she still loves you?'

'Yes,' Roker said miserably.

'Phone her, Jim. Promise me. This has nothing to do with our business.' He found himself on the verge of pleading because suddenly Roker's well-being was very important to him.

'Do you think it'll do any good?'

'It might. Don't take no for an answer. If that doesn't help, keep phoning her.'

Roker suddenly looked hopeful. 'By God, I will!' he cried.

Blake laughed. 'Now, get the hell out of here, I've got some sleeping to do.'

For the second time Roker headed for the door.

'And be polite to the Ivans on your way out,' Blake prompted, already dropping off into an exhausted sleep.

Years afterwards, whenever Roker thought of that meeting, he considered the odds against it happening the way it did. Yes, Blake was unpredictable. More so than anyone he had ever met.

VI

Jim Roker had not slept for thirty-six hours, but the adrenalin of humiliation and failure kept him wide awake. Slumped in a chair in the embassy code room, he was in no mood to hear Renway's brand of crow, he made no excuses; on the contrary, his dogged replies to the other's biting sarcasm had placed the blame squarely upon himself. In the end, spluttering with rage, Renway had rung off.

Roker asked the embarrassed operator to leave the room. It was Agency policy to record phone conversations in the field to forestall differences of opinion over what was said, so he settled back to listen to the recorded playback. Renway's voice came over like raw acid; he began by quibbling over the most trivial details.

Then Roker listened to his own voice trying to explain: *'We don't neglect things like that in the field,'* he replied. *'It's standard operating procedure. After we located Blake's hotel all the routine precautions were taken. The trouble was, they were already there, waiting inside the building.'*

'You walked into an ambush?'

'That's right. We learned afterwards that they moved in the same day Blake arrived… while we were still eliminating alternatives. The Russians are good at this sort of thing.'

'The Russians!'

Roker had to advance the tape here because of garbled noises on the other end. He ran it on to the point where Renway's voice came over loud and clear again. *'It was always a possibility that sooner or later he'd start working for them.'*

Roker heard his own bitter laughter come over the playback.

'Working for them? They're working for him.'

'The son of a bitch!' Renway's voice shrieked.

'I think he's blackmailed him.'

'Blackmailed who, for Christ's sake?'

'Yuri Yarabin.'

There was a brief silence while Renway digested all the implications. The voice was a trifle more subdued when he spoke again. *'That figures,'* he admitted. *'Blake would do something like that.'*

'Anything happening on your end?'

Renway took off again. '*Anything happening on my end? The roof's just caved in, that's all! You haven't seen the papers over here! Particularly those bastards on the* Washington Post. *Think they're on to another Watergate. If you bungle it again, you're through, Roker. Centre's already howling for your hide. I can't hold them off much longer. What happens now?*'

'Bombay's sealed. Roads, trains, planes. We've got men covering all exits.'

'*Once he steps out of that hotel, don't lose him. I don't care how many Russians he's got covering him; or Indian security people for that matter – you read me, Roker?*'

'Yes, sir.'

'*Stay with him wherever he goes, you hear?*'

'Yes, sir,' Racer's voice replied resignedly.

Renway worked himself up to another shout. '*You get yourself on the same plane, bus or train and, if that's not possible, contact the first stop – wherever that'll be – and make damn certain we've got men to cover him when he arrive. And another thing: next time don't miss. Centre wants him bad.*'

Roker switched off the machine. On the face of it, Blake was alone, one man against the security services of half a dozen nations. The reality was somewhat different. Thus far too many of them had people who for one reason or another were willing to help him.

Roker was confused. It was the old dilemma between loyalty to one's country or to one's friend. And of late it was becoming increasingly difficult to decide who was right, the Agency or Blake. He kept asking himself why Centre was taking such a tough line and at the same time why Blake was so unwilling to see anyone's point of view but his own. With all that – and Edith – on his mind, he got up, stepped out of the building, and didn't stop walking until he reached his hotel room.

On entry, he went straight to the phone, put through a call to his London number, and when he heard Edith's voice, he stood there, tongue-tied, unable even to say hello.

'Is there anyone there?' she was saying, having repeated it for the third time.

Roker finally stammered, 'It's… me.'

Edith was genuinely pleased to hear his voice. 'Jim? How lovely to hear you.'

She said a lot of other things, too; and so did he – commonplace things that people say to each other on long-distance phones when they are aware of the minutes ticking away and are either too embarrassed or too shy with one another to articulate what they really feel.

They were aware of one another's gladness and relief, of course, they knew each other too well for it to be otherwise.

Then he heard himself saying, 'I wrote to you tonight, you should receive the letter in a day or two.'

She said, 'Oh, Jim, what are we talking about, what are you trying to say?'

There was desperation there, and longing, and he felt the same. 'I love you,' he spluttered. 'It's been hell.'

'For me, too!' she cried, her voice wavering.

He remembered, 'Everything you said to me before I left was true.'

'Yes, it seemed to be the only way. It was better for us both.'

'Yes.'

'Yes, but it was hell. In the morning, when I went to bed at night – I don't know how I got through the days.' Edith started to sob.

Roker blew his nose. 'Edith, darling, I really do love you.'

'I never doubted that for one minute.'

'Oh, Edith.'

Reduced to trite declarations that were ancient when Zeus sat on the summit of Mount Olympus, they went on. What other words were there? Had they existed, two such adult people would have surely used them.

Half an hour and a week's salary later it ended much as it had begun: 'I love you,' they said, 'and I can't help it, can't live without you.'

Roker promised to write every day, and he did; so did she. But it wasn't what they said. None of it really mattered. What mattered was she would be there when he returned to London.

Tired as he was there was no sleep for Roker that night. He could only think of her and of his debt to Sam Blake for making him promise to phone her.

CHAPTER SEVEN

I

YURI YARABIN TOOK ONE HORRIFIED LOOK AROUND BLAKE'S room at the Rubicon Hotel and bellowed, 'How dare he? I'll have Tukaschev's head for this – it's a veritable slum.'

Blake asked, 'Who's Tukaschev?'

'He's supposed to find suitable accommodation for embassy guests. Peasant. But then, what can you expect from a Ukrainian?' He threw up both hands in disgust.

'Don't be too hard on him,' Blake laughed. 'Had his priorities right, like Fort Knox. Nothing could reach me here, except the bugs.'

Yuri, who was just settling into a chair, shot out of it like a man half his age. 'Bugs?'

Blake scratched himself. 'Try settling on the edge of the bed, my friend Roker didn't pick up anything there.'

Yuri was adamant. 'I prefer to stand, thank you.'

Blake lay back on his pillows. 'They're your arteries, suit yourself.'

Yuri wrinkled his nose. 'What's that dreadful smell?'

'Curry. Pungent, isn't it?'

'Revolting.'

'Home from home for the railroad crews; some of them bring their women along on the occasional trip. They cook in their rooms.'

'Let's get down to business,' Yuri snapped. 'You're leaving here tonight, by road to Delhi. From there we've arranged a flight on one of our aircraft to Teheran. From there, you're on your own, and, if you'll forgive me – good riddance.'

'What's that bag for?' Blake yawned, indicating a rather old-fashioned suitcase that Yuri had brought in and placed beside the rickety chest of drawers when he had first entered the room.

The Russian grinned: 'For your clothes – *they're* flying to

134

Cairo.' Retrieving the case, he placed it on the bed and proceeded to unpack it. 'Your replacements. You'll wear these to Delhi.' Radiating *bon ami* and good humour, Yuri scolded, 'Well, come on! I haven't got all night – get out of your clothes.' Blake looked balefully at the replacements that Yuri had heaped on his bed.

'You expect me to wear those?'

'What's wrong with them? They're clean and your size. Hang 'em up for a while, they'll lose their wrinkles.'

Blake gazed at the immaculately-dressed Russian. 'You wouldn't be caught dead in that outfit. Christ, I'll look just like one of your scalp-hunters.'

Yuri grimaced. 'Quite appropriate, knowing your reputation. Hurry, please. We haven't much time.'

Blake proceeded to get undressed. As each garment was removed, Yarabin folded it with care and placed it in the suitcase.

'One or two questions, Yuri, before we go.'

Yuri looked up like a man being asked for a loan. 'What is it now?'

'That letter of credit – you're sure it's okay?'

'Unless you attempt to cash it; it's genuine all right,' Yuri said stiffly. 'What else?'

'Who do I see in Geneva, assuming I ever arrive there?'

Yuri shrugged. 'One of my messengers. And remember, you burn that damned letter of yours in his presence or it's no deal.'

Blake nodded. 'I see, he'll have the letter of credit?'

'He will.'

Having finished packing Blake's clothes into the old suitcase, Yuri locked it and looked up to see the American, now fully dressed in the Russian substitutes, unhappily gazing at his reflection in the mirror over the chest of drawers.

Blake shuddered. 'God, what a sight!'

Yuri burst out laughing. 'Splendid. The living image of the late, unlamented Lavrenti Pavlovich Beria.'

'Thanks.'

'Don't mention it, Comrade. And to observe the niceties, I shan't either.' With that, Yuri picked up the suitcase and headed for the door. '*Now you owe me*,' he said, putting a wealth of meaning into the phrase.

Blake put a shapeless grey felt hat on his head to complete the ensemble. 'I'll remember that, friend.'

'See that you do.' Then his voice softening, he added, 'Take care of yourself, Sam. There aren't many of us old ones left. You were like a breath of fresh air.'

Before Blake could reply, Yarabin was already moving through the doorway.

II

In the course of his duties, Linderman was occasionally called upon to provide call girls for important contacts and he did this as he did everything, with thoroughness and dispatch. A man of the world, he had no qualms about this, accepting the fact that from time to time men needed women as they did food and drink. He screened his girls carefully, and, once he accepted them, he was reluctant to replace them with girls he didn't know. He disliked change simply because it was bad for security. Being human, he sometimes indulged himself, and invariably with the same girl.

She called herself Sandra but that wasn't her real name. That and her entire background were available in Linderman's file. She was twenty-four, from Scranton, Pennsylvania, a struggling method actress who had done summer stock and a couple of off-Broadway shows. She was also a beautiful girl in the modern mode, slim, tight-assed and long-legged. Looking fresher than her years, her hair was light brown, naturally straight and hung down over her shoulders.

Linderman, though quite incapable of having close relationships with anyone, nonetheless came as close to liking her as it was possible for him to do. When he was in New York, he availed himself of her services in a room he kept for her in a small residential hotel off lower 5th Avenue on the fringes of Greenwich Village. When Blake's message from Bombay was relayed to him on a scrambler phone, he was alone in the room. 'Telex from Bombay letter-drop,' the voice intoned. 'Got your pencil?'

Linderman never went anywhere without a pen and pad.

Replying in the affirmative, he proceeded to write down the string of numbers which were read to him over the phone. Later that night back at the safe house he decoded the conversation, which read: *Unable to establish true identity of Hans Reichter, an alias. Suspected connection with Baader-Meinhof. Need alternative aliases. Top priority. If you can help, better locate or pinpoint contacts, use letter-drop in Geneva.*

Later Linderman telexed another coded message to a contact in Hamburg who was a staffer on a prominent German news magazine. He then dispatched identical communications to others in Bonn and Amsterdam.

III

The car drove into a small clearing high in the hills on the outskirts of Geneva and stopped. In good weather it was a popular spot because of its unobstructed view of the lake. That day, however, a cold rain swept through the trees and a heavy mountain mist had settled over the city and its famous watering place.

The young man behind the wheel was neatly dressed, his hair was closely cropped and his name was Boris Tomov. Something of an athlete, in his mid-twenties, he looked like a corn-fed kid from Omaha rather than a KGB field operative. Blake sat beside him balancing Patel's briefcase on his knees. Friendly disposed towards the young Russian, he regarded him with some amusement. 'How old are you, sonny?'

Tomov turned to his passenger in some surprise. Brought up to beware of strangers, particularly foreigners, he shifted uncomfortably in his seat. 'Twenty-five, sir,' was the reluctant reply.

'You're older than you look.'

Boris regarded him blankly. The eyes were very clear and very blue.

'What's your sport, sonny?'

'My name is Boris, sir.'

'Okay – what's your sport, Boris?'

'I play ice-hockey... wing, sir.'

Blake patted him on the shoulder. 'Bet you're good, too.'

For want of a suitable answer, Tomov plunged a hurried hand into a pocket, produced a large manila envelope and handed it to his affable companion.

Blake announced gleefully, 'My letter of credit, I do believe.' He ripped it open and removed a neatly-folded sheet of heavy vellum paper. Spreading it out, he found himself in possession of an impressive document. There was a magnificent, beribboned seal embossed in gold, it was drawn on a large Swiss bank and made out to the sum of $2,500,000.

Tomov solemnly produced a receipt and pen. 'Will you sign, please, sir?'

'Forget the sir, Boris, you're becoming repetitive.' He readily obliged. Blake was enjoying himself.

The youngster, like so many of his countrymen, was a stoic. He waited patiently, but even this had limits. The American didn't seem to realise what was expected of him in return. He watched Blake slip the prized letter of credit into his briefcase and prompted, 'Don't you have something for me, sir?'

Blake looked aggrieved. 'My dear fellow, how remiss of me.' A fast grope in Patel's bag of goodies sufficed to produce another envelope.

In his eagerness, Tomov snatched it from his hand and pulled forth the incriminating document that could have put Yuri Yarabin in front of a Soviet firing squad. Before Tomov could read it he snatched it back again. 'Tut-tut, kid, roll down your window.'

The voice had hardened, the smile lost its warmth. The young Russian hurriedly fell in with the suggestion.

'Now burn it.' Blake tossed him a box of matches and handed back the paper. 'I wouldn't want it to reach the wrong people.'

'My orders, sir, were to bring this to my superior.' His eyes widened with alarm. 'If I don't…'

'I know, the Irkutsk Dynamos get another hockey player – *burn it!*'

Tomov's jaw dropped in astonishment. The face was hostile and the sudden pressure of the gun barrel was hurting his ribs. Blake gave it a vicious dig. The boy cried out in pain.

'Burn it, or I'll blast your guts out!'

After one or two frenzied attempts, Tomov managed to light a match. His trembling fingers held it to the paper and it burst into flames. When all but the tiny bit between his thumb and forefinger was consumed, his head lolled back on the seat. Blake reached over him and rolled up the window. Tomov was having difficulty with his breathing.

Blake put away the gun, mindful of another fresh young face back in Nice; like this one, eager, uncorrupt and dumped so unceremoniously aboard that plane back to Renway in London. Somehow it wasn't a satisfying thought. 'Look kid, it's a hard world,' he said, softening. 'I know the coach of the Toronto Maple Leafs, maybe he'd help. You ought to get out of this.'

Tomov's head came off the seat with a jerk, he was near tears. 'I'm not a traitor – you can go to hell.'

Blake sighed. 'Sorry, kid.'

'You're all the same, even on our side. Just because you're older, you think you know it all.' He kicked the starter, the tyres shrieked, the car swerved out of the clearing and roared down the hill. Out on the highway, he stammered apologetically, 'I'm sorry, sir, for losing my temper.'

Blake produced a pack of chewing gum. He offered a stick to Boris and took one himself. 'Forget it, kid. We all do that sometimes.'

Boris eagerly tore off the wrapper and shoved the gum into his mouth. 'Juicy Fruit!' he exclaimed gratefully.

Blake shook his head. 'Your favourite brand?'

Boris chewed happily. 'I like Spearmint, too.'

'I'll bet you do. Remember that basketball final at the Munich Olympics when we thought we'd won, but the Italian referee said no, there was still five seconds on the clock?'

Boris beamed. 'Then we put the ball back into play under our basket and our tallest player threw it the length of the floor and we scored a basket as he blew time – we beat you at your own game!' The young Russian sat there gleefully reliving the moment.

'...and we went into mourning, or UCLA did as they had provided most of the players.'

Boris almost lost control of the car in his excitement. 'It was a great day.'

'Almost as good as you losing the Olympic ice-hockey title to the Czechs a day or three later.'

For Boris it was an eclipse of the sun. Black night blanketed the bright sunshine of his morning. He moaned.

'You win some, you lose some, kid. That's the way it goes.'

After that they drove on in silence, Boris reliving the catastrophe. It was hard to believe that he was one of the new crop of KGB bionic men, honed to a hard edge by the most ruthless school in the world.

Boris suddenly remembered, 'I'm sorry, sir. I forgot to mention that I was instructed to ask if there is anything else we might do to assist you.'

Blake gave this some thought before saying. 'There might be, I'll need a couple of hard men who are quick with their hands. Know anyone like that?'

Boris's nod was energetic. 'We have several on the staff who answer to that description, sir. When will you require them?'

'I don't know yet. They've got to be fairly young, too. The type who could pass for gas-station attendants.'

'Yes, sir. Hard men, quick with their hands, young, who could pass for petrol-station attendants.'

'You got it, Boris. I'll let you know if and when I need them. It's a simple job but I'll have to brief them first.'

'They're accustomed to that procedure, sir.'

Blake studied him fondly. 'I'll bet.'

They rode on again in silence, the rain still pelting down.

IV

After Boris dropped him outside the American Express office in Geneva, Blake's first consideration was to check if there were any watchers about. Spotting none, he still stuck to the usual procedure, doubling back and forth on his tracks, then finding a crowd and losing himself in it. When he emerged, the coast was clear and he found himself near the letter-drop which was situated in a small tobacco shop on a quiet side street just off the town centre. Once inside, he gave the elderly clerk his code name and a minute or two later, carefully pocketing an envelope, he bought some cigarettes and departed. Being lunchtime the street was practically empty of both people and cars. Certain he wasn't being followed he took another roundabout route back to his hotel.

As usual, Linderman had delivered the goods. The message was brief and, decoded, read: *He's your man. Aliases Johan Krause, Mateo Ortega, Juan Camilo Mandala.*

It wasn't the first time, and certainly not the last, that Blake found himself wondering how Linderman did it. The man's sources were not only reliable but fast. What took weeks for most people, took him a mere matter of days. There were never any explanations, ifs or buts. If Linderman thought he could deliver, he said yes, if not, he said no. How? Somehow he always found people who could go directly to the source. Rarely were there third persons involved. In this case, Blake could only surmise that Linderman's contact was an active member of the Baader-Meinhof gang.

Linderman would employ backups of course. At a guess, he probably used as many as a dozen contacts, each unknown to the others. This was logical. It also required years of groundwork, the assembly of hundreds of contacts throughout the world, and contacts that Linderman himself checked for loyalty and reliability.

There was only one man, a Russian – code name Sobel – in the same street with him. Laymen would call it genius, those in the trade knew it was something else as well. Like everyone else in the Intelligence world, Linderman used the routine procedures: painstaking hard work, constant double-checking on both material and source, the process of elimination, never relying on a single contact, unshakable patience. But Linderman had a third string to his bow, the capacity of total recall. Anything read or heard was never forgotten.

Blake was impressed.

V

The main entrance of the Hotel Carleton was a fiesta of blazing neon lights and a maze of arriving and departing taxicabs. Inside, the foyer was crowded with people hurrying in and out of the public rooms and cocktail bar.

As Blake moved up to the porter's desk, someone brushed past and politely excused himself. To an ordinary person it would have meant nothing, but Blake knew straight away that he had been frisked. Evidently Reichter's security was being handled by professionals.

'May I help you, sir?'

Blake turned to the Porter. 'Yes, thank you. I'm Philip Barnes from Dubhai. I have an appointment with Juan Camilo Mandala of Barcelona. He is staying here, I believe.'

The Porter regarded him carefully. 'One moment, sir. I will call his suite.'

Blake allowed his gaze to travel slowly around the foyer. Unobtrusively stationed in places with a clear view of the elevators, stairs and entrances, he spotted four security men. It was well done. Only an expert could have recognised them.

Another one suddenly appeared at his elbow. 'Mr Barnes?'

Blake nodded.

'Would you accompany me, please. Don Mandala is expecting you.'

Blake followed him into an elevator. They stepped out on the twentieth floor. Another security man was on hand at the door. He led Blake to a private lift leading up to the penthouse suite.

As he stepped through the wide double-doors leading into the main lounge, he found himself alone with the man who was presently calling himself Don Juan Camilo Mandala and his chief accountant, a spruce bespectacled Swiss named Gunther Sterr.

Reichter possessed an extraordinary quality of repose. Physically, he never made an unnecessary gesture or move. In appearance he was indistinguishable from the legion of businessmen who thronged the hotel foyer downstairs. Neatly turned out in a grey business suit, his only sign of lavishness was a pair of highly-polished crocodile shoes. He wore no jewellery other than a silver wristwatch with a black leather band, and like so many successful men he was on the short side. Blake judged him to be about five foot six in height, weighing in the neighbourhood of one hundred and fifty-five powerfully-built pounds. Other than that he was olive-skinned and topped with thick black curly hair, which he wore closely cropped. Oddly, although he moved very little, he gave the impression of bullish strength and great energy. Further, his beard was heavy and probably required shaving twice a day. The eyes were furtive, the mouth humourless. Blake detested him at first glance.

Blake was waved to a seat. Settling down, he allowed his gaze to sweep the room, noting that the entire outer wall was a sheet of glass from floor to ceiling and the room itself was the size of a baseball infield. There was a running fountain playing on a pool full of goldfish, life-size statuary serving as flower bowls (all brimming with red roses) and settees that could have accommodated the boards of a dozen companies. The garden outside was floodlit, revealing green grass, trees and an enormous swimming pool. It was pure Hollywood. Hans Reichter, alias Don Juan Camilo Mandala, was a big spender.

Reichter settled into a small L-shaped sofa and beckoned Blake to a deep chair directly opposite. The Swiss seated himself beside his employer and placed Patel's letter of introduction, Barnes's passport and letter of credit in front of him on the coffee table.

Herr Reichter said in clear, concise English, 'You have double-checked all these documents?'

Sterr nodded, 'I have.'

'You find them genuine?'

'We have both written and oral confirmation regarding the passport from the American Embassy in London, the same from the Banque Commerciale here in Geneva regarding the letter of credit and Dilip Patel himself vouched by telex for his letter of introduction.' He added cautiously, 'These appear to be in order.'

This was the moment. If anything was going to go wrong it would be now. Blake felt his muscles tighten and willed himself to relax. There would be no escape from that room if they rumbled him now. The place was crawling with musclemen. One word from Reichter and he would be dead, if the German wanted it so. He certainly wouldn't hesitate if he did. Blake wondered how many men he had ordered to be killed, how many he had personally seen tortured to death, how many – several of them prominent politicians, rich industrialists, humble bank tellers, chance passers-by – had died because of him. And all because he, whoever he really was, hated what he termed the 'system' and had taken it upon himself to change it.

The icy chill of Blake's hatred spread slowly up his spinal

column. He was a fatalist. If it all stopped here and now, he had no choice but to accept it.

Reichter turned his head towards the entrance hall and nodded. The last of the security men on station there promptly departed.

Sterr was saying, 'As far as we can tell, Mr Barnes is who he claims to be, the personal representative of Mr Patel, based in Dubhai, Persian Gulf. We have also checked it with another source there. It confirms.'

Reichter gave this some thought, then fluttered a flaccid hand. 'Good. You may go.'

The Swiss inclined his head and walked briskly from the room. Blake might have been absent, not once had either one so much as cast him a glance.

Reichter managed the ghost of a smile. 'You understand, of course, Mr Barnes, that we must be careful. Now tell me, how soon would you like to conclude this business?'

Blake replied, 'Yesterday would do, but that's past, isn't it? Today's almost gone, too. Why not first thing in the morning?'

When Reichter laughed it sounded like glass being broken over a bed of petrified stone. 'Oh?' he crackled. 'Yes, most amusing, indeed.'

That little ball in Blake's wary old stomach tightened, informing him that this one was going to be rough.

VI

Although it was moving at high speed, the engine of the big Mercedes might have been idling, it was running so smooth.

Reichter worshipped power and speed, that was why he drove his own cars and flew his own aeroplanes. That morning he was driving and Blake was his only passenger. But they weren't entirely alone; here the security wasn't so subtle. But then, how could it be, on an open highway? The inevitable carload of security men was following close behind.

After the recent rains the weather had cleared to the crystalline sky and snow-capped mountain peaks of postcard Switzerland. It was a good day to drive.

Reichter switched on the radio. Blake was admiring the view. 'Pretty country,' he observed dryly.

Reichter pursed thin lips, 'It's a place.'

'You visit a lot of them?'

Reichter nodded. Articulate expression was exclusively reserved for business. He didn't indulge in small talk.

The radio warmed up in the middle of a news bulletin. *'…when the school bus containing the thirty British schoolchildren disappeared this morning…'* the voice announced in French.

It was difficult to tell whether Reichter was listening or not, his attention was focused on the road.

'…on the outskirts of Bradford, a midlands industrial town. Later the same day, an anonymous phone call to a London daily newspaper purported to come from an as yet unnamed terrorist group, revealed that it was responsible for the kidnapping…'

Reichter was rounding a long curve, his foot hard down on the accelerator. Blake glanced at the speedometer. They were doing over a hundred miles an hour. He glanced casually over his shoulder. The escort car was still there.

'…meanwhile British army units are assisting the local constabulary,' the announcement continued, *'in an all out effort to find the missing school bus and its occupants, all young children in the five to twelve age group…'*

'No holds barred,' Blake commented quietly. It was a simple statement of fact, something anyone might say on hearing such news.

Reichter asked, 'Is it ever any different in a war of liberation?'

Blake yawned. 'No, I suppose it isn't.'

'People get hurt, even young ones.'

Reichter didn't smoke, he chewed gum instead. The masticating jaws, an action indicative of indifference, reminded the American of bored shop girls.

'…It was also announced that the Home Secretary has visited the town. Now an entire nation, together with the anxious parents, wait for word from the terrorists. Back in 'London the envoys of several Third World nations have offered their assistance to the authorities should negotiations—'

Reichter switched off the radio. Blake kept his eyes firmly fixed on the road, relishing his loathing. Outside the sun was shining on a forest of green pine.

'What time is it?'

'A quarter to nine,' Blake told him.

A large sign loomed up ahead. Reichter eased into the appropriate lane and put his foot down on the accelerator. He was in a hurry to get to Zurich.

'Can you pull up somewhere? My bladder's bursting,' Blake asked apologetically.

'There's a station along the road a bit. I need gasoline anyway,' Reichter decided reluctantly.

A few minutes later they eased up beside a row of gas pumps. Blake was the first to get out. As he turned towards the men's room, the escort car drew up behind the Mercedes. A couple of overalled attendants passed him on his way inside. Neither gave any sign of recognition.

At the pumps, one checked the oil and water in the Mercedes and the other started to hose gasoline into the escort car. Neither took very long. Reichter stayed put but his bodyguards, their coats bulging with holstered guns, stepped out of their car to have a stretch.

The second attendant held the hose with one hand. He had secreted a small bottle of sugar in the palm of the other. It wasn't difficult to empty it into the tank along with the gas because he was an ex-pickpocket (rehabilitated by the KGB) accustomed to working with crowds. No one noticed it.

Moving around to the front, he lifted the hood, removed the oil stick, wiped it off with a rag and bent to replace it. It wasn't far from the sump to the horn and it took him no time at all to cut the wires connecting the latter to the horn-ring on the escort car's steering wheel. The clippers were small, fitted nicely into the palm of his hand.

Blake walked out of the station as one of Reichter's men paid the bill. A few moments later both cars were back on the road.

After a while, Blake glanced at his watch then up into the rear-view mirror where he saw the escort car rapidly vanishing under the brow of a hill.

The driver of this car sat helplessly behind the wheel. The engine bucked and wheezed, then stopped altogether. He pumped his foot on the starter and when the engine failed to respond, he banged a fist on the horn. Nothing happened. That wasn't working either.

The men piled out of the car.

'You two start walking,' one of them briskly ordered in German, pointing up the road. 'He's bound to stop when he discovers we're not behind him. Fritz, you come with me. If we hurry, we can get back to the station in a quarter of an hour.'

In the Mercedes, Blake had another look at his watch. The Russian ex-pickpocket was good at his algebra. Two cars are travelling at the same speed. How long does it take a substance like sugar to work its way up to the carburettor, and how far is it prudent for the other car to travel after the first one stalls? He decided to give it another minute.

Reichter was saying, 'Payment, you understand, is made the moment I sign the shipment over to you.'

'Providing the price of gold hasn't shot up in the last hour or two,' Blake replied knowledgeably. 'And why Zurich and not Geneva, there's an airport there, too?'

Reichter wasn't accustomed to such queries from mere company employees. He swung around impatiently. 'I felt like a drive, besides the venue doesn't concern you if it doesn't interfere with you carrying out your instructions.'

Deciding that the minute was up, Blake rasped, 'The hell it doesn't. You better watch it or I'll walk out of this deal – who do you think you're talking to?'

Reichter braked violently and swung into the side of the road, his mouth twisted into an ugly grimace. People simply did not speak to him that way. He glanced into his rear-view mirror then swung around to look out of the rear window to discover that his faithful watchdogs were nowhere to be seen. For some unaccountable reason, and at the precise moment when it mattered most, they had let him down. His reaction was violent, the language obscene. Being delivered in German, to Blake's ear it sounded even more so.

Blake didn't interrupt the guttural flow. He didn't take his eyes off him either.

Herr Reichter sat there, his face suffused from hairline to Adam's apple with an unhealthy shade of apoplectic purple.

He bellowed, 'Get out of my car!'

Blake lifted an amiable eyebrow. 'Did I say something to upset you?'

'Get out or I'll drag you out!' Reichter snarled, plunged and froze all in the same movement. Sprawled over the seat, he found himself staring into the stunted barrel of Blake's revolver pressing hard against the bridge of his nose.

'They won't be coming,' Blake announced flatly.

The German was bewildered. He hadn't had much time to think. First the insults, then the strange loss of his escort, now this? To an imaginative man, the muzzle of a gun barrel is an alarming sight, particularly when it is pressing painfully against one's own head and one has the good sense to suspect that the man in possession has no qualms about pulling the trigger.

'Get up and drive,' Blake barked.

Reichter got the engine going and the car swerved back on the road. 'Why are you doing this?' he managed to stammer.

The sudden turnabout was exacting a heavy toll on his nerves. He had a lot to lose.

'For money,' Blake lied.

'How much money?'

'A lot.'

'Ill pay you double.'

'That's not enough.'

Reichter's shrug was expansive. Now that they were talking the odds had lengthened. Rapidly gaining confidence, he waved a negligent hand. 'How much do you want?'

With the Reichters of this world Blake made statements, he didn't indulge in conversation. 'This is bullshit,' he began evenly. 'If I wanted money that Arab creep down in Nice would have coughed up all he had to stay out of that pigpen.'

Reichter all but lost control of the car. Blake had to reach over and steady the wheel. 'Who are you?'

Blake gave him a dig in the ribs with the gun and the German squealed, more out of fear than pain. 'Watch where you're going.'

Reichter's fear was an unfamiliar feeling and his body was unable to cope with it. The tremor started in his hands and rapidly spread to his arms and legs. He had enemies and this man could be representing anyone of a dozen. He was an American, he knew that much; he was also a professional, but a professional what? That bit about the pig murder could be a bluff, but if it wasn't it could be the end of everything. There was death in that tight face, unrelenting hatred. The hairs standing up on the back of his neck told him that much. It was doubtful that he could be bought off.

'There's a side road up ahead. It leads up into those trees.'

Blake indicated the place with his head. 'When you reach it, turn into it.'

Reichter stared, wide-eyed with terror; instinctively he knew he was going to die. 'Why are you doing this to me?'

'Because you're dirt.'

As they rounded a curve, the side road was plainly visible about five hundred yards along the highway. 'Slow down,' Blake ordered. Reichter noticed that his eyes didn't blink once. It wasn't possible? Not here? Not now? Such things happened to other people, mere names in newspapers?

When they reached the turning, Reichter swung the big Mercedes into a narrow dirt track. 'Why do you say that?' he stammered. The tremor had reached his throat, making it difficult to articulate his words.

'You kill,' Blake began softly. 'You kill innocent people.' Impersonal, devoid of emotion, it was a simple statement of fact.

Reichter burst out excitedly, 'That's a lie! I've never hurt anyone.'

'No, you get others to do it.'

'Never!'

'...or turn half-baked idealists into killers with all that shit about the clean new world they're fighting for.'

'No!'

'No? That Lufthansa airliner hijack in Majorca, the cold-blooded murder of Jürgen Schumann, its pilot – *where?* – naturally in front of the passengers, kids and all,' the voice droned on. 'Then out be goes – *plop* – like a sack of garbage, dumped on the runway at Mogadishu, Sudan, a hole in his head. But you wouldn't know anything about that and the fact that your Baader-Meinhof assholes butted in on the act. What you'd call Combined Operations, with those other halfwits who have the gall to claim they represent the Arab people.'

'You've got it all wrong!'

'Have I now? So what about all the other little acid trips your junkies got high on that you don't know anything about? For instance, Peter Lorenz, your Minister of Justice. Him you snatch, try in a kangaroo court, torture and kill. And that other poor bastard, Hans Martin Schleyer; his crime was cash. He had a boatload of it, and you wanted a chunk of it, so what do you do? You ransom him, collect a cool million, then shoot him anyway. For why? Because he made it in what you call the "consumer society" and anyone who does that, discounting yourself, deserves to die.'

'Please!'

'Sadistic killings, bank robberies, hostages, fatherless kids – *that pilot had three* – and all for what? Mindless idealism and your bank balance.'

'Oh, God – *God!*' Reichter wailed. 'You're insane!'

Blake paused, watching the progress of the car up the narrow trail. 'Well, hear this,' he resumed, 'bugs like you and those punks of yours deserve just what you dish out – no mercy, no trials, no cushy cells – you'll get only one thing from me… a hole six feet deep in the ground.'

Narrowly avoiding a large rock, Reichter moaned, 'You've got it all wrong!'

The voice went on like muffled drums at a royal funeral. 'But, then, you've never hurt anyone, you know nothing about anything, you only provide advice on how to rob banks and snatch millionaires; your killers know nothing about your gold smuggling and other side deals.'

Tears welled up in the German's eyes and dripped down over his face. 'Please,' he sobbed. 'For the love of God – please!'

Blake scraped the hard steel along Reichter's ribs. 'And why do you do this? For what else but hard cash. You've made millions – nobody knows how many but you and your bankers – you're very greedy. You also like power, the kind that can dictate who lives and who dies. But more than anything, it's hatred. You hate people, even the idiots who work for you. You're slime, Reichter.' Blake glanced through the windshield. 'Turn up into those trees,' he said, pointing out the way with the hand holding the gun.

The Mercedes bumped over some rough ground, then slid into a small clearing.

'Stop here.' Blake pulled hard on the hand brake. 'Now open the door and get out.'

Reichter lost all control of his limbs. He began to thrash about like someone in the throes of an epileptic fit. His eyes stood out from his head, flecks of spittle gathered in the corners of his mouth. 'No!' he pleaded. 'You don't understand – I help the oppressed!'

'Open the door.'

Reichter screamed. Like a man warding off a swarm of angry hornets, he waved his hands about, then hugged the wheel, the knuckles of both hands whitening under the strain. It would have taken two strong men to pry him loose.

But Blake was an old hand. He took his time. Bracing himself, he aimed carefully and brought the blackjack down just under the right ear. He didn't hit him hard, just enough to stun him for a while. When done by an expert, it didn't so much as leave a bruise; the soft-leather loaded with sand simply bent on contact with the surface it hit, unlike steel. And Blake was an expert.

Reichter slumped over the wheel. Blake had padded handcuffs taped to the calf of his leg. He ripped them off, slipped them through the spokes of the wheel, and clipped them on to Reichter's wrists. He wanted to minimise any signs of a struggle.

He stepped out of the car, moved around to the other side and opened the door. Lifting the slumped figure off the wheel, he pulled him down on the seat and as far out of the car as the cuffed hands would permit. He eased the lolling head down until it was resting just below the level of the door.

He removed the keys from the ignition switch, stepped around to the back for the can he had bribed the garage attendant in Reichter's Geneva hotel to slip into the luggage compartment. This contained two gallons of sea water.

He rummaged in a pocket for a small roll of transparent plastic and when it was unrolled, he emptied the contents of the can into it. Full of water it looked like a circular fish bowl.

Reichter started to moan. Not yet fully awake, his eyes fluttered open. Blake placed the bag just under his head, took a firm hold with both hands on the adhesive lip, stretched it over his head and on down over the bridge of his nose. 'Pretty, isn't it?' he said. 'When there's more of it, the water turns blue.'

He gave it one last tug. It slipped down over the rest of Reichter's face and when he released the lip it snapped tightly over the throat.

With his feet planted firmly on the ground, he straddled him and lifted the bag over his head. Blake sat back and admired his handiwork. Reichter looked like a deep-sea diver with some slight variations: his old style bubble-shaped helmet was transparent and it held the water in rather than kept it out.

'Come on in, the water's fine,' Blake joked. He was in a buoyant mood. Muffled sounds of splashing water and choking protests drifted up from inside the helmet. Reichter was trying to say something.

'That's right. You're dying. Now you know what it feels like. Not very pleasant, is it?'

Reichter's legs kicked violently. A foot knocked the radio out of its casing and it fell to the floor.

Blake glanced at his watch. 'Your lungs are burning, but not for long,' he chided. 'Someone like you murdered my daughter. Now you're paying for it.'

Blake grabbed him by the coat lapels and lifted him up to get a better view of his face. The water level had settled just above the hairline and little bubbles were trickling up from the corners of his mouth. The eyes were riveted on Blake. Some might have said there was a pleading note in their expression. The mouth gasped for air and inhaled water. The feet kicked a few more times, but soon the struggle ceased altogether.

Blake stood there looking at his watch. When he was sure that Reichter was dead, he gently lowered the helmeted head to the ground. He cut a small hole in the bag and let the water drain out on the ground. Then he hesitated, wondering if he had forgotten anything. Remembering what it was, he promptly removed the bag from the dead man's head, rolled it up into a tight little ball and slipped it into a pocket.

He found a handkerchief and wiped the water off the face and neck of the corpse. Removing the handcuffs, he dragged it to a nearby tree and propped it up into a sitting position against the trunk. He ran a comb through its hair, readjusted the collar and tie, then fetched the camera from the glove compartment in the car. Adjusting it for close-ups, he returned to the body and took some photographs.

Careful to leave nothing behind but tyre tracks, he drove out of the clearing.

Later that morning, the Geneva police received an anonymous phone call. 'You will find the body of Hans Reichter in a wood just above a village called Aubonne on the road to Zurich,' the voice informed them in flawless French. 'And, incidentally, that wasn't his real name. Neither was Juan Camilo Mandala, the one he registered under at his hotel in Geneva. And his home wasn't in Barcelona. One thing is certain, however – he was the active head of the Baader-Meinhof gang.'

VII

Within four hours of leaving Hans Reichter's corpse propped up against that tree in the Swiss forest clearing, Blake crossed the frontier into Italy at the town of Chiasso.

He cleared Passport Control on a forged Canadian passport. An hour later he reached Milan via the *autostrada* and checked into a safe house run by a reliable house mother, ex-Agency, and one of Blake's old friends. Three hours after this, the Geneva Police released the news of Reichter's murder to the press.

Guido Gretti was a rare bird. A native-born Milanese, he had begun life on the streets as a petty thief and had graduated south to Calabria to something less hazardous with the Mafia while still on the right side of twenty. Then, just prior to the end of World War II in Europe, and like so many of his kind at that period, he abruptly found himself doling out American Army food rations to the hungry populace of Naples. From this it was only a hop, skip and jump to the SOE (The American Army Intelligence Service) simply because the Mafia had run the only organised resistance to the Germans in that vicinity and the Americans at this point in time badly needed their assistance to root out known collaborators.

Gretti, a boisterous extrovert, was a rarity in the secret world because, being a larger-than-life character, it was his nature to attract attention to himself. But somehow he had survived. Now, three and a half decades later, and much to Blake's surprise, he was still alive. After much back-slapping and elephantine embraces, Blake found himself sitting in a chair with Gretti producing the inevitable bottle of *Grappa*.

The Milanese emptied his first glass at a single swallow as if he was drinking tap water and exclaimed, 'Now, my friend, I have news for you.'

Blake tried to emulate him with the contents of his own glass and when he finished coughing, managed to observe, 'From Linderman?'

'*Si.*'

'The news?'

Gretti refilled the glasses. 'Those prisoners who survived the airport shooting in London. British counter-intelligence interrogated them.'

Undecided whether it was the *Grappa* or his own excitement which caused his blood to quicken, Blake leaned forward, but managed to keep his voice steady. 'And?'

'The prisoners were tough, they didn't get much.'

'They must have got something.'

'Yes… something,' Gretti nodded complacently.

'*What* for Christ's sake?'

'The German. He let slip that they were an execution squad, working for somebody called Habib Yasli. Heard of him?'

Blake froze. 'Yes. He used to operate out of Iraq, training recruits in sabotage. This German? Can you be more specific? What else did they get out of him?'

'Not much, other than what I've said,' Gretti shrugged.

'Did they discover where Yasli's operating from now?'

'Not exactly.'

'What do you mean by that?'

'Linderman has another source, who says he's running a training camp in the Lebanon.'

Blake shot off his chair and, this time, he did the embracing. 'I'll need a safe route to the southern Adriatic, to somewhere near Brindisi, then a boat out to Cyprus. From there it's less than a hundred miles to the Lebanon.'

Gretti considered it. 'When?'

'Today, if it can be arranged.'

'It'll take three days, maybe longer.'

Blake refilled the glasses. 'But you can do it?'

'*Si.*'

'Tell Linderman he can reach me via the letter-drop in Nicosia, Cyprus.'

'*Va bene.* Anything else?'

Blake drained his glass and relaxed back in his chair. 'Yeah, give me another belt of that firewater.'

Guido happily obliged.

'All right if I bunk here?'

The Italian's grin was like his nature: affectionate and spontaneous. 'I wouldn't have you stay anywhere else, *amico.*'

Much later that night, Blake put a call through to a safe phone in London. He asked them to relay a message the following morning to Miss Monica Riley and gave them her office number. The next day he stood by in a public telephone booth in the Duomo Arcade, and at the appointed time, Monica rang through.

'It's me,' he said by way of hello.

'Sam! I felt it in my bones it would be you.' Attempting a breeziness that didn't quite come off, she went on, 'Woman's intuition – how's Milan?'

'Damp. Busy?'

'Not so busy I can't talk to you. It's been ages since I last got a squeak out of you.'

Sam said gently, 'It wasn't possible, but that doesn't mean that I haven't been thinking of you. You know that, don't you?'

'Sam, I can get a few days off. With any luck I could get a flight out of here in the morning... what do you say?'

'No, it's too risky.'

Monica insisted. 'Don't be silly. You forget, I've done a few tricks in the field myself. I'm not exactly a novice. Come on, darling, for once in our lives let's think of ourselves.'

Blake hesitated. It was tempting, and what she said was true.

Also, Centre was tracking one man alone. A couple travelling together might confuse them. 'I don't know,' he replied carefully. 'Why not wait till things settle down a bit?'

Monica's voice went cold. She became quite formal, even polite. 'I see. Very well. But if I don't come now, I don't come at all – *ever*. Bye, now.'

'Wait a minute! If it means that much to you…'

'Get off the fence, Sam. I'm sick and tired of waiting for the phone to ring, wondering what's happening to you – do I come or don't I?'

'Okay. Come if you must. But this is no pleasure jaunt. You come on strong when you want something – I surrender.'

He tried to laugh it off but it stuck in his throat.

'Darling!'

'But not for a day or two. There'll be a ticket in your name at the Air Italia office in London. I might not be in Milan, but wherever I am the place will be marked on the ticket. I'll meet you when you fly in. You talk to no one about this, understand?'

'Oh, Sam,' she cried. 'I do love you so.'

'A minute ago you sounded like a tax collector!'

When he rung off, he stood there for a moment wondering why he had let her talk him into it. Once she arrived she couldn't help becoming involved. But despite all this, his head felt light. His heart sang, *Monica is coming!* He could think of nothing else.

Only later that night did it occur to him that her arrival might turn out to be a luxury that neither of them could afford.

VIII

Jim Roker sat in the bar thinking how much the Gazzera Club had changed. The Nile was still there; flowing placidly outside the window, and the bustling streets, the monuments, the shabby buildings, the noisy trams – these were as he remembered them in pre-Nasser Egypt when the British Foreign Office had virtually run the country and the late King Farouk was monarch in name only.

Roker's Egypt had been forged by the languid pen of Lawrence Durrell in *The Alexandria Quartet* where the beautiful people had been modishly decadent in four languages and as many religions. The leisured idle of five continents had lazed in jasmine-scented gardens, French was their *lingua frama*, Greek the argot of shopkeepers, Arabic the tongue of the *Fellaheen* masses who waited on their tables and scrubbed their floors. All this had ended with the abdication of the King and Nasser's revolution; now only the over-crowded city remained. Foreigners were found at the Hilton, and Gazzera itself was the unofficial officer's club of Sadat's army.

Roker asked the barman for a refill. He returned with a telephone as well as the replenished glass. It was Renway and he was in one of his bilious moods. 'Where the hell have you been? I've been trying to reach you for days.'

'I've been here,' Roker flared irritably. 'He's holed up in another fleapit in the old quarter. We can't get near him, the place is crawling with legmen.'

Renway countered primly, 'They can't be Russians. Sadat booted them out months ago.'

'What the hell difference does it make who they are? They're there, that's all I know.'

'But how do you know it's Blake?'

'Because I saw him board the plane myself in Bombay, surrounded by KGB security men.'

'How close did you get to them?'

Roker glanced along the bar. The place was empty except for the bartender, who was serving a solitary newcomer at the far end. Nonetheless, he lowered his voice. 'Close enough. They pulled up at the terminal in two cars at the last minute and hustled Blake through to the VIP lounge, then straight out to the plane – a Pan-Am flight from Singapore bound for Rome via Bombay and Cairo.'

Renway cut in impatiently, 'Did you have a man on that flight?'

'How the hell could I? Flights go out of there for Europe all day long. I can't cover them all. Next, I suppose you'll ask me if his name was on the manifest.'

Renway pressed on, ignoring the sarcasm. 'You said it was Blake – did you see his face?'

'No, but it was him all right. He was still wearing the same clothes he had on when I last saw him at his hotel in Bombay. As soon as they got him aboard it taxied out to the runway and took off. I had no authority to stop it…' It was no good. As he was speaking, Roker realised that he had been had by one of the oldest dodges in the business, so moth-eaten it wouldn't have fooled a novice on his first day in the field – passing off a decoy in Blake's clothes. Miserably, he said as much to Renway, concluding, 'Then I phoned Cairo, alerted our people to meet the plane, and flew out on the next flight myself. You know the rest.'

Oddly enough, Renway didn't crow; he was too worried for that. Instead he asked, 'When did you last see him, then?'

'Last Wednesday… just a week ago.'

'He certainly didn't waste any time,' Renway snapped, the anger creeping back into his voice again.

'Why, what's happened?'

This time the other exploded. 'Don't you read the papers? While you've been sitting on your ass in Cairo, he's been on the rampage again here in Geneva, committed another murder! I want you on the first flight out of there, Roker, and I don't care what you have to do to get on it. I'll be waiting at the airport when you land.'

Roker stared at the phone. Renway had rung off. It was a fitting end to what had been a frustrating day.

IX

They were seated in the back of a taxicab which was stuck in a traffic jam halfway between Geneva and the airport.

Renway was fuming. 'Move it!' he shouted at the phlegmatic driver, who merely turned, mumbled something and shrugged. An imported worker from Istanbul, his knowledge of English was negligible. Renway slammed his ample bottom back on the seat. 'What did he say?'

'*Kismet*,' Roker said tiredly. He wasn't in the rosiest of moods himself.

'What the hell does that mean?'

'Fate.'

Renway besought the roof. 'Jesus Christ, what a world!' He picked up a pile of newspapers and dumped them on Roker's lap.

'Before you do anything, read these. This time the balloon's gone up for real. All-night sittings at the Security Council, Congress baying for blood, pinkoes picketing the White House, and everyone blaming us.'

Roker hunched his shoulders, 'It'll all die down in a day or two.'

Renway scowled, slamming a large manila envelope on top of the newspaper pile. 'You think so? Have a look at that.'

Roker pulled out a glossy photograph of Hans Reichter propped up against the tree. He looked very dead. The words *How did he die?* were scrawled across the top in Blake's handwriting. Roker stuck it back in the envelope.

Renway was in a bitter mood. 'He had the gall to send that through the ordinary mail, addressed to me personally. Next he'll be sending flesh samples!'

'What do we do now?'

'Find him, goddamn it, before he kills everybody on that crazy list of his.'

Roker lifted his eyes from a lurid headline. 'Not in Geneva. You know Blake. He would have cleared out the same day.' Renway was chewing his lips. 'We'll find him.'

'Same channel?'

Renway's nod was emphatic.

X

Maurice Boule, a portly Swiss Intelligence official, was on hand to greet them in the Coroner's office when they arrived. A pipe-smoking burgess from the canton of Basel, he greeted Renway like an old friend. He smoothed his well-oiled, sparse hair (combed sideways across his head to hide a large bald spot, with plump fingers and shook hands with Roker.

'It's your man Blake, all right,' he said puffing his pipe. 'Reichter's bodyguards recognised him directly they saw his photograph. But there's still no trace of those two at the service station.'

Renway impatiently brushed this last aside. 'You'll never find them. Blake only uses professionals.'

Boule's small blue eyes lit up with amusement. 'Ours or theirs?'

Renway shook his head. 'No Russians this time. Whatever they owed him you can bet they paid helping him find this last one. He wouldn't risk going to them again.'

Roker didn't agree but he kept it to himself. In his present mood, Blake was capable of anything. That at least was predictable.

'Well, whoever they were, they were good,' Boule said. He invited them to accompany him down the hall to the morgue room. Like most of its kind this one was clinical, with a well-scrubbed stone floor, a sink, an antiseptic odour and a large freezer containing a couple of dozen drawers covering one entire wall. Here bodies awaiting autopsies were stored.

As Boule ushered them into the room they saw the coroner and his assistant, both wearing white coats, bending over a body on the dissecting table. The coroner saw them and beckoned them to join him at the sink where he proceeded to scrub his hands. He was a precise little man with a fresh complexion and protruding ears. After the introductions, he said, 'Extraordinary, his clothes weren't even wet yet the autopsy indicates that he drowned – in salt water, of all things, and this in Switzerland, some three hundred kilometres from the sea. Extraordinary!'

Renway asked, 'Was there anything else – bruises, cuts, that sort of thing?'

The coroner finished wiping his hands, folded the towel neatly and placed it carefully on its rail. Like most Swiss he was meticulous in such matters. While they waited, he thought over what he was about to say with rather ponderous deliberation, at last announcing, 'Other than some slight bruising behind the right ear and along the rib cage, there isn't a mark on the body.'

Boule nodded. 'The bruise behind the ear. Probably a sandbag. Even a hard blow leaves little trace on the skin.'

Renway and Roker readily agreed. 'He thought of everything,' one of them said.

A phone rang and the coroner's assistant went to pick it up.

Boule called to him, 'If that's another newspaper, I'm not here.' He turned to the others. 'They've been plaguing me ever since I got up this morning – salt water, indeed!'

Outside he took them to a taxi-stand. Renway warmly shook his hand. 'Thanks, Maurice, I appreciate your keeping his name out of it.'

Boule nodded. 'Where do we get clearance in the event I have to reveal it?'

'Only Centre can give us that,' Renway said carefully.

'And Centre is God,' Roker added. He was looking at a large poster in front of a nearby news-stand, It read:

BRITISH SCHOOLCHILDREN STILL MISSING. TERRORISTS
NEGOTIATE WITH GOVERNMENT FOR THEIR LIVES

Maurice Boule followed his look, said kindly, 'You're thinking that perhaps your former colleague isn't so wrong after all.'

Roker nodded, 'That's exactly what I was thinking, you've read my mind.'

Renway was in a hurry to return to the airport and climbed into the nearest available taxicab. Roker followed and Boule stuck his hand through the window by way of goodbye. Both shook it, then the taxi shot off into the heavy rush-hour traffic.

Renway said straightaway, 'What the hell did you say that for?'

'What?'

'That crap about Blake not being wrong.'

'I meant every goddamn word of it,' Roker said grimly.

Renway raged, 'I guess if anybody is going to kill that son of a bitch, it's going to be me! And hear this: from now on out, where you go, I go – got it?'

CHAPTER EIGHT

I

THE OLD ROAD FROM PERUGIA TO ASCOLI WOUND STEEPLY up into the mountains of the Apenn Marchigiano and of late it wasn't often used: drivers preferred the smooth surfaces and straight tunnelled runs of the new *autostrada*. Blake and Monica were bound for a small Adriatic village called Porto d'Ascoli where their passage had been arranged on a fishing boat to Cyprus; he prudently avoided congested areas where he would most likely run into police patrols.

He was driving the car Monica had hired in Bergamo and she was sitting beside him with a large road map on her lap. The going was bumpy, full of hairpin turns and littered with potholes.

Monica was feeling the strain. 'We'll never make it at this rate. Can't you drive faster?'

Blake had to slow right down. A large hole was looming up ahead. Fortunately it wasn't deep. He patted her knee, 'Relax. It isn't a scheduled run. They agreed to wait.'

Both lapsed into one of those dreaded awkward silences they had been enduring since her arrival. That was only two days ago, but it seemed more like a month for Monica. She had been left alone most of the time and when they were together, Blake had been preoccupied.

Right then he was concentrating on his driving and she was gazing idly out the window. Then Blake broke the silence, dropping it casually like a stranger remarking on the weather. 'You should have stayed in London. If the Agency knows its job – and it does – this place could be crawling with hit teams... I don't like it.'

Monica's eyes watered, a thing they had been threatening to do since her arrival. She had never seen him so edgy. He wasn't like the man she knew at all. She just managed a husky, 'Thank you.'

'I should have known better – Christ! What have I done with my brains?'

'It's nice to know I'm wanted.'

Blake whirled around, his face pale with anger. 'You've no right to say that, and you know it! You're a professional, you know the risks, so don't play the little woman with me. One false move and both of us could end up on a morgue slab!'

He slammed the gears into low to climb a steep hill. Monica found a handkerchief and blew her nose. Outside the patchy mountain scrub, as if in response to their mood, took on an aspect of gloom. For all they knew, there could be armed men behind every bush.

Blake broke the silence roughly. 'I suppose you want to know everything?'

Monica took her time. She fumbled in her handbag until she found a cigarette. Whatever happened, she was determined to keep a clear head and her feelings under firm control. Hysterics didn't work with Blake, he simply withdrew into a brooding hostile shell. Lighting her cigarette, she turned to him. 'I think I know most of it already. You know how things get around, particularly in the circles we move in. Nobody really knows, of course, but there have been some shrewd guesses.'

Blake asked indifferently, 'What are they saying?'

'Some of it's pretty wild.'

'How wild?'

'That the Agency's got a contract out on you.'

Blake nodded. 'That's right. What else?'

'If you've been reading the papers, you know.'

'What do you think?'

Monica took a deep breath, hoping against hope. 'You did it – all by yourself.' Despite her resolution, her eyes filled. 'Oh, Sam, tell me you didn't, *please!*'

Blake slowed for another steep curve. 'You're right. I personally killed both of them. You also know why, so we needn't go into that.'

She reached out and touched his arm. 'Sam, if you're

identified by anyone outside the Agency, you know what'll be said, that you were acting on their orders. Too much is involved, they can't have that. The government can't afford to be linked with something like this, it has too much to lose. For God's sake, stop now before it's too late!'

Now that he had told her, he felt better. Brightening, he leaned over and pecked her cheek. 'I can't do that. I knew all this would happen before I started out – I'm committed, right to the end.'

'Yes,' she said bitterly, 'on a morgue slab.' Hurt and angry, she turned away from him. 'If that's the way it is, why did you allow me to join you?'

Blake slowed down to a crawl for another tight turn.

'Because I need your help. You insisted on coming, nothing I could have said would have stopped you. You're no novice in this business, you've helped the Agency before, so why not me now?'

In a single furious moment, Monica dropped his arm and slid as far away from him as she could get. He wasn't going to get away with that. The more she thought about it, the angrier she got. 'So that was why? Not because you missed me. Oh, no, that would be too much to ask. You don't give a damn about me and never did. Christ, what a fool I've been! You can go to hell!'

Blake said nothing. An old stager, he waited for her to cool down.

Furious, she wrenched a handle on her door, but it was the wrong one. 'Stop this car, Sam, I want to get out!' Then she burst into tears.

Blake went on driving until she cried herself out, as the saying goes, then passed her a handkerchief. 'That's not true and you know it. You know how I feel about you, how I've always felt. You also know that I've got other things on my mind just now, like finishing this thing, and survival. Now, are you going to help me or not?'

'What do you want me to do?' she asked, blowing her nose for the second time that morning.

Blake stopped the car and swept her into his arms. 'I love you,' he whispered. Then much later on, he remarked, 'Why is it always so much better after a row? I've never been able to figure that one out.'

'You didn't tell me what you wanted me to do.' Monica remembered. She was repairing her make-up with the aid of the rear-view mirror.

'Nothing you can't handle. There should be a contact in Beirut. I've got to hole up somewhere, I can't chance being spotted on the streets. You can move around the town for me. I'll give you the details later.'

'Why not now?'

'I don't have them yet myself. That information should be waiting for me in Nicosia.'

'Letter-drop?'

Blake ran his fingers through her hair. 'You do ask a lot of questions, don't you?'

She pushed his hand away. 'I've got to know what's happening, Sam, if I'm going to be able to help you.'

He found himself staring into a pair of very open violet eyes. She was anxious and eager to help. Blake kissed her again.

'I know,' he mused.

'Nothing else?'

He shook his head. 'Apart from your company, no. Don't worry, I'll get you back in one piece somehow.'

'I don't give a damn if I never get back, Sam, and well you know it.'

Later on, she looked out at the passing ravines and steep cliffs hemming them in on both sides of the road. 'It's hard to believe that this is Italy. It's so primitive, not a house for miles, nothing.'

Blake pulled her close. 'No Holiday Inns, no junk food. What the hell, we're in the wilderness.'

She inched up and kissed him under the chin.

Monica was looking very beautiful at that moment, with the sun doing all kinds of nice things to her tawny hair. 'What did you tell them at the office?'

She sat up. 'That I needed a vacation.'

'Trouble?'

He liked the shape of her lower lip when she frowned.

'From me, plenty. They owe me, I haven't had any time off for ages.'

'You just walked out?'

'Right in the middle of a sentence. Jake had to finish the article.'

'Jake?'

'My new editor. He loves me. It was marvellous when you called. I kissed the phone.'

'You never answered my question?'

'Umm?'

'Why is it always so much better after a row? I'm not kidding, I really want to know.'

Monica pursed a pair of inviting lips. 'The Chinese say that anger is a good aphrodisiac.'

'And they should know.'

'Positively.'

Up ahead about six miles (two as the crow flies) a repair crew was filling a deep hole in the middle of the road. There were large warning signs and red lanterns positioned around the site to inform motorists that work was in progress. When the hole was filled it was tarred down and a heavy roller drove up to press down the loose gravel. Two men appeared with a large wire reel connected to an explosive device that had been placed just under the surface of the recently repaired hole.

They let it unwind behind them as they struggled up towards the summit of a steep hill.

There was an air of urgency about the operation, and directly the hole was resurfaced the roller was driven off to a siding and parked in a roadside shed. The signs and lanterns were hastily removed and, aside from the gleaming patch of tar, it was just another stretch of empty road.

The foreman beckoned his men to disperse, some to various hiding places along the hill, others down into the deep ravine below the road.

The pair with the wire reel finally reached the top but they didn't have time to rest. One of them – Renway – slipped a pack off his shoulders and pulled out one of the old-type detonators equipped with a long wooden-handled plunger. It didn't take him long to attach the wire-ends from the reel to the power points on the detonator. The other – Jim Roker – had taken up a position on the summit of the hill and was scanning the road through a pair of binoculars.

Down on the road and about a mile away, Blake was rounding a sharp bend with something more than his customary caution. He didn't know why but he was beginning to feel uneasy. Perhaps it was tiredness. They had only stopped once since leaving Bergamo early that morning and then only for half an hour. His feeling seemed to be contagious. Monica was sitting bolt upright beside him, her face tight with anxiety.

Blake patted her knee. 'You okay?'

'This road is like a merry-go-round. I feel dizzy.' Her face was damp with perspiration.

Blake looked down at his shirtfront. It was wringing wet.

'Once we clear this stretch, it straightens out a little.'

Monica kept staring out of the window at the passing hilltops. There was no breeze and no sound other than the steady hum of the engine. Overhead the clouds were low and moving fast. 'Must be windy up there,' she remarked absently.

Up above on the hilltop, Jim Roker spotted the car as it cleared one of the curves. He held it in his binoculars until it vanished around another bend.

Renway called, 'Any sign of him yet?'

'He just rounded one of the curves,' Roker called back. His voice sounded unnaturally loud. He wasn't positive but it seemed that Blake wasn't alone. He hurriedly readjusted the focus and waited for the car to appear again. When it did it was much closer than it had been before. Roker looked again, now he was certain. There was a woman sitting beside Blake and she looked familiar.

Renway's voice was a nervous croak. 'Where is he now?'

The woman seemed to be looking straight at him as the car cleared the last bend. Roker's eyes bulged with horror. 'It's Monica! Jesus Christ, Monica's in that car with him!'

There was only one chance now and Roker didn't hesitate. He did the only thing he could do – he began to flick the binoculars up and down. The odds were a thousand to one against them seeing the flashes as the spasmodic sunlight reflected off the thick lenses. Then the car vanished around the final bend. When it rounded that it would reach the straight. From that point on it was a bare two hundred yards to the tar patch.

Roker found himself shouting, 'You're going to kill her, too!'

Renway sat on his heels, squatting beside the detonator, both hands poised on the plunger. He barked, 'Drop your arm when he reaches the patch!'

'You bastard!' Roker yelled, desperately juggling the binoculars. 'Monica, for God's sake – *look!*'

When she spotted the flashes, Monica screamed, but it was too late to stop. All Blake knew was that he must avoid that tar patch. He swung hard on the wheel.

There was a wailing screech from the tyres as Blake put his foot down hard on the brake pedal and the car lunged towards the shoulder of the road and the emptiness beyond. It swerved sideways along the very edge, skidding along the loose gravel, its inner-wheels just touching the outer edge of the tar patch.

'You son of a bitch!' Roker roared, launching himself into a headlong dive to stop him, but he was too late.

Renway put his full weight behind it and rammed down the plunger. Down on the road, the patch dissolved into a great geyser of flying gravel, dust and macadam. Lifted by the impact of the explosion, its front wheels surfacing first, the car bounced, swerved crabwise, straightened, bounced again, its engine revving, its tyres wailing, all the while managing to stay upright, then – still intact – it shot out of the dust. A huge plume of flame blossoming out of its rear end, the rattling wreck, shedding bits and pieces in its headlong plunge, swerved into another bend and vanished altogether, trailing a cloud of billowing smoke.

Roker and Renway stood confronting each other. 'You knew she was in that car, didn't you? Well, it didn't make any difference – they made it.'

Renway smirked, 'Maybe they had a little help.'

'What do you mean by that?'

'That's an old dodge, the sun reflecting off a pair of binoculars. You didn't think I'd fall for that, did you?'

'I don't give a good goddamn what you think, not after this, you murdering bastard. I'm through.'

'You're under orders, Roker, you will do as you're told, same as the rest of us.'

'You would have killed her!'

Renway turned away. Centre wasn't sympathetic to failure. He could see a lifetime of hard work dripping down the drain. It wasn't a comforting thought. 'I did what I had to do,' he said.

Spluttering with rage, it took the younger man a moment to get the words out. 'That's the phrase that covers everything, isn't it?' he jeered, spinning away. He started down the hill on the run, stumbled on a loose stone and lost his footing. Scrambling back to his feet, he lurched on in a headlong rush down the hill.

Renway started after him. 'Where the hell do you think you're going?'

Roker stopped dead in his tracks and whirled around. 'I've strung along until now because I honestly thought Blake had to be stopped. But don't ask me to stomach this, orders or no orders! I won't stand by and watch you kill somebody like Monica – get yourself another boy!'

Breathing hard, Renway reached him as Roker turned to continue his flight down the hill. Holding on to his arm, he blurted, 'All right, suppose *you tell me* what you would have done – in *my* place, Roker, not *yours*?'

Roker made a start but Renway cut him short before he could get it out. Rage, frustration, guilt: they were all there in his expression. '*How else can he be stopped?* You know him better than I do, you tell me how to stop him without killing him and I'll do it!' Renway grabbed him by the shoulders and started to shake him. '*Damn you! You know it can't be done.* Now go!' he shouted, pushing him. 'If that's what you want – piss off! I've had a gut full of your lily-livered conscience!'

Roker took a last despairing look down at the gaping hole in the road and wheeled off in the opposite direction. He didn't even turn his head, he kept on going.

Renway made no further attempt to stop him. One of the men (young Page) scrambled up to him. The blood had drained from his face and he stood unsteadily on his feet.

Renway growled, 'What the hell do you want?' Page stammered weakly, trembling with repugnance at what he had just seen down on the road. 'I think the car escaped, sir... what was left of it.' He held up a mangled chunk of metal. 'This was the exhaust pipe. He can't have gone far. I've sent out two vehicles to pick him up.' His eyes were following Roker's retreating figure.

Renway grunted. 'Don't worry about Mr Roker, Page, he'll

come around.' But they were only words. Renway was too concerned with his own prospects to give a damn one way or the other. Right then he was wondering how long it would take Centre to dispatch one of their hatchetmen to London. It wouldn't be pleasant if that happened.

II

From somewhere beyond her securely-locked front door, Edith Roker could hear the voices – a lot of people in a room, enjoying themselves – a shout, now and then sudden laughter. It made her feel more alone than ever. She had just put down the phone. Jim had rung her up from somewhere in Italy. It had been a worrying conversation.

Edith had never known what exactly he did at the embassy although she suspected that it had something to do with security in one of the departments. Not that she hadn't asked. But he had soon made it clear after their marriage that he wasn't at liberty to talk about it; it was policy, that was all he could say, and she soon learned that it was best not to talk about it.

The trouble had always been his sudden departures and protracted absences. This made it difficult for both of them and eventually led to the break-up of their marriage.

There was no other woman, she was convinced of that. And now he was alone in some foreign room and deeply troubled. He needed her and there was nothing she could do to help. And in that brief telephone call he had revealed things about himself that years of marriage had failed to do.

Edith wanted to rush to his side, to comfort him, advise him, lavish the love that he had never given her time to give.

'I've quit,' he had said. 'Walked out. I'm through.'

Edith had received this bit of news with mixed feelings. Compassion for his despair, gladness that now, possibly, they may have a future together.

Part of the time he had been incoherent, some of it she didn't understand when he wasn't; but never once did she worry about their prospects, his loss of a pension, or so-called practical matters like that. It simply never occurred to her, so complete was her concern for what it was doing to him.

'Why don't you come home?' she suggested. 'Right now. Just get on a plane and fly out of there. I'll meet you at the airport.'

'I'm so sorry,' he said. 'For everything, all the things we missed together because of that goddamned job.'

'Darling, come home. We'll sort it out somehow.'

But no, he wasn't able to do that. There was something he had to do first, something involving Sam Blake, who was in another place. Jim had to find him, to explain things. 'I love you, Edith, and I promise it won't take long, and when I come home it will be for good. I'll never leave you again.'

He had been desperate and, most worrying of all, bewildered. Her heart had gone out to him. 'I'll be here,' she had promised. 'Waiting. Come as soon as you can.'

III

At the Hotel Konstantos in Nicosia, Cyprus, Blake tossed restlessly in an overstuffed chair by the closed window shutters, oblivious to the racket down on the street. He sat there with his eyes closed waiting for his head to clear. With each unfamiliar sound his brain reeled in confusion, his entire body ached. The whole thing had been a nightmare not dissimilar to the ones that had plagued him in the British hospital after Janis's death. He hadn't slept properly for three days, two of which had been spent in a tiny airless cabin on a tossing boat. He was neither awake nor asleep, merely floating in a limbo of uncertainty and unanswered questions. He didn't remember much of what had happened back in Italy on the road to Ascoli. There had been Monica's scream, he remembered that, then the explosion, the noise of the engine, the screeching tyres, the showering debris and the fire, but little else. Somehow he had coaxed the battered wreck to the rendezvous with Gregorios, a leather-faced little Cypriot fisherman, who had been delegated by his captain to meet Blake, under the new bridge, which fortunately had only been a couple of miles down into the ravine from the scene of the explosion;

then the tortured wait for darkness with Monica moaning in delirium, followed by the interminable drive to the little port and, finally, to safety on Sergiou's boat. They had been lucky. Neither had been touched by the fire in the back of the car.

Like most autumn storms in the eastern Mediterranean, this one had arrived without warning and departed as suddenly. Monica had been in great pain but Sergiou's rough weathered hands had been gentleness itself. Blake hadn't been much help so the big fisherman had set the bone himself and wrapped it into a pretty good makeshift of a plaster cast. Two days later she had crawled up into the sun suffering more from a hangover than a fractured arm, neat *ouzo* being Sergiou's substitute for a suitable anaesthetic to deaden the pain.

Blake rose carefully for fear of waking Monica, peacefully asleep on the bed, and lifted the shutters just enough to see down to the street. Sergiou had a couple of his men watching the place outside, but the uneasiness persisted. The trouble was, he didn't know the town nor the island, and his knowledge of Greek being non-existent, he felt vulnerable.

To make matters worse, his movements were restricted. For the next twenty-four hours he could do nothing but wait. Alternative transport to Ghazir, the closest port of entry to Beirut in the Lebanon, was notoriously unreliable, especially now with the Turks in possession of a good part of the island. Anything could happen, he might be stranded there for weeks. Air transport was out because the airfields were too well guarded by the occupation forces. But then, his options were limited. Cyprus, because of its position, lying less than a hundred miles off the Lebanese coast, was the only place he could go to ground in with any degree of safety, despite the fact that it was crawling with Palestinian refugees from the fighting in Lebanon. Blake knew from experience that not all of them were genuine. Because of the confusion resulting from the sudden influx of such numbers, it wouldn't be difficult for the various extremist groups that proliferated in that area to slip in agents, or murder squads. Now was the time for hiding, and waiting, until Sergiou could get him out to the Lebanon.

There were also other problems, namely how long it would take Monica to get well enough to travel. He couldn't move her until her temperature came down. Then there was the position of their room, unfortunately situated on the second floor, facing onto a busy street, directly above the bar, a popular hangout for well-heeled refugees from Beirut. This was too close for comfort because there was always the possibility of being spotted. It wasn't a happy situation, but he had encountered worse, and as long as they remained where they were, they had a reasonable chance of leaving in one piece.

Monica moaned in her sleep. He crossed the darkened room to the bed and placed another wet towel on her forehead. She opened her eyes and saw him leaning over her.

'Feeling better?'

'I'm starving,' she whispered. 'I could eat a horse.'

Blake brightened. 'How's the arm?'

'The swelling has gone down, I can feel it. Sergiou's a lovely doctor.' She puckered up her lips. 'Kiss?'

He obliged, mindful that they were considerably cooler. Her temperature was almost back to normal. 'We'll have to wait a while. Petros will be some time with the food.' Then he remembered the broth sitting on the bedside table. He fed her with an overlarge spoon.

'Umm, delicious, darling, and so cool,' She greedily swallowed it all.

'Any pain?'

She smiled, 'Not much… just a dull ache, that's all.'

Blake settled carefully on the side of the bed. 'We're lucky to be here at all, it was as near as dammit back there.'

Her eyes grew large and luminous in the shadowed room.

'Sam?'

'Try not to talk.'

'Just tell me – who are these people? Can you trust them?'

Blake said gently, 'They're friends from the old days.'

She persisted. Monica was worried. 'Yes, but *who* are they?'

'They worked for Grivas. *Organosis-X.* A kind of EOKA intelligence unit for unification with Greece. Don't worry about them.'

Blake saw that she was asleep. He tiptoed back to the shuttered window.

IV

Sergiou's hulking body sprawled deep in the chair and Blake and Monica sat stiffly on the bed, facing him. A moonbeam lit up the pattern of the shabby carpet. There was no other light in the room. For Blake it was like a prison. He hadn't left it since the moment they had arrived six weary days earlier. Outside the *khamsin* was blowing and the sand of the Sinai Desert was sifting through the shutters. When they walked on the stone floor it was like treading on sugar.

Blake was irritable. 'How long is that thing going to blow?'

Sergiou's big shadowed bulk shrugged. 'In Italy the *Spaghetinos* call it the Sirocco, yes?' He took another deep swig of Krasi and waved a ham-sized hand. Sergiou was in his usual bubbling mood. 'On Pelopannisos we call it something else, but you *Englezos* wouldn't be able to pronounce it.' His laughter echoed alarmingly along the fly-specked ceiling.

Blake had given up trying to explain that they were Americans and not Englishmen. 'Christ, it's hot in here. Doesn't it ever cool down? The twenty-fifth of November and you could fry eggs on the street.'

Sergiou announced proudly, 'Always nice and warm, yes. In winter we swim. The water never gets below sixty degrees. That is good.'

Blake snapped pettishly. 'When do we leave?'

Sergiou's big white teeth flashed in the gloom. 'Tonight, when the moon sets, my friend. This time tomorrow you'll be in Beirut. You leave it to Sergiou.'

Monica leaned forward excitedly, she was much better. Sergiou had sneaked a doctor up to the room and he had replaced the big Greek's masterpiece with light splints. Like Blake, she was eager to see the last of the stuffy room. 'Then what are we waiting for – let's go!' she burst out happily.

Sergiou flashed those teeth again. He was very fond of the *Englezos* lady. He leaned over and lifted one of the shutters.

Below the street was black and empty. Even the bar was silent, the last customer having departed an hour earlier. But Sergiou was cautious. He would move when he felt it was safe to do so, not before.

It was past three when the moon dropped behind the sloping olive groves outside. They moved rapidly out into the empty hall, found the service stairs and emerged a few minutes later from the back of the building. Some of Sergiou's men materialised out of the darkness, led them down a black alley and up through a grove of cypress trees. Here they waited for one of Sergiou's friends, who he said knew the local hideouts. When he finally arrived the sky was already brightening over the tops of the hills. He was a grizzled old peasant wearing a ragged *funstanella*, a kind of short ballet skirt, over heavy baggy trousers. After exchanging swigs of *Krasi* and much voluble conversation and waving of hands with Sergiou, they started off again, moving up a steep rise covered with pine trees.

Breasting the rise, they found themselves on a small plateau bisected by what looked to be goat tracks. An open farm truck was waiting and with much shouting and laughter, they all clambered aboard. Sergiou's basso boomed out of the lightening shadows. 'Now we ride, *Englezos*. We be there soon.'

A minute or two later, as they rattled down the steep track, Blake wasn't so sure they would arrive anywhere. 'Tell him to slow down, Sergiou.'

Monica clutched his ann. 'Oh, God, what if we go over the edge of one of these cliffs?'

Blake sheltered her in his arms. 'Try closing your eyes and a couple of "Hail Marys". Right now we could use a miracle!'

Her prayers evidently answered, the truck rattled down the last steep hill and braked on a sandy beach. Sergiou motioned for silence and they all jumped down on the sand.

From there it only turned out to be about a mile's walk to the boat, which Sergiou had prudently anchored close offshore in a small cove some three miles northwards along the coast from the village of Trikoma. When they reached it the sun was already burning the sand and Antonis and Markos, two of Sergiou's men, were on hand with a fragile-looking rowboat. Both had shotguns slung over their shoulders. Everyone save Blake and Monica burst into a torrent of excited Greek.

Blake smiled reassuringly at Monica. 'Are you okay?' He didn't like the tired shadows under her eyes.

She hugged his shoulder and looked up smiling. It didn't quite come off. 'Why shouldn't I be – this is the last lap, I'm feeling fine.'

Somebody shouted, 'Everybody down!' Blake grabbed Monica and dropped to the sand. The others quickly followed.

Somewhere near there was a rapid burst of machine-gun fire. Blake hugged the sand. It was an ideal spot for an ambush. His eyes moved warily along the low ridge encompassing the beach. Sergiou crawled up beside him, so close Blake could smell the garlic on his breath. The big mobile face was sporting a joyful smile. 'Don't worry, *Englezos* – it's only Gregorios.'

'Who?'

'You remember. He met you under the bridge in Italy. I had him bring them here.'

'For what?'

'The ambush.' The big Greek shrugged. 'It's good to be careful. Yes? Sure enough they come.'

Blake paled at the thought of what could have happened to Monica. 'But how did they know I was here?'

Sergiou nudged him in the ribs and winked. 'You know the Greeks. They like their *Krasi*, then they boast to their women. They find it hard to keep secrets.'

Blake felt the anger rising right up into his throat. 'You knew about this?'

'But of course. Niki, our guide, he told me when he join us on hill last night outside hotel. He very old, wear *funstanella*, but he hear and see good. These men. *Spaghetinos*. Here for dig, they say. But they have many guns instead of shovels. Niki, he tell them he's busy, sends one of his sister's sons – Gregorios. They ask many questions about man like you, then we know.' Sergiou brought a stiff finger across his throat, a gesture that was as old as his race.

Blake saw three men emerge from the ridge. They wore rough civilian clothes and carried modern weapons. One of them stood apart from the others. He lifted his cap and waved. It was Gregorios.

Sergiou said, 'Come with me, *Englezos*.' They got up, hurried to the men on the ridge, and everyone started to shout at once in Greek.

Sergiou turned to Blake. 'Down there, *Englezos* – you see?' Blake followed his nod down into a shallow trench just below where they were standing.

There were three dead men lying there, their young faces already covered with flies. One had died from a blast in the chest, another had a gaping hole in his stomach, the third the back of his head a slithery mess of dripping brain tissue and bone splinters.

'We emptied their pockets,' Gregorios said, nodding a cheerful hello to Blake. 'From over there.' He pointed out to sea in the general direction of the invisible Italian coastline. 'They had Italian passports, but could be from anywhere.'

Adopting an expression often seen in church when the collection plate is passed, the big Greek spoke earnestly, 'Too bad, we might have asked them who they were before we shot them.' Sergiou burst out into a gale of booming laughter at his own joke.

The situation had that innate touch of Levantine madness. 'What else did he ask him?' Blake managed soberly. It was that way with the Greeks, you had to be philosophical.

Sergiou shook his magnificent head. He didn't know, nor judging by his expression, did he care very much. He showed his teeth again, one of solid gold in the centre of the top row. It gleamed like a cut diamond in the sun. He took Blake's arm and pointed towards a rowboat bumping in the surf. 'Young Markos will stay behind and bury them after we sail,' he said. Blake hurriedly emptied his pockets and handed him a large wad of Cypriot currency. 'That ought to be enough for his hotel bill until you return.'

Sergiou's broad grin was a many splendoured thing. Blake turned to Gregorios and his two companions. 'Much obliged,' he said, shaking their hands. 'If I knew Greek I'd say something more appropriate to the occasion. Instead all I have to offer is a great deal of hard American cash.'

They all grinned, not understanding a word, then Blake turned and hurried down to Monica waiting beside the boat. He felt the nausea boiling up from that hard knot in his stomach. The other was the bitterness. The Agency had a lot to answer for, using a young kid like Page on a job like this. He recalled their chat in Claud's car back in Nice when they were driving him to the airport. It was a hard end for the boy – lying in a sandy trench somewhere with no chest and a face full of flies. Renway should have known better.

V

Blake stood beside Sergiou in the tiny deckhouse, watching the glistening reflection of the full moon on the water. They were moving along the Lebanese coast some five miles offshore and Sergiou was manning the wheel. Monica was sleeping below in Sergiou's cabin.

Sergiou pointed to a distant light that was blinking at intervals through the haze that hugged the shoreline. 'That marks the Ghazir channel we shall pull into, *Englezos*,' he said, checking their bearing on the luminous compass-card in front of the wheel.

Blake asked, 'How far is it from Beirut?'

'Not far… no more than twenty-five kilometres,' Sergiou smiled, his teeth gleaming in the moonlight. 'We have someone waiting with a vehicle.'

'Where did you learn your English, Sergiou? You speak it pretty good.'

'From the *Englezos* soldiers on Crete.'

'During the German occupation?'

Sergiou's deep laughter echoed around the limited confines of the deckhouse. 'They occupied the towns – we controlled everything else; the mountains, the roads, the villages – you'd never catch them in any of those places at night, *Englezos*, and Crete is mostly mountains.'

'You gave them a hard time?'

The big Greek cheerfully crossed his throat with a forefinger. Then he remembered something else. 'You know Niki, our guide last night, the one who warned us of the *Spaghetino* ambush on the beach?'

'You mean the old guy in the skirt?'

Sergiou was offended. 'Please, *Englezos*, you speak of our *funstanella*, not some woman's petticoat. In Greece it is as old as time.'

Blake patted him fondly on his enormous back. 'I beg your pardon, old friend. I meant no disrespect. What about him?'

Good humour fully restored, Sergiou announced importantly, 'He had two messages for you. He picked them up in Nicosia yesterday at a... a...?' Sergiou groped manfully for the right word, but it wouldn't come. He muttered something under his breath, probably some Greek obscenity.

'At the letter-drop?'

Relieved, Sergiou's frown was replaced by one of his more animated smiles. 'Yes, *Englezos*, that's the word. My English is not as good as you think. He gave them to me, I studied each word, then burned them right away. Don't trust words on paper.' He tapped his large skull. 'Better in here, it's safer.'

'Okay, what did they say?'

Sergiou knitted his weathered forehead, then repeated the first message like a child reciting a nursery rhyme it had only recently learned: '...let me... know... where to reach you... knowing... Monica... was in car... Renway... still... blew it up... I... quit... want to... join you,' Sergiou faltered, then hastily concluded, 'reply Salerno, Jim!'

'Was there anything else?'

'No, *Englezos*. That was all. Once I learn, I never forget,' Sergiou frowned, offended again that Blake could question his memory. But curiosity rapidly overcame his injured feelings. 'Who is this Jim?'

'A friend.'

'He knew you were in Nicosia?'

'Not necessarily, no.'

Sergiou was bewildered. 'But, if he didn't, how did he know where to write?'

Blake replied patiently, his mind on Roker. 'He knew I was travelling south in Italy when I ran into that land mine, the rest was routine procedure. He drew a large circle around that spot on a map, then sent identical messages to all the letter-drops within its circumference, figuring that one of them would reach me sooner or later. Simple system, usually works.'

'I see,' Sergiou said brightening. 'On the road he was with you in the car?'

'Nope. He was up on the hill, waiting for the mine to explode.'

Sergiou was scandalised. '*Englezos*, you call him a friend?'

'The best. For a while there he had a loyalty problem, but I suspect that's been overcome.'

'Overcome?'

'Once he tried to shoot me, but first he remembered to forget to put shells in the gun. I've got a hunch he saw Monica in the car just before the mine went off. That probably decided him...'

Thoroughly bewildered now, Sergiou lapsed into helpless Greek. 'You *Englezos!*' he bleated. 'You're crazy! You will tell him where you are so he can try and kill you again?'

'What's that?'

'Forgive me, my friend,' Sergiou said in English. 'You trust him?'

Blake didn't say anything straightaway. He sat there gazing out on the moonlit water, then he nodded, 'With my life... and the other message?'

Sergiou began to repeat the painful process all over again. When he finished, Blake thanked him and went below to Monica in the little cabin.

She was lying on a bunk, her face a pale oval in the dim cabin light. Blake settled on a rough wooden bench bolted to the deck alongside a small table.

She sat up, wide awake and expectant. 'Are we there yet?'

'Not quite. I've got our contact in Beirut, name's Mahmoud Farak. Repeat it, please.'

Monica dutifully obeyed in a strained voice. It was clear she hadn't fully recovered yet. 'Mahmoud Farak.'

Blake jumped to his feet. His expression softened. 'Sorry, darling. This can wait till later.'

'No, I'd rather get on with it.'

Blake stood there looking down at her, concern and guilt etched all over his lean features. 'You're sure?'

She smiled. 'I'm sure – Mahmoud Farak.'

'Lebanese banker!'

She repeated it.

'First you will go to the Union Bank Swiss. I'll give you all the addresses when we arrive in Beirut. There you will collect a banker's order for a large sum of money. Then you will take it to Farak at his bank. You will ask for him personally, speak to no one else.'

'Two questions, darling. I might need authorisation at the Swiss bank.'

He nodded. 'You'll have it, in code, in my handwriting. They've been briefed. My New York agent doesn't forget details like that.'

'And Farak. How do I approach him?'

'I'll give you written clarification.'

'Again in code?'

Blake nodded.

'What then?'

'He'll give you a sealed envelope, containing his adherence to certain instructions he received from New York. With any luck, he will already have carried them out.'

'Nothing else?'

'That's it. You're sure you're all right?'

To show that she was, Monica repeated it all back to him, word for word.

Blake kneeled beside her bunk. 'You're a real pro. And I can't pay you a higher compliment than that.'

He didn't mention Roker's message. That was something he would chew over to himself before he decided what to do.

VI

It was never easy to tell just what Habib Yasli was thinking because the scholarly face never permitted itself anything other than an expression of deep concern. That morning, however, his feet let him down. He couldn't sit still.

Despite the chilly mountain wind outside, the bunker was stifling. Habib Yasli didn't believe in ventilation and was partial to electric heaters, as many as he could stuff into the restricted space of the cubicle. Asaf Barakat sat there reading that morning's edition of his newspaper, dreading the cold he would feel when he stepped out into the late November mountain weather.

The apprehensive little banker, Mahmoud Farak, the only other visitor present, was devoutly mumbling over his worry beads. Both raised their eyes from time to time to see Yasli pacing the floor – and waited uncomfortably for him to speak. He stopped beside his table and turned to face them. His manner was formal, the words clipped and to the point. Further, he spoke with the dogmatic conviction that tolerates no disagreement. What he believed was irrefutable; when he acted, no matter how horrific the consequences, it was done for the benefit of mankind. 'Typical of the Establishment press,' he confided to his audience of two. 'All lies, of course. Hypocritical sensationalism. It speaks for itself. A police cover-up. Undoubtedly done in connivance with the American State Department. I shall hold the Swiss government responsible. Comrade Reichter is a great loss, but others shall take his place.'

Barakat risked an opinion. 'But the Swiss are a cautious people. Their policy of neutrality in all such matters involving foreign nationals is well known. I very much doubt they would enter into such an arrangement.'

Yasli raised a pontifical hand. 'Enough! They were involved, and, further, I shall personally see that they are punished for it!'

Barakat shrugged and lapsed back into silence. Yasli yanked back his chair and sat down, each gesture a rebuke that his judgement should be questioned. Then Mahmoud Farak, lifting his eyes from his worry beads, found himself speaking. 'These assassins... no one seems able to stop them. Think of yourself, Habib. Yours is the only other name on the list. He's bound to come out here and make an attempt on your life.'

Yasli bounded to his feet. 'Nonsense!'

A pretty young female soldier in shapeless khaki dungarees entered with a coffee tray and placed it reverently on Yasli's littered table. He ignored her and she hurriedly withdrew. 'Nonsense,' he repeated. 'There's certainly more than one man behind this. We know what's going on. American, British, French, Russian... now even Greek intelligence is involved. Do you honestly believe that this happened by accident? Face the facts; everyone's against us, including our so-called brothers in Damascus and Cairo. We have only ourselves.'

Barakat didn't agree. 'Then how do you explain this?' He got up and placed a sheet of paper on the table. 'That comes from a reliable source in Geneva and it informs us that even the Americans are hunting this man; together with every other security agency in Europe. All have orders to shoot him on sight. One man. If we can discover his identity I suspect that it would prove very embarrassing for someone. He's not an ordinary man. Ruthless, professional and capable of anything.'

Yasli fluttered a dismissive hand. 'You have been summoned here today to consider something far more important to our cause than idle speculation. I refer to the recent abduction of those schoolchildren in England.'

Barakat interrupted, 'I want it put on record that I for one am against this action.'

Yasli ignored him and carried on. 'This is war and we are alone. How many of our children did the Syrians and Maronites kill in Beirut in one day? We shall do what we have to do to regain our land, nothing else matters. Every man who has fought for our cause held in European prisons will be released, assembled in London, and flown to freedom. Those are our demands. If they try to trick us, the blood of those children will be on their hands.'

Barakat hotly protested. 'On the contrary, it can do us immeasurable harm at a time when world opinion is beginning to swing in our favour. We must stop it, now. Think what would happen if, God forbid, one of those children is harmed! Where will it end? We kill the children, they kill you and our men who survived the London Airport operation. It can't go on. We should cooperate with the European authorities in stopping this madness, not oppose them.'

Mahmoud Farak squirmed in his chair. '...To be fed like swill to swine... to drown where there is no water?'

Barakat shifted uneasily under Yasli's hypnotic gaze. 'You don't begin to understand the power of the press,' he murmured stubbornly.

'Oh, but I do,' was the calm reply. 'You forget: my name, and not yours, is on that list. If I didn't, what is the point of the struggle? It would be much easier, would it not, to give in to the Zionists, pack up and go home? Unfortunately, however, as a

Palestinian I don't happen to have one.' With this he got up and crossed briskly to the door.

Barakat and Farak were eager to leave now that the meeting had so abruptly terminated. They wasted no time in joining him.

'And I can assure you,' Yasli concluded dryly, 'that I have no intention of being fed like swill to the swine or drowned where there is no water.'

VII

The City Council in Beirut was in two minds about the rebuilding of the ruined city. Some wanted to bulldoze what was left into the sea and start from scratch; others were more cautious, they advised something more piecemeal to enable them to carry on business during the reconstruction, and as a result of the dilemma little was done. A shanty town of hodgepodge shacks and shabby jerry-built structures sprouted up like fungi along the once-proud boulevards. It was like London after the Blitz, but on the cool, windswept day that Monica drove into the place, she hardly noticed. A foreign correspondent accustomed to war-torn cities, she was inured to such sights.

After parking the car, she moved purposefully along the busy streets showing little signs of her recent ordeal. Other than the silk sling supporting the fast-healing arm, there was nothing to distinguish her from other European visitors that were beginning to return to the city.

Breezing into the bank she stepped up to the teller's cage and slid an envelope addressed to Mahmoud Farak under the grill.

'Is Mr Farak in?'

The teller, a young female relative, nodded.

Monica gave her a warm smile. 'Kindly take this to him right away. I'll wait.'

The girl nodded, and slipped promptly through a door at the end of the room. Monica didn't have long to wait. In a minute or two the girl returned: 'He'll see you now, miss,' she said, in surprisingly good English. Then politely escorted her down to the temporary vaults in the basement. Shyly introducing Monica to her boss, she ran appreciative eyes over her clothes and promptly departed.

Mahmoud Farak was equally accommodating. Time was precious and he wasn't one to waste it. He scurried up with a chair and invited her to be seated.

Monica thanked him and sat down. 'You are Mr Mahmoud Farak?'

He attempted a timid smile. 'Thank God you've come. I was getting worried.'

He raised both shoulders in a self-pitying shrug. Monica gave him one of her brightest smiles. 'My pleasure,' she said.

'Do forgive the mess, madam. There is so much to be done, the war you know… but we do what we can. Soon things will be liveable again.' He seated himself behind his desk and fumbled for his worry beads.

She sat there, fascinated by his tiny, prehensile hands. 'Shall we get down to business?' So saying, she opened her bag and drew forth the draft she had earlier been given at the Union Bank Swiss. She asked coolly, 'Don't you have something for me, too, Mr Farak?'

He hurriedly scanned the bank draft, then folding it carefully, placed it in the inside pocket of his coat. 'Of course, forgive me, madam. I have it right here.'

He fumbled in a drawer and handed her a large envelope heavily sealed with Sellotape. She stuffed it into her bag.

Farak stepped to the door and flung it open. Outside, the passage was empty. Hurriedly closing it again, he turned to her, his face bathed with sweat. 'The contents of that envelope, madam, were difficult to come by; indeed, at times extremely hazardous. But everything they require is there. The receipts for the rented properties, the helicopter, the crucial maps of the town headquarters, the encampment and all the other items listed in the request. They will find everything in order.'

Monica glanced around the room. 'Do you mind if I use your phone?'

Farak was horrified. 'Not here – please! Yasli trusts no one, he monitors our calls. It's more than our lives are worth.'

'Of course. How careless of me.' Instead of rising to leave as Farak expected her to do, much to his chagrin she settled back into her chair.

Working rather frantically on his worry beads, Farak croaked, 'Is there anything else you require, madam?'

She bestowed her sweetest smile on the frightened little man. 'Forgive a woman's curiosity, Mr Farak, but you don't appear to be the kind of man who would get himself involved in this sort of thing. May I ask why?'

Farak cocked his head, listening for noises out in the passage. When he heard none, he launched into his favourite lament. 'Appearances can be deceiving, particularly here in the Lebanon.' Dropping his voice, he went on, 'We are Arabs, we love our country, we have roots here, ties, and they ruin us with their insane demands. They sabotage our firms, they threaten our lives, or worse, brand us as traitors unless we pay their blood-money. Believe me, it is not only the Zionists we fear. These people come here, they try to take over the country, they call themselves freedom fighters, the liberators of Palestine, and the whole world hates us for their crimes.'

Farak rose unsteadily to his feet and shuffled to the door to listen again. Regretting her question, Monica got up to leave. 'I'm sorry, Mr Farak. Please excuse my impertinence. I really didn't mean to offend you.'

Farak hardly heard. 'I'm not alone, madam. There are many like me here in the Lebanon. These others care nothing for freedom. How can they – they're Marxists, their masters live in the Kremlin.'

Out on the street, she thought of trying a phone kiosk, then she saw the watcher. He was a young Arab with hair curling down over his shoulders and wearing a T-shirt with the University of Texas boldly emblazoned over his chest. She moved straight to her car and drove off. He followed on a motorcycle.

VIII

Monica wasn't surprised. She had been expecting something of the kind all morning. The opposition was professional, whichever faction it belonged to. This particular man could be working for any one of a dozen agencies who were hunting for Blake, and right then it didn't matter which. Her decision was simple: lose him as soon as possible and extend Blake's freedom for a little while longer. She had no doubt that his days were numbered.

She was a good driver, and Beirut at that time of day wasn't a difficult place to get lost in. She pressed her foot hard down on the accelerator and the car shot down the street and swerved around a corner, scattering a street full of protesting pedestrians.

There followed a succession of mad dashes, haphazard twists and turns, terminating at last in a jammed market area. Abandoning the car, Monica promptly lost herself in the crowd.

An hour later, after doubling on her tracks twice, she appeared in the office of the garage (where she had rented the car on the night of their arrival) informing the clerk that after shopping she had returned to where she had parked the car and found it missing.

He was sympathetic in a puzzling mixture of French and English but she got the drift of it. 'It happens all the time nowadays,' he explained. 'Don't worry, it'll turn up when they've had their joyride, they usually do. We'll find it on a street somewhere. In the meantime, we'll rent you another one.' This was what he meant; what he said sounded like the clacking of an excited cockatoo.

When later she drove out of the garage there was no sign of the motorcyclist. She waited until nightfall before returning to Blake.

She found him asleep on the terrace of the small villa Farak had found for them overlooking the distant ruins of the city presently shrouded in darkness. He slept soundly despite the chill and the noise of the news bulletin coming over the radio. It was a BBC overseas broadcast regarding a news blackout ordered by the government concerning terrorists shortly to be assembled in London upon release from jails all over Europe. It seemed that a proposal had been put forward by a neutral mediator suggesting an exchange for the missing schoolchildren.

Monica switched off the radio and perched on the edge of Blake's bench seat, tickling the end of his nose with Farak's envelope. 'Hi,' she giggled.

He swept her into his arms, mindful of her injured arm.

'How do you manage it?'

'Go back to sleep.'

'Aphrodite emerging from that seashell.'

'Wasn't that Venus?'

'One and the same, different name.'

She hadn't seen him like this since Janis's death, relaxed and one might even say happy. 'Bet you say that to all the girls.'

'When you were younger, you were really something. Now you're even better than that.'

'Fact?'

'Fact.'

'Tell me more.'

'How do you manage to remain so goddamned beautiful, and what took you so long?'

'I was tailed.'

'By whom?'

'A young Arab on a motorcycle.'

'And you lost him?'

'I had to dump the car and rent another one. Waited until it got dark before risking it happening again.'

'Describe him.'

'Hair down to his shoulders, white T-shirt with some university written all over it.'

Blake laughed, 'Good, you taught him a lesson. His name's Haroon and he works for me. I don't like you wandering around that town alone. Angry?'

She shook her head. 'You might have told me, that's all.' At that moment she wondered how much he really trusted her, but knowing what his probable response would be she didn't show it. Blake was a hard man. She changed the topic instead.

'Aren't you going to ask me how it went?' she asked, handing him the envelope.

'How did it went?'

He loved to hear her laughter so she didn't hesitate. 'Fool!'

He kissed her. 'How was Farak? They tell me he's a timid man.'

'Terrified. Just like that mouse in the cartoons, only not so cute.' She felt the pressure of his hand on her shoulder and knew she wanted him right then and there.

'I always feel sorry for Tom the cat,' he yawned. 'He's the perennial loser. I'm told our little mouse gets the job done.' He settled back sleepily on the cushions with Farak's envelope in his hand. Before he could open it, his eyes closed. 'Give me another hour,' he murmured, 'then wake me.'

Monica wasn't very successful in smothering her disappointment; the lovemaking would have to wait until later. 'Oh, Sam!' she cried, 'Oh, Sam.'

She sat very still on the edge of the seat, lost in the contemplation of that beloved face, asking herself how she could possibly carry on if anything happened to him. He couldn't last much longer. That incident on the road in Italy had convinced her of that. Eventually they would succeed. She struggled to hold back her tears, then remembered the envelope. She thought of retrieving it from his fingers, but changed her mind. She didn't move, sat there waiting until she was certain he was asleep, then she slipped silently into the house.

In the bedroom, she inched the door closed then put an ear against it. She stood like this for a long time, listening. The trouble with Blake was that one could never be sure.

When she was satisfied that she wouldn't be disturbed, she moved to the window to check if there was anyone outside. She was well aware of the risk she was taking, but time was running out – it had to be done. She detested herself, even at this late hour she wasn't entirely convinced that she was doing the right thing. But what was the alternative? Better that he should remain alive than the other. With mixed feelings, she took a firm hold on herself, crossed to the bedside phone and dialled the number.

The phone rang only once before the voice on the other end came through on the receiver. 'Yes, who is it?' Renway asked impatiently.

'Me,' Monica said softly. 'This is the first chance I've had to phone. He has me followed everywhere. I'm with him now.'

'Where? We need the address.'

'First your promise,' she insisted icily. 'I want no repetition of what happened in Italy and Cyprus, you bastard. No harm will come to him – will you swear to that?'

Renway blurted impatiently, 'Of course!'

'Your word of honour?'

'Goddamn it, how many times do I have to tell you? All right, my word of honour – we only want him for the debriefing. What's the address?'

She saw the hand press down on the cradle, cutting off the call, and looked up into Blake's face leaning over her shoulder. He gently took the phone out of her hand. 'You're getting rusty, pet.'

They regarded each other quietly. There was no point in hiding their feelings now.

'Who are you working for this time?'

Monica shrugged. 'What difference does it make? They're all hunting you now. You've got to stop this, Sam.'

'So I've been told.'

She moved away from him, fighting hard to keep her feelings under control. 'How long did you know?'

Blake seemed amused. He said lightly, 'Didn't, until now.'

'But you must have suspected something, the way you had me followed everywhere?'

He shrugged. 'Procedure. I do that with everyone.'

Angry despite herself, and utterly female, she flared, 'Even me?'

He said softly, 'Even me, if I could manage it.' He settled on the edge of the bed and regarded her with his usual tenderness. 'You want me to toss in the towel, like the rest? Cry uncle? Please pull your knives out of our backs – is that what you want?'

Monica bit her lip and turned away. She couldn't bear to see him like this.

'Close the airports, stop flying altogether, right? But then they'd start blowing up the trains. We can't close everything, can we? They're thick as roaches in a sugar sack, liable to turn up anywhere, even on school buses.' He got up and crossed to the door, admitting the young Arab who had followed her on the motorcycle. He nodded to her politely then looked at Blake.

Blake introduced them. 'Monica, meet Haroon, a friend of mine. Haroon, this is Monica, another friend of mine.'

Monica stood there, rooted to the floor. She tried to smile but her mouth refused to respond.

'I want her out of the way for three days,' Blake added as an afterthought. The strain was beginning to show.

Haroon reminded him, '...or for longer if necessary.' He was very circumspect for one so young. Also, having been educated by Jesuit priests, his English was good.

Blake pondered the problem for a moment or two, then concluded, 'Treat her well, and when I send word, put her on a plane back to London.'

Haroon took her gently by the arm and led her to the door. She turned back to Blake. 'I'd have turned you in, Sam,' she murmured shakily.

He moved to her and stood very close. 'I know.'

'Betrayed you.'

'Uhuh.'

'You don't seem to care?'

'I know why you did it.'

'Sam! Oh, Sam… my feelings haven't changed.'

'I know… mine haven't either.' He knew the signs. She had been through too much: that business on the road in Italy, the broken arm, the fever in Nicosia, the ambush on the beach. And all for him, to save him from himself. He had to comfort her. 'You'll be all right. Just don't worry. When this is over, I'll come to you, I still owe you that vacation on Cape Cod, remember?'

Her look was loving, her feeling one of despair. For her he was already dead. 'Oh, God – must it end like this?'

He held her tight. 'Take my word for it – it won't.'

She' clung desperately. 'Renway's our only hope. He promised me nothing would happen to you. All he wants is the debriefing and to stop the killing, nothing else.'

'He's got his orders, I can't give up yet. We're in a tough business.'

Her voice began to waver. It was like holding a broken doll. 'Did you mean all that out on the terrace just now?'

'Every word.'

She raised her head. He kissed her hard. She broke away, her face wet with smeared eye make-up. 'Thanks. I love you, too.'

Blake watched them go. He stood there for a long time, staring at the empty doorway. Everything he had was outside climbing into the car with Haroon. He wondered if he would ever see her again.

He looked down and saw that he was holding Mahmoud

Farak's envelope. Switching on the lights, he ripped it open and began to scan its contents.

Skimming rapidly through an exhaustive list of equipment which had been secured for him and other details relating to the purchase of a second-hand truck, a fiat rental and a warehouse, his flagging interest was restored by the little banker's reference to Habib Yasli's twin brainstorms – the Heathrow Airport massacre and the kidnapping of the British schoolchildren. Farak didn't mince words. He held him solely responsible for both and was convinced that unless his demands were met every child held hostage would be killed.

The effect of these revelations was instantaneous. One moment he was on the edge of exhaustion, the next his veins were humming like electric wires. All doubts regarding his recent acts were dispelled. His hatred, again a living entity, nourished his soul.

Sam Blake was back in business.

CHAPTER NINE

I

JIM ROKER WAS JUST A FACE FLOATING IN THE GLOW OF THE dashboard. Sleepily aware of the recent war ruins speeding past on both sides of the road, he glanced at his watch. It was three a.m., and being November they had at least three more hours of darkness.

Blake was driving the old truck with great care and slowed right down to avoid a bump in the road. He was in a baiting mood. 'You know your trouble, don't you?' he goaded, 'You'll never be anything but an Eagle Scout.'

Roker kept his eyes straight ahead, fully aware of what his friend was up to. He didn't bother to reply.

'You never really liked the field, which is your way of saying you've never managed to overcome a natural aversion to cold-blooded murder. Now you've joined up with me – it's not logical.'

Blake was a good prodder. Roker could no longer remain silent. 'To begin with, I was convinced you had to be stopped,' he said.

'To begin with?'

'Oh for Christ's sake,' Roker blurted angrily, 'I'm here, what more do you want?'

'I like things spelled out. That way I sleep better nights.'

Roker spread his arms. 'All right,' he sighed, 'I had orders to kill you. I didn't like it but I was prepared to carry them out...'

Blake was way ahead of him, he broke in, 'But 'you didn't appreciate Monica being thrown in for good measure?'

Roker's large homely features tightened. 'That's right, but there was something else. Monica was a friend, that was personal. When I saw that Renway was willing to kill her to get you, I had enough.'

'And the something else?'

Roker faced him grimly. 'That missing school bus in England. All those little kids. And those crazy bastards will kill them if they don't get what they want. That can't be right. They can't be allowed to get away with that.'

Blake regarded him for a moment in sober silence. 'Don't worry. They won't.' Then returning his attention to the road, he continued in his bantering mood. 'So where does that leave you? You walked, blew it, your whole career up the spout, for a principle.'

Roker listened, reliving that moment up on the hilltop with Renway when he saw Monica in the car with Blake.

'So you burned your bridges to climb into my boat – Public Enemy Number Two. Now they'll come gunning for you.'

'That's about it,' Roker agreed.

'I can understand that.' Blake slowed for a steep curve. 'But why join me? You've got too much to lose.'

Roker threw up both hands in exasperation. 'Why go on with it? I'm here. Now you can sleep better, okay?'

Blake eased the vehicle to the side of the road and stopped.

When he turned to him, Roker caught one of those rare glimpses of the real man behind the façade. Blake was grateful and he didn't mind showing it. He said softly. 'I never doubted you for a second, you big ape. For all your shilly-shallying, I knew you'd come sooner or later, and I'm damned glad you did. Now let's get the show back on the road.'

Turning into a side track fringed on both sides with un-tended cornfields, the old truck drove on until it reached a boarded-up factory building that had escaped the recent shelling. Blake drove into the yard and pulled up in front of some large double-doors. He handed Roker a key and waited for him to get out and open them, then drove inside.

What light there was filtered in through the slats covering the large windows, revealing long rows of machines and high shelves running the entire length of the building. These shelves were piled with various plastic articles, including toys, dishes, kitchenware and furniture. Both men stepped around to the back of the truck, removed several heavy, five-gallon drums and carried them through to a small back room.

When these were neatly stacked in a corner, Blake crossed to a table and switched on a flashlight. Roker joined him, spreading out a neat, hand-drawn map of Beirut buildings and city streets. Both men bent over to study it.

'Where are his rooms?'

Roker indicated the spot on the map. 'The halls, immediately above and below, are well-guarded. Yasli's party occupy three entire floors.'

'And we are where?'

'Directly across the alley on the top floor. Their roof is just opposite our front window.'

'How long did Farak rent it for?'

'For long enough,' Roker said.

'How wide is the alley?'

'Just under twenty feet.'

Blake raised his eyes from the map. 'It isn't going to be easy.'

Roker considered it. 'If he's alone in his room, it's possible. If he isn't, we'll have to shoot our way out.'

'Maybe we ought to wait a while?'

'No, we'll never get a better chance. Back in his compound, we'd have to take him by assault and that would require at least fifty well-trained men and more luck than there is in the world, assuming everybody's asleep.'

'You're willing to risk it then?'

Roker favoured him with one of his rare light-hearted smiles.

II

The colours of the sky had a quality that can only be found in the Mediterranean. The bright glow of a set sun hugged the black hills as the motorcade sped through the rubble of the old Arab Quarter and braked to an abrupt halt in front of the Aleppo Hotel. Old-fashioned, with an inner courtyard and six floors, the Aleppo was situated in the centre of Beirut's Muslim enclave and catered exclusively to the inner-circle of Yasli's extremist paramilitary organisation.

Heavily armed with automatic weapons, the outriders spilled off their vehicles and formed a tense semi-circle around the entrance as Yasli and his entourage stepped out of a Land Rover and hurried into the hotel. Other armed men moved to cover the alley, some hurried up to the roof: in moments the place was completely encircled by troops. It was a disciplined security exercise.

Across the alley from the Aleppo stood a modern apartment block that had sustained extensive damage from small arms fire, but this had been repaired and many people had moved back into the building.

In the excitement generated by the motorcade's arrival, few paid much attention to the small pickup truck that drove up and turned down the ramp leading to the underground garage beneath the apartment building next door.

Down in the garage, Blake parked the truck and followed Jim Roker to the elevator. They stepped out on the sixth floor, moved down the hall to a door leading to one of the apartments, unlocked it and entered.

Blake crossed directly to a long picture-window and closed the blinds, then Roker found the switch in the entrance hall, turned on the lights, and moved through to join Blake in a large open-plan apartment. There were no walls separating the living room, a functional kitchen and the dining area. These were separated by waist-high partitions. There were two doors leading to bedrooms, each of which had its own bathroom. The furniture was mixed; part modern, with a few pseudo-antique pieces scattered here and there throughout the complex. It looked what it was: expensive, impersonal, rented.

They worked steadily at previously assigned tasks with an unhurried familiarity betokening total professionalism.

First, Roker went to a small closet in the entrance hall and removed parts of a lightweight aluminium ladder, a small block and tackle, a sack of small triangular wooden blocks, a hammer, two leather gun cases, the parts of a Jacob's Ladder and a small black suitcase. When the closet was empty, Blake helped him carry this equipment into the living room where it was placed in a neat row under the window.

Blake opened the suitcase and removed a roll of black adhesive tape, a pair of scissors, a package of cotton-batting, a tin of black shoe polish, a small medical chloroform tin, a blackjack, binoculars and a pair of handcuffs. These were laid out on the dining table.

Blake helped Roker assemble the Jacob's ladder. Two small metal arms with screw-clamps and a frame containing a ratchet-wheel were promptly fitted together and placed in readiness beneath the window.

Blake removed the parts of two sub-machine guns from their cases and put them together while Roker ran the block and tackle rope through the Jacob's ladder ratchet-wheel. When this was accomplished, he rubbed heavy grease on the rope to minimise noise when it was used.

When every item of equipment had been checked by each in turn, the two men crossed to one of the bedrooms. Both were dressed in ordinary street clothes. They slipped on black overalls over these, placed dark-blue stocking caps (equipped with eye-holes when they were pulled down over the face) on their heads, and changed into black tennis shoes. Retaining their street clothes was a precaution in the event things went wrong and they were forced to run for it. If this happened, it would take less than a minute to remove the overalls.

There were still a few final details to attend to in the living room. Blake oiled one of the machine guns, carefully wiped it, fitted a drum to the magazine and placed it beside the other one under the window.

He strapped a heavy leather safety-belt around his waist while Roker put the aluminium ladder together, then Blake moved to the table and carefully stuffed the adhesive tape, the chloroform tin, the shoe polish, the cotton-batting, the handcuffs, the blackjack and the scissors into his pockets.

Roker switched off the lights. Blake opened the window blinds. He checked his watch, Roker joined him and slid one of the windows open. Roker found the binoculars, adjusted the focus and trained them down on the alley. When he nodded, Blake lifted the ladder to the window sill and pushed it over to the Aleppo Hotel's roof directly opposite. He helped Roker lift the Jacob's ladder onto his back, slung one of the guns over his head and helped him onto the ladder.

Blake took the binoculars for a final check of the alley and the

Aleppo's roof. When he signalled the all-clear, both pulled the
stocking caps down over their faces, adjusted the eye-holes, and
Roker started to inch himself across.

As he reached the Aleppo's roof, Blake tied the sack of wooden
blocks to his safety-belt, slipped the hammer under it, slung the
machine gun over his head, the coil of rope over a shoulder,
hoisted himself up and proceeded to cross the ladder. When he
reached the other side, Roker pulled the ladder after him. Blake
paused to catch his breath. Roker carefully laid the ladder beside
the low balustrade that ran the length of the roof.

Both men heard the voices, dropped to their knees and froze.
They waited, trying to locate the direction they were coming
from. Roker lifted a cautious head. As the moon hadn't yet risen,
it was a black night. Blake handed him the binoculars. These were
fitted with night lenses. Roker scanned the entire roof twice
before he finally spotted them.

There were two men, standing on the front side of the roof,
leaning over the railing and looking down on the street. Their
voices were a steady monotonous drone, they were both smoking
cigarettes and had their machine pistols slung negligently over
their shoulders.

Roker squeezed Blake's ann. Blake took the glasses and had a
look himself, then joined Roker down in the shadows.

'Shed that weight and work around to their left, I'll go the
other way,' he whispered, then crept off.

Careful not to make the slightest sound, Roker took some
time to get the heavy Jacob's ladder off his back. When he finally
managed it, he slipped into the shadows behind a skylight, then
crept on all fours, hugging the railing, making slow progress
towards the front of the roof.

The guards hadn't moved and although he couldn't see them,
he was able to home in on their voices. He inched along until he
was within leaping distance, then waited.

It was a difficult problem. These men had to be dealt with in
total silence. Roker braced himself for the spring and waited.
Blake would move first – there would be no signal.

. When it happened, Roker didn't have time to think. Where
there were two shadows, suddenly there were three. He sprang,

brought the butt of his gun down hard and heard the crunch of splintering bone. When he looked down, the two guards lay slumped beside the railing, the sparks of a cigarette glowing in a head of hair. He bent down and patted them out with his hand.

Blake whispered in his ear, 'They're done for, come on.'

They had gone over the floor plan of the hotel many times and knew the precise spot where they had to set up the Jacob's ladder. Habib Yasli had two adjoining rooms on the fourth floor facing the alley. One he slept in, the other was used as an office, and both faced out onto the same terrace. But before they did anything the skylights and the door leading onto the roof had to be secured.

There were four skylights. Blake emptied the blocks out of the bag and, to minimise noise, wedged them into the cleats with the butt of the hammer's wooden handle. Roker did the same with the door leading onto the roof. When they finished, they were jammed solid. Nobody could open them from the inside.

Roker retrieved the Jacob's ladder and carried it to the chosen spot on the railing where Blake helped him clamp it home. When this was accomplished, Blake slipped into the looped seat, crawled over the balustrade, and started to let himself down over the side of the building.

Roker kept a hand on the ratchet, controlling the speed of the rope passing through the pulley. Blake's descent was safe and slow, it took him two minutes to reach Yasli's terrace. When his rubber soles touched the floor, they didn't make a sound. He tugged once on the rope and vanished into the shadows.

Roker pulled the looped seat back up to the roof and sat down for a long wait. He settled alertly into the shadows beneath the balustrade, cradling the gun, his finger on the trigger guard. He couldn't afford to relax, not now, when they were so close. All he could do was pray that no one took it into his head to come up and relieve the guards. He looked at his watch. Twenty-five minutes had elapsed since they had first climbed onto the roof.

Down below, the terrace was suddenly flooded with light. Blake was kneeling in a corner behind a large potted plant. When nothing happened, he inched forward until he reached the French windows leading into Yasli's office. Lying flat on his stomach, he risked a quick look inside. The window was covered with lace curtains but he could see two heavily-armed guerrillas, one stretched out asleep on a sofa, the other slouched in a deep armchair idly perusing a magazine. Blake inched back to his hiding place.

There was another set of French windows leading onto the terrace and the room beyond was in darkness. Blake inched forward, step by step, until he reached it, then he lay doggo for a minute or two until he was sure that his presence hadn't been noticed. He pressed an ear against the glass and listened. He heard nothing.

It took him a full minute to reach a standing position and another two to press down the handle and nudge the door open a couple of inches, then he froze. He remained poised there for a long time, straining to detect the slightest sound in the room. Then he caught it. Bedsprings! Barely discernible but rhythmic. Blake nudged the door open another few inches and slipped into the room.

The sound of the bedsprings was more audible now, and as his eyes became accustomed to the deeper darkness of the room, he could just make out the figures of three people lying on the bed. Two of them were making love and their breathing became more disjointed and increased in volume as they laboured towards their climax. The rhythms of the bedsprings took on an urgency they hadn't had before, and Blake broke out into a wild spasm of mute laughter. If it was Yasli, he was certainly a durable lover.

He could see quite clearly now because his eyes had become accustomed to the darkness and the light from the other room was filtering in from the terrace. Resolved to take a firmer grip on his sense of humour, he reached into a pocket and eased out the blackjack. At that moment the other girl climbed out of bed and sleepily trotted off to the bathroom.

She fumbled for the switch and when the light came on she saw Blake. Her jaw dropped in horrified amazement. Dressed as he was, his face covered with the stocking cap, he must have presented an alarming sight. And that he was there at all – even more so.

In the space of two fleeting seconds, he saw it all. The naked plumpness, the flawless olive skin, the wide dumb-founded gaze.

When she opened her mouth to scream, it was too late, the chloroform-soaked cotton ball had already closed on her comely face. The struggle was brief and when she slumped, he eased her gently to the floor. Then he switched off the light.

They say that endurance is an admirable quality, a sentiment with which Blake at any other moment would have heartily agreed: the lovers were still at it when he crept back into the bedroom.

The couple were lying in the traditional position, both oblivious to the world. A bulldozer could have rumbled through the room and they wouldn't have noticed it. Blake didn't make any noise at all. He simply materialised beside the bed, raised the blackjack and brought it down just behind the man's ear.

The girl – unaware of the dead weight – gasped with pleasure. She moaned, 'Come on, come on!' in frantic Arabic.

Blake had to bite down hard on his lips to stop the laughter.

Slowly becoming aware of her partner's lack of cooperation, her eyes fluttered open.

It is doubtful that she ever saw Blake or even recovered her senses before the chloroform sent her into a deep sleep.

As he switched on the flashlight, even the hardened Blake felt the triumph of the moment. Lying helpless and stark naked on that bed was the most fanatical killer of them all, a man the Israelis would have given a King's ransom to lay their hands on – none other than the notorious Habib Yasli himself.

But Blake didn't stop to congratulate himself, he had too much to do and he did it as if he had all the time in the world. First he found Yasli's clothes, green denim Army fatigues. He dressed him in these, then blacked his face and hands with black shoe-polish. The unconscious Yasli was lifted, draped over his back and held in a fireman's lift with handcuffs. Blake had taken the added precaution of scaling his mouth with adhesive tape, and even that was the right colour, matching the shoe polish.

The terrace was uncomfortably like running the gauntlet. Spotlighted like a performer in a circus, he was an easy target for the two guerrillas in the other room and, if they missed him, there was a hotel full of others who would come baying like hounds at the first sign of trouble.

When he reached the railing, he found the Jacob's ladder

already dangling above his head. Evidently Roker was just as anxious as he was to get out of there.

Blake got himself seated into the loop and signalled Roker to winch them up.

When he let go of the railing, they began to swing like a pendulum, scraping the flesh off their elbows on the hard wall. It was a dicey moment, with nothing between them and the hard ground but air.

The ratchet-wheel protested, then clanked home. They began the slow ascent, foot by foot.

They dangled there, a hundred feet above the ground.

Looking up, he saw Roker leaning over the roof; it was a sight he would never forget.

Roker seemed to be everywhere. He winched them to the top, pulled them over the balustrade, unlocked the cuffs, lifted the stunned terrorist leader off his back and helped Blake to his feet. He removed the blocks from the skylight and the roof door, careful to stow them back in the sack.

Blake undraped the Jacob's ladder and removed the marks left by screws with a piece of sandpaper. Both checked the roof to make sure that nothing had been left behind.

Roker kneeled down, Blake lifted Yasli onto his back and again secured him with the handcuffs.

As it turned out, crossing back to the apartment was the easiest part of the operation.

Roker went first, then Blake followed with the Jacob's ladder firmly strapped on his back.

Climbing through the window, they lay where they landed. Yasli began to snore.

Blake was the first on his feet. He took the binoculars and had a good look at the Aleppo Hotel. He checked the roof, the terrace of Yasli's suite and the alley separating the two buildings. Nothing was happening anywhere. Yasli's disappearance was still undetected.

It took them five minutes to change clothes and pack everything back into the bags and another fifteen to carry it – including Yasli – down to the basement and stow it under a heavy canvas tarpaulin in the back of the truck.

'Did you check everything?'

'They won't even find a matchstick.'

Blake shuddered. 'I'm getting too old for this sort of thing.'

When they pulled up out of the garage and turned into the street, all was peaceful.

'What do you think?'

'What is there to think? So far we're in the clear. With a little luck…'

'You make your own luck.'

'Not always. You draw to an inside-straight, that's luck.

Then you're beaten by a flush – that's fate. You can't make that.'

'You're a cynic.'

'It's kept me alive a long time.'

'What the hell do you believe in?'

'I just told you. Fate. It's all written – *Kismet*.'

'Just so you believe in something. Christ, I'm starving.'

Blake rummaged in the glove compartment and produced a large chunk of garlic sausage, a good cut of cheddar cheese and a loaf of French bread. 'Help yourself.'

After he had eaten, Roker leaned back on the seat and lit a cigarette. For a non-smoker that was unusual.

III

Driving into the factory building and securing the large double-doors, they lifted Yasli out of the truck and carried him past the cluttered shelves and machines. Blake didn't switch on the flashlight until they reached the room at the far end and deposited the terrorist beside one of the moulds.

They moved to the heavy drums they had earlier stored in one of the corners. Each contained five gallons of Acrylic resin, a liquid substance used in plastics manufacture. There was also a can containing one gallon of Paroxide solution. When used in conjunction with the resin, the result was a rock-hard piece of fibreglass.

They lugged the drums to the mould where they had left Yasli. He was awake now, but his feet were bound, his wrists secured and his mouth covered with adhesive tape. Only his eyes moved and these were expressive. Other than a few muffled protests, he made no other sound.

Blake produced a hypodermic and a small phial with a rubber cap. Plunging the needle through the rubber, he filled it, bent down over Yasli and unbuttoned the man's sleeve. 'Give me some more light,' he muttered. Roker obliged.

Yasli's large brown eyes reflected the bright stream of light and there were more muffled protests as Blake inserted the needle and injected him.

Rising to his feet, Blake dryly observed, 'New drug called Immobilon. Deadens the nervous system. Works fast, paralyses the entire body. Beauty of it is he can hear, see, think, knows exactly what's happening to him. Isn't that right, Yasli old son?'

Roker was horrified. 'But, why? You're killing him, isn't that enough?'

Blake could have been commenting on the weather. 'He's been a busy little bee. He organised the slaughter at Heathrow Airport that killed Janis,' he said simply, 'to say nothing of the small kidnapping of some thirty innocent school-kids in England. Now untie him and take that tape off his mouth. We don't need it any more.'

Roker roused himself and did as directed.

'And wash that muck off his face. He's got to be nice and clean where he's going. There's a piece of soap, a towel and a canteen full of water in the truck.'

A few minutes later, they propped Yasli up on a box. Roker washed the blacking off his face. Yasli sat there, mummified, his eyes staring straight ahead with burning intensity. Also, from his vantage point on the box he had a clear view of everything, including the interior of the mould.

When the last drum had been emptied, the syrupy liquid reached within a few inches of the top. Roker found a large wooden paddle and stood by while Blake emptied the Paroxide hardener into the mould.

'Start stirring,' Blake said. 'And put your back into it.' Turning to Yasli, he explained, 'More you stir it, harder it gets.'

Both watched in silent attendance as Roker paddled. Blake

voiced a thought in a pleasant tone. 'You had no qualms about killing my daughter, I have none about killing you. Fair enough, isn't it?'

Roker was beginning to struggle with the paddle. He angrily exclaimed, 'If I don't pull this thing out pretty soon, I won't be able to get it out!'

'Time for your bath.' So saying, Blake lifted Yasli off the box.

Roker removed the paddle and stepped aside, avoiding Blake's eyes. 'If you don't mind,' he said, 'I'll wait out there in the truck.' As he hurried out, Blake eased the paralysed terrorist down into the mould. Due to the hardness of the mixture it took him some time to submerge.

Blake felt no jubilation, not even a sense of relief. Deep hatred left little room for other feelings. He simply stood there, watching him sink, his eyes locked on the other's unblinking stare. 'It's not often a man can be present at his own funeral,' he reflected amiably. 'They'll never be able to chop you out of this without disfiguring your remains. Like the Pharaohs, you'll last thousands of years, only better. If they ever dig you up, you'll look just like you do now, clothes and all. Isn't modern technology wonderful?'

So it came to pass that the American and the Palestinian – each a zealot in fruitless quest of the Holy Grail – faced each other in silent confrontation for the last time.

For Habib Yasli, his final moments were, if not painful, certainly frustrating. A brilliant crowd-puller enamoured of the sound of his own voice was denied the traditional last words, a man of action was reduced to a state of helpless suspended animation. Only his hatred, primeval in its intensity, rose triumphant and flooded through the room.

The other might have been injected with the debilitating drug himself, he stood so still, his unblinking eyes fixed on those of his victim, his own hatred equally tidal. 'Going... going...' he murmured.

Below, in the mould, the thickening substance oozed at last into the nostrils and the face slowly settled beneath the surface, its bulging eyes riveted on its tormentor.

The man of bronze above, sighed, 'Gone.' Remaining there, reluctant to drag himself away. But everything has its end. At last he moved from the room, no doubt pondering the lie that certain learned mandarins had foisted on their fellows in days long past when they decided to rewrite the Bible, entitling it the New Testament.

Quite unlike Moses poised on the summit of his mountain, brandishing his tablets of forked lightning, and laying down the Law, they had more enlightened ideas. Man had come on a bit, they claimed. He no longer demanded an *'eye for an eye, a tooth for a tooth'*. That was the business of oculists and dentists. And he no longer struck down his enemy with a stone axe, they scolded. Rather he brought him to the feet of Solomon and hired lawyers to argue the pros and cons of the case.

'Turn the other cheek,' they proclaimed. *'Forgive thine enemies. Revenge is not sweet, it turns to ashes in your mouths.'*

'Bullshit!' lamented Blake; lamented because his joyful parting from the late Habib Yasli had been so brief.

Now he had only the small-fry to attend to.

IV

It was difficult to remove the large fibreglass block from the mould, but once it settled on the cart they had no trouble getting it to the side of the truck. It took more time than they liked to set up the block and tackle and place the chains around the block, but once this was done it didn't take long to hoist it up and ease it down gently on the platform. It proved to be a tight fit, leaving just enough room to crawl along the sides and cover it with the tarpaulin.

As they drove out of the factory, Roker noted the time on his watch. The embalming process and the loading had swallowed up the rest of the night. The eastern hills were already ablaze with the rising sun.

Blake's tone was casual. 'We don't have very far to go, five or six miles.'

Roker looked out his window. He wasn't overly fond of Blake at that moment. 'Why drive at all? They could have come to the factory.'

They were moving out into the desert at a leisurely forty miles per hour. 'Too close to town,' Blake remarked sleepily, 'better further out.' He gave Roker a quick sideways look. 'You okay?'

Roker grunted, unsmiling, 'I'll live, I guess.'

'Sorry you came?'

'I didn't bargain on this.'

Blake was chewing on a piece of stale bread. 'You saw a side of me you didn't like?'

'That's putting it mildly.'

'To kill is one thing, to enjoy it another?'

'You said it, not me.'

'I'll go further… you didn't think I'd ever do such a thing?'

'You're goddamn right, I didn't.'

'It was like a horror comic… or worse?'

'Much worse.' Roker turned to him. 'It was medieval. Christ, man, we're living in the twentieth century.'

Blake purred, 'The most medieval of all. The difference is I'm more at home in this glorious epoch than you are. When in Rome do as the Romans do.'

'Jesus Christ, don't you feel *anything*?'

'Yeah, a little tired, but after a few hours' sleep I'll come bouncing back like a babe. It's like going to confession. You come out with a lily-white soul and feeling ten years younger. Tomorrow I'll show you the sunny side of my nature.'

They didn't speak after that and when Blake turned into the sandy field there was a helicopter parked right in the middle of it. It had a crew of two and it took all four of them to shift the heavy tarpaulin-covered block into its storage compartment. Roker noted the military markings on the fuselage but didn't ask questions. The crew were Arabs and could have come from any one of six or seven Middle Eastern states. Why they were there didn't interest him, he had enough on his mind.

When they were ready to leave, Blake returned to him. 'When you dispose of the truck, you know what to do?' he asked quizzically, searching his eyes.

Roker nodded, 'Yeah, get the hell out of Lebanon, and fast.'

'You have everything you need?'

'Yes.'

Blake smiled, extending a hand. 'See you when I see you, then. If I'm late, don't worry about it – I'll show up eventually.'

Roker tried to return his smile, but he wasn't very successful. He did, however, unbend sufficiently to shake his hand.

'Okay.'

'I'll understand, if you're not there, Jim.'

Roker flared, 'I'll be there dammit, now you better get going.'

V

The enclave was heavily fortified. Deep tank ditches lay just beyond the high steel-mesh fence surrounding the enclosure and numerous artillery emplacements could be seen further up the hill, trained down on the Maronite positions in the valley below. The place was bristling with newly-arrived guerrillas fresh from training centres in Iraq. These men were Russian-trained and well supplied with the latest Soviet equipment.

It was an uneasy peace and no one on either side expected it to continue. For the moment it seemed that the Arab nations, spearheaded by Egypt and Syria, were bent on reaching an accommodation of some sort with Israel. The Carter administration in Washington appeared to have reached an understanding with Presidents Sadat and Asad resulting in a frantic build-up of arms and troops on both sides. What had begun in Jordan in September 1971 and continued in the Lebanon from 1974 through to the present day would be brought to its final solution, which in plain words meant the total extermination of the Palestine Liberation Movement, together with its various extremist offshoots, chief of which was Habib Yasli's extremists. The final showdown was about to begin.

The eager faces ranged around the blanket were very young. Children, who had been born in refugee camps throughout the backwaters of the Middle East, to whom the word Palestine was a rallying cry or a curse on their elders' lips rather than a place, were once again being persuaded to die for the cause.

Overhead, the late autumn sun was already shining down on their heads and the dissembled parts of the gun were warm to their instructor's touch. But all this was forgotten in the excitement engendered by the sudden roar of the engine overhead.

Someone cheered then others took it up. Ill-disciplined, deaf to their instructor's shouts, the youngsters jumped to their feet and, like the children of Hamlin, scampered off in pursuit of their Pied Piper, the Soviet-made helicopter.

The machine banked steeply and dived, losing altitude fast. Then skimming the trees it began to hover some ten feet above the ground.

The young men came running and soon the compound was packed with cheerful faces. The crewmen up in the machine wrestled with the heavy object in the open door, then gave it a final nudge. There was more loud cheering as the object fell heavily to the ground.

Overhead, the helicopter started to rise and gain forward speed. Soon it was lifting over the trees, circling, returning again at greatly increased speed.

But few on the ground paid it much attention, the general interest was now centred on the object in their midst. More youngsters joined the throng and the circle tightened around the strange object glistening in the sun. The light-hearted cheering slowly subsided, fading to stunned silence. Happy enthusiasm gave way to bewilderment, then to disgust, finally to howling rage.

The object itself was perfectly transparent. Looking much as he had in life, his scholarly face tightened in a thoughtful frown, his arms out flung like an orator at the climax of an impassioned speech, stood their beloved leader, Habib Yasli, hovering in space, his heavily-shod feet in free fall, suspended in aspic, stilled forever in his glassy sarcophagus.

Overhead, the helicopter zoomed into a steep climbing turn over an adjoining hill.

VI

Police Constable Bert Crawford gazed along the solid rows of impounded cars and scratched a closely-shaven chin. 'Always the same on Thursday nights, bleedin' late shoppers,' he complained. 'Drivers think their bleedin' cars 'ave been nicked and we get all the work.'

His partner, PC Ron Richards, another stalwart of the

Elephant and Castle Car Pound, tipped back his cap. 'Friday mornings is always a bind, you know that.'

''Ad any awkward ones yet?'

Ron had a boxer's nose which had been running freely that morning. He gave it a good blow. 'About average. One old biddy – sixty if she was a day – screamin' 'er bleedin' 'ead off. Right old cow... Well – wot are we waitin' for?'

It turned out to be a busy morning. Regulations required that all unclaimed vehicles had to be searched. Bert and Ron cleared twenty-six by ten o'clock. The twenty-seventh was a 1968 Cortina Sedan. Ford products being easy, Ron got the door open with the third key on his large ring, then went around to the back and unlocked the luggage compartment.

'Christ!' he cried. 'Hey, Bert, come 'ave a butcher's at this!'

By the time Bert reached him, Ron's face had gone ashen. 'Poor little bleeder!'

The body of a dead child was stretched out in the luggage compartment, its head resting on the spare wheel. It was a boy and, judging by the look of him, he couldn't have been more than twelve or thirteen. He seemed asleep and there was no odour of decomposition or visible signs of violence on the body. 'Hasn't been dead long,' Bert said. 'Where did they pick up the car?'

Ron ran his eyes along a list on his clipboard, 'Blimey, it was found right in the parking lot in Scotland Yard! Arrived here last night. Wot's that pinned to 'is jacket? Don't touch it, don't touch nuffin'!'

Bert leaned down and read a crudely-lettered note written on a piece of lined paper that had been ripped out of a school exercise book.

'Well, wot does it say? Can't you read it?'

Bert leaned in closer, straining his eyes. 'Says *"There will be one killed"*,' he read laboriously, *'"every other day until our demands are met!"* Christ, 'e must be one of them kids from the missing school bus!'

'Dirty bastards!'

'Them blokes, whoever they are, that's been knockin' off them terrorists. I know who I'd 'elp, if they came to me!'

Ron was already running towards the cashier's hut. 'Stay right there, mate – I'm callin' the Murder Squad!'

VII

What happened was no surprise to anyone although it resulted in a public uproar of unprecedented proportions. The inhuman barbarity of this cold-blooded murder, together with the tender age and innocence of the victim, sufficed at last to wake the great British public from its complacent sleep.

The case of the missing schoolchildren had dragged on too long. Officialdom, faced with the threat of another oil embargo, dithered. Public opinion, bedevilled by unemployment, inflation, and the forthcoming election, was preoccupied, and a small group of mindless men, driven to desperation by official ineptitude, lost their heads.

Their demands hadn't altered since the beginning: stubbornly refusing to compromise, they would accept nothing less than the immediate release of all 'freedom fighters', whatever their nationality or crime, held in West European jails. Further, these men would be assembled in London and flown by an aircraft belonging to a nation sympathetic to their cause to a secret destination.

The British Government was given four days to comply. If they failed, every child (there were thirty-three still missing, discounting the one already dead) would be killed.

VIII

Renway was in a cautious mood. For once he didn't roam around the office; he sat glued to the edge of his chair in an attitude of gloomy attention, hanging on to every word being uttered by his VIP visitor from Centre HQ in Washington.

Never one to mask his feelings, he felt and looked inhibited. He knew exactly where he stood in Centre's books at the moment – squarely behind the eight ball.

His visitor, Milton Voss, was old school, a dyed-in-the-wool bureaucrat, a manipulator, a born procrastinator, above all, a survivor. Dealing with him was like treading on eggshells. Voss was dangerous. Securely seated at the top table, privy to all decisions taken at the very highest level, he ranked roughly number five in the pecking order.

Somewhere in his early fifties, skeletal, bald, he had recently spent a small fortune on a hair transplant that hadn't quite come off, the general effect being that of an underfed greyhound topped with a poodle mop. Not entirely devoid of a male ego and understandably feeling put upon by fate, be wore a perpetual frown. To a military man, he was an alien species. 'Sorry to intrude,' he was ruminating, 'but Centre asked me to drop in on my way through London. I really see no reason why there should be any difficulty in finding a solution to the problem.'

'I see,' Renway replied, waiting for the axe to drop.

But Voss didn't drop it, at least not yet. Like a praying mantis about to swoop on an unsuspecting fly, he pursued his theme. 'Quite obviously Centre wants the Blake business settled, but I'd be less than frank if I didn't mention that two somewhat divergent points of view are developing at home. Let me put it this way, Colonel, there are those who now believe that, for the moment, it suits our purposes to soft-pedal on Blake and concentrate on the safe delivery of those children. Do you understand?'

Renway couldn't believe his cars. Such a turnabout in the Agency wasn't only bewildering, it was unheard of. He sat there grimly, hesitating to comment, managing a distracted nod. He thought of saying, 'Nothing succeeds like success', but muzzled it.

'Priorities, you see… we must be flexible. My instructions are to assist the authorities here regarding a successful exchange. The children must be rescued first, then we shall decide what to do about Blake.'

Renway gulped. 'I see,' he said, which of course he didn't. He did however manage a rather rueful, 'The British might not welcome our interference.'

'Not if we approach them in the right way. I know them rather well. I have an acquaintance or two in their Foreign Office who could be amenable.'

Renway coughed. Losers didn't argue with senior operatives from Centre.

Voss ran a well-manicured hand over his mop. 'Is MacNalley still our man in Libya?'

'He was on station in Tripoli last I heard from him, why?'

Voss hunched his narrow shoulders. 'Colonel Ghadafi might be prevailed upon to cooperate, even at this late stage. He wants those Mirage fighters rather badly. We might expedite matters with the French. How well does MacNalley know him?'

Renway blinked. 'I don't see where this is leading. MacNalley used to get on fairly well with him, but lately... I don't know.'

'He's still International Oil's senior representative out there, isn't he? He must have access to some of his aides. He couldn't function otherwise, and they need him to keep their revenues pouring in.'

Renway started to object but Voss sped on, undeterred. '...the object being to convince Ghadafi that it's in his interest to assist us in freeing those children. MacNalley must speak to him, it's the only way, and it must be done quickly, before any more of them are killed.'

Despite everything, Renway made an honest effort to be reasonable, but he was determined to go down fighting. 'The question is, how?' he began. 'Let me tell you this: a reliable source within the government has already informed me that the British Cabinet has information – which for obvious reasons they haven't leaked to the press – that Ghadafi has already offered the terrorists political asylum. He's done it before and he'll do it again, but whether he'll do it this time is problematical. It may be a blind. But if he doesn't, you can be damned sure that he's arranged it somewhere else. Why do you think they're insisting on using a transport belonging to – how did they put it – "a nation sympathetic to their cause"? I'll lay odds that it'll be one of Ghadafi's planes for two reasons: one, he has a pathological distrust of the West; and two, once that plane is airborne he can direct it anywhere he wants it to land. Ghadafi's crazy. He won't lift a finger to save those kids, Mirage fighters or no Mirage fighters, if he sees a chance to make us eat crow. It's a waste of time.'

Surprisingly, Voss gave in. 'I suppose you're right, it always was a long shot. Forgetting Ghadafi, let us consider what they're asking.'

'An arm and a leg...' Renway began.

Voss waved him into silence. 'They want everyone held in European jails on terrorist charges, regardless of nationality, freed, brought to London, exchanged for the children, and flown out to some refuge in the Middle East or Africa. They hold the aces. The British have nothing to bargain with. They'll have to get off the fence. If they delay much longer it will be too late.'

Forgetting his caution, Renway let rip. 'Sure! Then what happens?' He slammed a fist hard down on his desk. 'Don't forget that some of those terrorists took part in the Heathrow massacre. When they attempt to board that flight, Blake is going to be there and he's going to blast them to hell, even if he dies doing it. I know him, believe me, that's what he's going to do. He has already murdered three men in cold blood, do you think he's going to stop now?'

'No indeed,' Voss exclaimed, doing some table-thumping himself. 'And what is more, we're counting on it. The question is *where*?'

'Wherever they attempt to fly out from, where else? I'd bet my bottom dollar on it – he'll be there!'

Voss wasn't so sure. 'Maybe, maybe not. Possibly it's occurred to him that he'll have a better chance if he catches them where they land.'

Renway doubted it. 'Odds are against it. If he does it that way, he could miss them altogether. They could set down in Libya, Algeria, even Uganda. Don't forget, Idi Amin is even crazier than Ghadafi. And there are other places, any one of those tin-pot African Marxist states. He won't chance it. He'll come here.'

Unruffled, Voss suggested dryly, 'But just suppose he decides that London is too risky and waits in Libya – the most likely place – instead? You've already said that he has the funds and the facilities to find the men and mount an operation of that scope. Why should he try to penetrate security here when he can do it a lot easier there? Just sit back and wait for them to fly his target to him. It would be an adroit move.'

'Without MacNalley's knowledge? You're asking a lot.'

'You've already reminded me how determined he is,' Voss insisted, a brittle note creeping into his voice.

'I just don't think he'll do it like that.'

'But he might?'

'He won't. Out there, even if he was desperate enough to try it, he'd be surrounded by Ghadafi's army. You couldn't get a cockroach through to that plane if it touches down in Libya, which I doubt, because it's too obvious and anyone who says otherwise simply does not know Blake.'

Voss realised that Renway would soon be asking him to make a decision and he was feeling decidedly uncomfortable.

Renway, sensing this, started to speak very fast: 'All right, hear me out, and if you don't agree, we'll do it your way. I'll help with the British or anyone else for the sake of those kids. First, Blake – and now maybe even Roker – will come to London. He's not about to pass up a chance like this, an entire plane-load of terrorists. No. He'll come here and, some way, he's going to get onto that airport. Remember, he won't be working alone. He'll have plenty of help, even in high places, that's the way he has functioned so far. No use switching fields at the last minute either, or using duplicate aeroplanes, he'll take all that into account.'

'And the British authorities?'

'They'll be more concerned than we are that nothing goes wrong if they decide to go through with it. They'll lay on a whole armoured battalion, together with bus loads of armed police. The entire area will be cordoned off, patrolled by tanks and armoured cars.'

'And you think he can penetrate that?'

'Yes. This isn't Libya, it's practically his own home ground. He'll get in somehow and I want to be ready for him when he does.'

'You've considered that he might get in before the place is sealed off?'

Renway's smile was positively sunny. 'I have. That airport will be turned inside out every eight hours.'

Voss demurred. 'You make it sound very plausible, however…'

Renway held his ground. 'It's your decision. What's it to be?'

'You expect the British to give you that much latitude? They're usually rather sensitive when we are involved.'

'You said it yourself earlier. They can be persuaded if we're delicate enough. They'll be grateful for all the help they can get, even from us, if they go with the terrorists' terms.'

Voss wasn't entirely convinced. He stood there diffidently, like an underfed stork that had strayed into the wrong roost, a pose he often used to good effect.

'Well?'

'If something goes wrong?'

'I'll take full responsibility.'

'It's a big decision to make.'

'If I'm wrong, it's my head, not yours.'

Voss hesitated, suspecting that Centre might have other ideas about that. 'It's chancy…' he hesitated, 'very chancy…'

'*Yes or no?*'

'Very well. We won't interfere. Do it your own way,' the man from Centre sighed.

IX

Nothing was announced to the media until every prison in western Europe had been emptied of terrorists and these had been flown to London. An entire wing at Wormwood Scrubs' prison was cleared for the arrival of sixty-seven prisoners. An anonymous Third World government hastily agreed to supervise the exchange. The Home Secretary himself was supervising negotiations with the kidnappers of the schoolchildren.

It had taken the death of one small child to goad the reluctant leaders of the besieged democracies into action. Once again, and predictably, the forces of law and order capitulated to the forces of violence.

CHAPTER TEN

I

THE UMAR IBN AL KHATTAB OASIS IN WINTER WAS AN inhospitable place. It was also isolated. A few wind-driven date palms, stagnant water in a crumbling well, the remains of a stone shelter, nothing else. Once a busy place, the advent of a road running down from Djeneier, a Tunisian village (the nearest human habitat some fifty miles away), had made it redundant. Caravans (now truck fleets) nowadays only stopped there in emergencies, but on the rare occasion Bedouins camped there to rest their goat herds and water their camels.

Blake fell in love with the place. He holed up there for nine days while he waited for word from Linderman's contact in Tripoli. For him it was ideal. A mile or two from the Libyan frontier and few people ever visited the place.

Impervious to the bitter winds which blew continuously from dawn until sunset, Blake wasn't idle. He used the time to think. He got himself together, put his house in order, and Monica loomed large in his plans. A hurried phone conversation in Tunis a couple of weeks earlier had established her in good health, back safe in London, and none the worse for their experience. The dream – to be together as soon as possible on that place in New England.

Blake did his soul-searching, mostly flat on his back in his sleeping bag, gazing the nights away at a black velvet sky ablaze with stars. He couldn't get enough of it. It took him back to the plains of North Dakota and a child's wonder at the universe. They were all there as he remembered them: Spica, Regulus, Antares the Red Giant in surely the most beautiful constellation of them all – Scorpio. Aldebaran and Betelgeuse, Castor and Pollux the twins. Blake soared to all the happy yesterdays and hopeful tomorrows. Could it just happen? Could the whole goddamn cosmos be simply a blending of gases? It wasn't possible. So, like all those before him, Blake measured his own importance in the scene of things.

Not so Jean Jacques Runier, his erstwhile guide, cook and bottle-washer. He hated every moment of it, and as the days wore on he grew more morose and silent. For Jean Jacques's joy was an asphalt street lit by neon signs and peopled by girls who danced in discos. Deserts were made for sandflies and dromedaries, certainly not people. Jean Jacques felt very sorry for himself.

During the day, while waiting for the sun to set and the Big Show to begin overhead, Blake passed the time hunting for ancient patties of camel dung and donkey chestnuts to keep the fire going or simply sheltering from the wind. Jean Jacques suffered in silence.

On the ninth day they sat huddled together under the same blanket to keep the driving sand out of their faces. 'When's it going to stop?' Blake wondered. 'Or does it blow like this all winter?'

Jean Jacques wasn't amenable to conversation. He said darkly, 'You should be grateful it lets up when the sun goes down.'

'What sun? I haven't seen it for a week.'

The Frenchman flung another chunk of camel dung on the fire. '*Merde!* What a stink. And you like it here?'

Blake's grin was blissful. Like a matron from Appleton, Wisconsin, he enthused, 'It's so romantic. Those desert sheiks, their white chargers. How can you be so pedestrian?'

Jean Jacques couldn't bear it, he muttered a rapid series of blasphemous obscenities at the world in general and Blake in particular.

The American was offended. He took umbrage, unable to resist prodding such cloying self-pity into something more demonstrative. 'You *pieds noirs* are all alike,' he goaded. 'All you think of are your comforts. You're more Arab than anything else, yet you have the gall to call yourselves Frenchmen!'

These were fighting words, as Blake was well aware.

Frenchmen born in Algeria resented the tag their countrymen at home had hung on them and when they were reminded, it usually ended in a brawl. But Blake was saved by the sudden appearance of a car materialising in the oasis.

They grabbed their weapons and hit the dirt and didn't surface until the lone driver identified himself by the simple expedient of shouting louder than the wind. Deliverance.

Linderman had at last come through with the goods. Decoded, the message read: *Idris el Awal Airbase, Tripoli. Youssef. Egyptian engine mechanic. When you get there, wait, cafe outside perimeter. He will find you, pass instructions and ID papers. MacNalley.*

Blake's first impulse was to laugh but it was rapidly smothered. MacNalley? The Agency's veteran Middle-East hand? Even he had gone over to Linderman. He felt the hairs prickle on the back of his neck. Or had he?

Time would tell...

II

The military airbase at Idris el Awal, one of a chain stretching across the Mediterranean coastline from the Tunisian frontier to the Gulf of Salurn in Egypt, had the customary quota of Soviet-made MIG fighters parked in neat lines across the tarmac.

A large jet transport was drawn up in front of one of the hangars being serviced by mechanics with the legend LIBYAN AIRWAYS stencilled in bright red letters across their backs. Up above them, the sloping green windows of the control tower reflected the light of the rising moon. Out on the windy perimeter, an army jeep patrolled the guard posts. Security had been stepped up in the past few days and some of the sentries were accompanied by Alsatian guard dogs. Other than this, and the activity described above, there wasn't much going on.

One of the mechanics, a balding Egyptian under contract to Libyan Airways, shouldered his toolkit and made his way up the boarding-ramp into the transport. Inside, he moved swiftly past the steward's pantry and slipped into the men's lavatory. In that confined space, he found a panel and proceeded to fit it some three feet below the ceiling. Already cut to size and painted the same colour as the original, it was hinged like a door and equipped with a spring-catch. After securing the panel with large screws, he climbed up inside to test it for size. When it was pulled shut, the false ceiling looked genuine. Dropping to the floor, he produced a walkie-talkie. 'Are you receiving me?' he asked.

Blake's voice came over clearly from the other end. 'How's it coming?'

'No trouble. It'll be a tight squeeze, but you'll manage it.'

'There'll be a careful check, suppose they spot the false ceiling?'

The Egyptian was adamant. 'They would have to know something about aircraft design. I'm a cabinet-maker by trade. There are no visible joins. I've covered them with plastic wood and the paint is a perfect match. It will pass all right.'

'Any sign of MacNalley?'

'None. The place is forbidden to all foreigners other than permanent staff like myself. Good luck.'

Switching off the instrument, the Egyptian retrieved his toolkit and stepped out into the passage.

Outside, Blake slipped out of the shadows and moved down a road running along a line of hangars. He was dressed like the mechanics in white Libyan Airways overalls and had a toolkit slung over his shoulder. He seemed at home in his surroundings and didn't turn his head as a patrol jeep sped past. He wasn't overly concerned, having already been stopped at three guard posts to have his papers examined. They were excellent copies.

He walked for several minutes until he reached the last hangar in the line, then made his way towards the tarmac. When he saw the transport, he turned into a darkened doorway.

Rummaging in his pockets, he found a can containing a dog repellent called *Anti-mate* and carefully sprayed his clothes and shoes. A liquid substance favoured by dog owners to spray bitches on heat, it was also popular with drug smugglers who used it to put off the dog-addicts belonging to Customs services searching for marijuana.

Blake waited in the doorway until the mechanics finished their work and drove off, then strode out to the big transport.

He moved up the boarding ramp and stepped inside.

He made his way along the corridor and slipped into the lavatory. There was a compartment beneath the sink containing a parachute harness and chest-pack. Blake reached up and released the false ceiling.

He opened his toolkit, lifted the tray and removed the two dismantled parts of a miniature machine gun, together with a pair of ammunition clips and a small explosive device equipped with a timing mechanism. This last item was Blake's insurance policy. He had read somewhere that a Korean airliner, having strayed off course into the Soviet Union, had been shot up by Russian fighters and, despite rapid depressurisation, not a single passenger had been sucked out of the aircraft. Blake wouldn't chance it happening again.

The gun was a revolutionary weapon called the MAC II. The product of an American small-arms designer who specialised in sophisticated weapons, the MAC II was 8½ inches long without its stock extended, capable of firing 1,200 rounds a minute. The main feature, apart from its small size and weight (56 ounces), was its lightweight silencer. It was a formidable weapon.

Stepping up on the sink, Blake lifted himself through the opening and taped each article separately to the ceiling bulkhead. He forced himself to work slowly. It had to be right because once the aircraft was airborne he would have no room in that cramped space to rectify errors.

The Egyptian had done his job well, had forgotten nothing. He had even remembered to fit a small ledge along the bulkhead to accommodate the chest-pack. This left the harness. Blake dropped back to the floor, adjusted the straps, and buckled it on.

Replacing the tray, he fastened the lid, took the toolkit out into the corridor and placed it on one of the seats. The Egyptian had agreed to return it to the tool-room in the morning.

Blake moved back to the lavatory, secured the chest-pack on the ledge, and hoisted himself up. Bracing his shoulders and feet against the opposing bulkheads of the tiny compartment, he reached down and released the spring. The false ceiling banged shut.

He lay there wondering what he had forgotten. He had sufficient food and water stuffed in his pockets to last him for two days and an empty plastic bottle when he had to urinate. If the flight was delayed and he had to remain there for longer, it couldn't be helped. He would have to stick it out. It was like lying in an upper berth on a train.

III

The Airport Authority at Heathrow in London had never before mounted such tight security. Special Branch men armed with rifles were positioned on the roofs of the arrival and departure buildings and uniformed police and detectives in civilian clothes were numerous in all the departments that had anything to do with incoming or outgoing passengers.

Outside, it was even more noticeable. All roads leading into the airport were blocked with barriers, Army half-tracks and armoured cars patrolled the aprons, heavily-armed soldiers waited in open trucks parked at intervals along the entire length of the tarmac. Even a tank lumbered past, an officer wearing earphones standing erect in the open turret. This being the festive season, a time dear to the hearts of all Englishmen, such a formidable array of military hardware seemed incongruous amongst the colourful Christmas trees that dotted the airport both inside the terminal and out in the grounds. Nothing, not even the present emergency, was permitted to interfere with that.

Milton Voss, the man from Centre, was standing with Renway beside the latter's car. 'Impressive,' he muttered laconically as a heavy troop-carrier lumbered past. He didn't appear to be the same man Renway had been so wary of at their first meeting. This Voss was bursting with confidence and obviously intent on getting the job done, and Renway was anxiously aware of it. Exuding sweetness and light, he remarked lightly, 'No Blake yet? Sure you've checked everything?'

'Repeatedly. And they're still checking, even the drains,' Renway replied uncomfortably. He stood stiffly, his eyes moving from one spot to another with nervous little flicks. 'He's here all right, I can smell him.'

A youngish department aid hurried up to them. Pausing to catch his breath, he blurted, 'There's been a last-minute hitch, sir. The Home Secretary is on an open line to the kidnappers, who now refuse to release the children until the plane carrying the prisoners is airborne and out of British air space.'

Renway nodded. 'Thank you. Anything else?'

The other glanced at Voss, uncomfortable to be in the

presence of one of the exalted ones from Centre. 'Nothing else yet, sir, no.'

'Right. Let us know if there are any further developments.' As the awed youngster backed off, Voss inched closer to Renway's shoulder. 'No problem. They just have to wait another half-hour, that's all, because I don't think Blake is going to show.'

Curbing his growing frustration, Renway cautioned, 'If he did now, he'd be a bit early, wouldn't he?'

'I'll say one thing for you, Colonel. You're a glutton for punishment.'

Renway said mirthlessly, 'All part of the job. We take the rough with the smooth.' As they climbed into the back of the car, he said to the driver, 'You know the drill. Move it.'

Out on the M4, the main road running from London to Heathrow Airport, the vehicles of the convoy were moving at high speed. Led by a pair of motorcycle outriders, a troop-carrier full of helmeted soldiers and an armoured car, a large bus containing the prisoners sped past a roadblock, followed by a second armoured car and two more troop-carriers. Further on, the convoy turned into a side road leading to one of the isolated areas of the airport.

As Renway and Voss stepped out of the car at the far end of one of the runways, they found the entire area cordoned off with soldiers. There were two tanks positioned on either side of the wide concrete strip and their guns were trained on the wire fence enclosing the eastern boundary of the airport complex.

The convoy thundered up and turned into the field.

Voss commented dryly, 'To use your own words, Colonel, not even a cockroach could creep through that.'

Renway was beside himself with anxiety. Behaving as if he expected Blake to suddenly materialise out of thin air, he snapped, 'Don't be too sure, they're not in that plane yet.'

Some two miles away, Flight Control up in the tower had given a Libyan Air Force transport clearance to land. This aircraft had priority over the customary incoming flights decked up above in layers, circling in their traffic patterns, waiting their turn to land. It was a clear day, visibility was unlimited, and the big transport made a smooth landing, continued on to the far end of the runway and taxied off into a parking strip.

The bus containing the prisoners drove promptly up to the transport, and, flanked by tight lines of soldiers on either side, the men began to file quickly out of the bus and up the boarding ramp leading into the transport.

They were a mixed lot. Some barely out of their teens, others in their late thirties. A few wore neat conventional clothes, others more colourful hippy gear. The latter were unshaven or bearded and many had hair trailing down over their shoulders.

All but three, easily distinguishable because of the noise they were making, were subdued, bewildered by the abrupt prospect of freedom. The jubilation would come later when the shock of their sudden release wore off. Unlike the others, the three young men were making the most of it. Stopping midway up the steps, they turned and waved arrogantly to the silent troops. One was a young Japanese, the other a dead ringer for the late Che Guevara, the last a young German with pale yellow hair and a blond beard. If Blake had been there he would have recognised them immediately because all three had participated in the devastating massacre almost a year earlier at this same airport. They were faces he wouldn't easily forget.

When all were safely inside the aircraft, the boarding ramp was wheeled away and the four powerful jet engines came to life. Even at this late stage, security was firmly maintained. As the big machine rolled out on the runway, it was escorted on either side by armoured cars. Then the engines whined and it started to move. In moments it gathered speed and its angle of ascent was steep as it roared into the air.

Renway and Voss didn't take their eyes from it until it vanished overhead. Renway turned abruptly and climbed into his car. Voss promptly joined him in the back seat. 'Well, that's that, then,' he said mopping his forehead with a large silk handkerchief. 'From Centre's point of view it's a damned good thing he didn't show up.'

Renway sat there in a state of acute shock. The inevitable hadn't happened. Somehow Blake had missed it. His mind a whirl of confused emotions, he lapsed into a dull torpor.

Voss even found it in himself to be sympathetic. 'Don't feel so bad. Now that it's out of our hands, I don't give a damn what Blake does. At least Centre won't blame us for it.'

Renway roused himself. 'When do I get chucked to the wolves, or do I have time to pack?'

'My dear fellow, you did all that could be expected of you and more. The fact that you can't read another man's mind doesn't alter the fact that you were prepared in the event he did come,' Voss reminded him expansively. 'Furthermore, I shall say just that in my report. He's in Libya, holed up on that airbase, waiting for that plane-load of crackpots to land – and that's where MacNalley's going to dig him out.'

Up in front, the driver switched on the radio and both men paused to listen as the announcer's voice flooded into the car. '...*It has just been reported that the missing children have been found in their school bus in Bradford a few minutes ago. They appear to have been well treated and relieved that their long ordeal is at last over. Further bulletins will be announced throughout the day as more reports come in.*'

As the relieved driver switched off the radio, Voss continued as if there had been no interruption. 'You're going back to where you belong, Colonel, to administration. You're not field and never have been. You report to Centre as soon as you can get back to Washington, and you should welcome it. People like Blake are best left where they belong – out in the jungle rooting out man-eaters like themselves.'

Renway sighed, 'And the condemned man ate a hearty meal.'

IV

When the No Smoking sign was switched off, the passengers unfastened their seat belts. It was a jubilant crowd. Everyone started to talk at once. The chatter was animated, high-pitched and in many languages because they came from many parts of the globe. They were the freedom fighters and they had all been directly involved in the war. They had hijacked airliners, robbed banks, kidnapped high personages, murdered, maimed or held hostage those they decided were guilty of crimes against the 'people' or had just simply got in the way in the course of one of their assaults, reduced airports in Rome, Tel Aviv and London to smouldering ruins – each had made his mark somewhere on the complacent silent majority.

They had one thing in common: bitter hatred for constituted authority. All were True Believers and their heroes were Fidel Castro, Che Guevara, Mao Tse Tung and the late Abdul Nasser. All clung steadfastly to the Marxian maxim that only violence can destroy a decadent society.

The names were legend. The Baader-Meinhof Gang, Black September, the IRA, the Red Brigade of Italy, the Popular Front for the Liberation of Palestine, the *Tupamaros,* the Red Army of Japan – they all had followers on that aircraft flying to refuge in Colonel Ghadafi's People's Republic.

The Jap, the German and the olive-skinned 'Che' occupied the front row of seats immediately adjacent to the emergency escape hatch and facing onto the steward's pantry. Whooping like Indians, they indulged in their elated horseplay.

By contrast, it was very quiet in the men's lavatory. Blake was up in his cubicle marking the time on the luminous dial of his watch, calculating that the transport would soon be flying over France. He put his ear to the bulk-head and when he heard no sound down in the lavatory, he released the spring, dropped to the floor and latched the door.

He reached up into the opening and wrenched the machine gun parts off the ceiling. When the gun was assembled, he fitted a clip into the breech, pulled the chute-pack off the ledge and clipped it on the chest-hooks of his harness.

The timing mechanism on the explosive device took a moment to set. There was a clock face with only one hand calibrated in minutes like a modern egg-timer. Flicking the switch, he activated the clock. In three minutes the device would explode.

He opened the door and stepped out into the passenger compartment. He stood there, silently facing the long rows of seats. The Jap and his friends were the first to spot him. Slowly the chatter died throughout the compartment as the others became aware of his presence. Blake looked out over a sea of stunned faces. Nobody moved, all eyes were riveted on him and the muzzle of his gun.

Edging quickly to his left, so close he brushed 'Che Guevara's' outstretched feet, he pulled hard on the red handle attached to a panel marked EMERGENCY EXIT. As the door vanished the harsh sound of rapid depressurisation filled the cabin.

Stunned silence dissolved into panic. They started to shout, to fight their way out of their seats, to run down the aisle. Blake was the first to be sucked out. The Jap clung desperately to his seat, but the force of the depressurisation pulled him out after him. Then he was followed by the screaming German and 'Che Guevara', after him, bits of luggage, clothing and anything in the immediate vicinity of the open hatch that wasn't firmly secured.

The aisle was piled high with squirming bodies and the screeches of the doomed resounded in the confined space of the compartment.

Blake didn't release his chute straightaway. He let himself drop in free-fall for a good thirty seconds before he pulled the little handle. Then he saw the blossoming fireball before he heard the sound of the ear-splitting explosion. Although he was some distance away, he could see what he took to be bits of twisting fragments spinning out in all directions from the centre of the explosion. When it cleared, there was nothing.

Blake floated slowly towards the earth far below.

EPILOGUE

IT WAS A WARM DAY. BLAKE SETTLED BACK IN HIS CHAIR AND asked the waiter to bring him another drink. His shirt was sticking to his skin, but the view more than compensated for this slight discomfort.

The water out in the bay was turquoise green blending beyond the harbour to deep blue. Overhead a gentle breeze rustled the palms. There was no one on the beach because the tourists hadn't yet heard of the place, just a few fishermen drying their nets.

Blake also ordered another drink for his friend Jim Roker who was sharing the table, catching up on the baseball scores in a week-old copy of the overseas edition of the *Herald Tribune*.

'How does it feel?' he asked, lifting his eyes from the page, 'Now that it's all over and you've settled your account?'

'The point is, I haven't,' Blake said bleakly. 'Nothing will ever bring Janis back.'

They left it at that. Roker returned to his baseball scores. Blake stared with empty eyes out at the water, wondering where they would go next. There weren't many places left.

Printed in the United Kingdom by
Lightning Source UK Ltd., Milton Keynes
137579UK00001B/73-90/A